TALES OF SLEY HOUSE 2025

In Memoriam

Jon Lasser
(1975 – 2025)

TALES OF SLEY HOUSE 2025

EDITED BY LILLIAN EHRHART

ISBN: 978-1-957941-24-0

Cover design and interior illustrations by Ranxvrus

Interior design by Dreadful Designs

Edited by Lillian Ehrhart

First Edition

2025

MEET THE SLEY SIBLINGS

GENEVIEVE – THE YOUNGEST SLEY SIBLING IS A CHAMPION OF DIVERSE VOICES AND FEMINIST LITERATURE. THE LIVES SHE MOST CARES FOR ARE HER PLANTS, A VARIETY OF SPECIMENS FROM THE WORLD OVER, NOW THRIVING IN HER GREENHOUSE, WITH THE POWER TO BOTH HEAL AND KILL. LIKE HER SPECIMENS, GENEVIEVE IS A RARE BREED. COLD AND CALCULATING, PATIENT, AND A LOVER OF STORIES OF REVENGE, JUSTICE, AND THE DARK FORCES GAINING CONTROL.

CHARLES – THE MIDDLE SIBLING SPENDS AS MUCH TIME GROOMING HIS MUSTACHE AND HIS STYLE AS HE DOES IN THEIR FATHER'S OLD LIBRARY. HERE, HE IS SURROUNDED BY ANCIENT VOLUMES. GRIMOIRES DEPICTING ANCIENT RITUALS AND MAGIC, FIRST EDITIONS OF NUMEROUS CLASSICS OF LITERATURE, AND OF COURSE, THE COLLECTIONS OF STORIES FROM AROUND THE WORLD. BE THEY STORIES OF MYTH AND LEGEND, CRYPTIDS OR GHOSTS, CHARLES RELISHES IN THEM ALL.

RG – THE ELDEST SLEY SIBLING HAS DONE MORE THAN READ HIS FATHER'S COLLECTION OF ANCIENT GRIMOIRES. HE HAS PRACTICED THEM, DABBLING IN THEIR DARK ARTS AS A PAINTER MIGHT IN OIL, RG HAS SPENT YEARS, A FORTUNE, AND HIS OWN HEALTH SEEKING ULTIMATE POWER. STORIES OF MAGIC, OF THE VASTNESS OF SPACE AND THE ELDRITCH HORRORS IT MAY CONTAIN, AND STORIES POWERFUL DEMONS AND OTHER DIMENSIONAL INTRUDERS PIQUE HIS INTEREST MOST, FOR HE SECRETLY WISHES TO UNLEASH SUCH THINGS ON THE EARTH.

CONTENTS

COME AND GATHER AROUND THE FIRE, CHILDREN, FOR I'VE GOT AN EVIL YARN TO SPIN, SO DASTARDLY, IN FACT, IT MIGHT JUST WRAP AROUND YOUR THROATS AND LEAVE YOU GASPING FOR MORE! I'M JUST KIDDING, OF COURSE. YOU CAN TRUST ME, AND I PROMISE I'M NOT CROSSING MY FINGERS BEHIND ME BACK (HEHEHEHEHE . . .). SO GRAB A SEAT FOR TONIGHT'S CREATURE-FEATURE ABOUT A LEGENDARY OWL THAT HAUNTS THE APPALACHIAN WOODS. IS IT REAL? OR IS IT A WILD FIGMENT OF COUNTRY-FOLK IMAGINATION? STICK AROUND AND FIND OUT. IN FACT, STAY AS LONG AS YOU LIKE, YOU MIGHT JUST GET SO COMFORTABLE THAT YOU NEVER WANT TO LEAVE. DON'T WORRY, WE WON'T LET YOU!!! HAH-HAH!!

COME SEE THE AMAZING HOLLER OWL

J.B. McLAURIN

She still couldn't believe she'd agreed to the trip. But, in the end, she'd figured she owed him for all the double dates and couples' weekends. Tom wasn't the type to kick and scream. He was a born people pleaser. Liked to keep the peace. Plus, on the dates, and the weekend trips to cabins and resorts, he'd always brought his best. Agreeing, at a moment's notice, to have drinks with her best friend's boyfriend of the month or to head out of town and get paired off with a stranger so Hannah and her best friend could gossip and make prosecco disappear. Tom had always been game for whatever, because he knew it made her happy, and the time had finally come for her to respond in kind. But God help her, Hannah never thought it would come to this. Not in a million years.

"So how much longer?" she asked.

From behind horn-rimmed glasses, his brown eyes crackled with excitement. "We're about twenty minutes out." As he air-drummed on the steering wheel, she realized his beard had gotten longer; it was sprouting some gray too. She'd been too busy at work to notice. "Damn, this is exciting."

They were deep in the backwoods of West Virginia. Far from any trace of civilization, winding through the hollers and mountains. It had been miles since she'd seen another car or gas station. They had well and truly entered the land of bumfuck nowhere, and in keeping with the customs of such forgotten territory, her phone had no service. Which, honestly, was to be expected: Was there a state more rural and backwards than West Virginia? Mississippi, perhaps. Honorable mention to Alabama.

"The sign should be coming up around this bend," Tom said.

As promised, a derelict sign, similar to the rectangular ones alongside the interstate, appeared up ahead. But unlike the billboards with a lawyer promising to get you a quick check or with an arrow directing you to the nearest adult superstore, this one was much lower to the ground. And it looked like it'd been stolen from a junkyard down the street from the house in the *Texas Chainsaw Massacre*.

"Lovely sign," she deadpanned.

"Oh, it's just part of the park's rustic charm."

"You got the *rustic* part right."

Faded rainbow-colored letters, akin to the garish font on a Ringling Brothers poster, heralded the name of the region's famous cryptid: *The Amazing Holler Owl. A creature that can tell your future! Forget the Mothman. Let the Holler Owl dazzle you with prophecy!!!*

Giddy, Tom turned down a bumpy dirt road. Overgrowth, brambles, and thorns scored the sides of the car. "Well, I guess you can cue the banjo."

"Oh, stop it. This place isn't that bad. Look, it's not Point Pleasant, but it's still an attraction that draws people."

Only a diehard cryptozoologist like her husband would think that comment made sense. Point Pleasant was home to the infamous

Mothman. The so-called harbinger of doom. A winged humanoid creature that—if you believe the lore—predicted the collapse of the Silver Lake Bridge, which claimed dozens of lives back in the sixties. You could say the Mothman was the Taylor Swift of cryptids. Well, maybe not. That crown probably better rested on Bigfoot's head. In any case, here was the state of affairs: Yes, her husband was a self-proclaimed expert on cryptozoology. Yes, this had been a helluva struggle for her to accept. But over time, she finally said *Fuck it.* He was good to her. Brought her coffee in the morning. Made her sandwiches for lunch (always slicing them diagonally, which made them taste better). Always made sure her water bottle was full and on her nightstand before bed. If obsessing over make-believe creatures was his thing, then she was here for it. Plus, she knew Tom was a nerd the moment she met him. It was part of his charm, and it made her feel safe. Thus, she found herself on this backwoods road, bouncing up and down, constant crunch of gravel grinding her eardrums.

"Can't wait to see what our guides look like."

"Well, that part I can't defend," he said, laughing. "I doubt they attract college kids like Disney and Universal. I imagine they will be of the unwashed variety."

"Oh, like at a Phish show," she ribbed. Tom had followed Phish on tour with some friends in college. When he'd shown her a few songs, she'd replied: *People pay to see this?* She'd looked the band up online and seen the legions of the unwashed at their shows. Like Woodstock '69 with more edibles, worse music, and hippies rubbing shoulders with frat boys. Not her scene by a country mile. "Except, you know, like a Phish show where they keep marriage within the family and make homemade meth."

"Is there any other way to make meth?"

"Fair point."

∞

When the woods opened up, a squat cabin appeared down in the valley. On approach, Tom cracked the windows; the coarse, yet comforting, smell of hickory wafted in. Tracking down its source, she saw smoke pluming out of the cabin's chimney. It wasn't quite winter yet, but it had been trending colder lately. The temperature was supposed to plummet tonight. They'd brought thick coats, gloves, and toboggans just in case.

Getting closer, she saw a gaggle of people, dressed in tan button-down shirts, jeans, and boots, milling around. They looked cleaner-cut than she'd expected. Almost like workers at one of those ranches out west where rich people went to get the pampered version of working the land. Where were the grease-stained men in overalls? The barefoot children chasing around a mangy dog? Behind them: a row of trucks with the Holler Owl emblazoned on the side. Under it was the company's name—Keel Tours LLC—a phone number, email address, and the symbols for Instagram and Facebook. They were online? Who'd a thought.

"See, babe, not as bad as you thought," Tom said, parking the car. "The sign is just vintage. They keep it up for nostalgia. Diehards like me love it."

Nodding along, she undid her seatbelt. Then got out, ready to get the show on the road. All she had to do was suffer through the museum in the cabin, a trip into the woods, and then a quick cocktail hour where they'd drink Holler Hooch (Lord save us in our hour of need) and eat Owl Burgers. He'd reassured her dozens of times they weren't made with real owl. And now seeing the guides dressed professionally, and the work trucks that were freshly washed and from this century, she actually believed him.

∞

"Welcome, welcome y'all," the guide—tall, wiry, and handsome—beckoned. "We'll gather over there on the porch. Y'all are it for today."

Tom leaned in and whispered, "That's great. Won't have to wait for any stragglers."

Stepping onto the porch, she realized the two other men—big, country-fed types—weren't there anymore. Where'd they go?

Next to the main guide was a woman—could be in her twenties or thirties. Hard to tell with these Earth-child types. She was tan, freckled, and slim, likely from a steady diet of granola and long days hiking in the woods. She and her boss wore their cracked, sun-damaged skin proudly.

"Glad to have y'all. My name's Jesse and this is Brenda. We're the main guides here at the Holler Owl Park."

Great, great, Hannah thought. *Let's get this thing moving.*

"Tom, right?" Jesse said, gladhanding the hell out of her husband. "Man, I'm glad you finally made it. I feel like we're old friends at this point."

Confused, she looked at Tom. "Friends, huh?"

"Tom loves to email questions about the HO-HO, as we call him. Your husband could practically work here at this point. Hell, he probably knows more than I do."

"Yeah, I thought there were more of you," she commented, genuinely curious about where the others went.

"Will and Samuel have to go prep the main attraction. It takes a while to get it set up and rolling." He held his arm out like a showman at a circus, ushering them toward the cabin's front door. "Brenda and I handle the historical aspect of the tour. Y'all ready to learn all you can about the HO-HO?"

"Yeah right, good luck showing or telling me something I don't already know."

"You're right about that, partner."

Like old high-school buddies at a reunion, they laughed together, then high-fived.

Jesus Christ.

All the while, Brenda stayed quiet. Lips pursed. Focused. Must just be wound a little too tight, Hannah thought.

She followed her husband and their tour guides into the small museum. Visions of prosecco and the charcuterie board waiting back at the hotel danced in her head.

☙❧

For a museum, the room was tiny, cluttered, chock-full of Holler Owl memorabilia. Framed newspaper articles detailing local sightings lined one wall. The accounts predated WWI. There was a shelf containing pottery and papier-mâché renderings of the cryptid. Some large, some small. Some nothing more than sticks twined together with leather. All of them bore a resemblance to the wooden statue in the center of the room. Jesse said his father had hand-carved it. Turns out Holler Owl Park was a family operation. And had been for generations. Hannah was baffled as to how they survived. Where was the money? She and Tom were the only ones there today. And yeah, they'd overpaid (she'd been too embarrassed to tell her friend the price), but it wasn't anywhere near enough to sustain a business. Not even close.

Stretching up to the roof, the thing dominated the room—lorded over it, actually. Temporarily, Jesse's reedy drawl faded away, as Hannah beheld the famous creature: Its frame was wiry, skeletal, thin in the hips but wide in the shoulders, with impossibly long arms;

swatches and tendrils of sinew and flesh oozed down off its face and body like batter; a few wisps of hair coiled down from its skull, thin and scant, like the hair of a malnourished beggar; its massive jaw stretched back almost to a ninety degree angle, displaying rows of misshapen teeth that looked like tusks; and of course, the large round eyes like an owl's, looking down at her, at once wise and vacant.

She walked a circle around it, wanting to take in everything. Long wings, clamped tight against its back, formed a heart stretching down to its wide feet.

Wings. Tom had never mentioned wings. Well, that wasn't fair. She probably just hadn't been paying attention. The wings reminded her of one of Tom's other favorite cryptids—the Mothman.

Such fine detail. Jesse's father had been a master craftsman; the level of precision took her breath away. This belonged in the Smithsonian, not holed away in the armpit of America.

"Beautiful, isn't it?" the woman remarked. She of the freckles and granola diet. She was next to Hannah now. She was short and petite, but her piercing eyes belied her small frame.

"God, yes," she responded, awestruck. "How long did it take him?"

"He worked on it every day for two years. And was able to finish it before he died."

Then, without another word, she winked at Hannah, spun on her feet, and walked away.

What an odd little woman.

She heard a back slap, then Jesse and her husband were by her side. "Yeah, took Pop two years—day and night—to get this bad boy done. But it was worth every second. It was his gift to this place before he passed."

The statue's spell had finally worn off. It was beautiful, no doubt, but the show needed to go on.

"He got it just right," Jesse continued. "It really is the perfect monument." All the folksiness had drained out of their guide's voice. And he was staring at the winged creature with that peculiar mixture of awe and reverence disciples display for religious figures. She recognized it from her childhood, when her parents had dragged her to church: the manic ecstasy of the congregant. It'd scared the hell out of her as a kid. That look on the congregation's face wasn't love. It was obsession.

Their guides kept staring at the "monument" for who knows how long, causing Tom to look at her and mouth, *I'm sorry.*

Hannah decided to start walking toward the door. Maybe some movement would shake them from their reverie.

It worked.

Jesse turned to them. "So, y'all ready to head into the woods?"

಄಄ಊ

"So this is where Noble Parks saw THE HO-HO in 1926. Right here at this very spot." They were standing on a precipice, overlooking a forest-covered valley. It was late afternoon; the sun's orange-yellow light dappled and shimmered through the leaves above and painted the valley below. "He told friends and family the owl's back was to him at first, then on approach, it turned and looked at him and plumed out its wings like a peacock."

She had to give it to Jesse, he was a born showman. Tom was hanging on every word. She still wanted this thing to keep moving along, but hard as it was to admit, the quirky romance of this place had swept her up a bit.

Jesse continued: "Then he said the man-bird opened its mouth wide—incredibly wide—and Noble told his family he could see things in it. Things that were impossible."

"Like what?" Hannah asked, thinking *Why not? We're already out here.*

"He said he could see his future right inside that creature's mouth, like watching a silent movie. His actual words were: 'It was like watching a movie about my future.'"

She laughed. What a bunch of bullshit. "Did they even have movies in the 1920s?"

"Of course," Jesse said. "Silent movies date back to the late 19th century. Hell, *Nosferatu* came out in 1922," he declared, chuckling.

"Well how did Backwoods Noble see a movie living out here in the middle of nowhere?" She looked to Tom for support and found none: He gawked at her as if her cellphone had just rung in a crowded theater.

Rude. She was being rude. This was their passion. It was petty of her to belittle it.

"Don't think it happened, huh, Miss Hannah?" Oh, she didn't like him sliding a Miss in front of her name. She didn't like that one bit at all. Fucking hillbilly.

And to think, she'd been feeling bad about poking fun at this guy.

But now wasn't the time to make waves. This was for Tom, not her. Couple more stops and then they would be back at the cabin, sipping world famous Holler Hooch. "No, no, no, not saying that. It's an entertaining story is all. Just thought it was funny." A pretty lackluster salvage effort, but it was all she could muster.

"Okay." He nodded and pointed back at the woods. "Next stop's a couple minutes that way."

෬෫

"Now this is where the most infamous event with the HO-HO happened."

They'd reached a clearing; the dirt was smoothed over, stepped on thousands of times, and bordered by mismatched boulders.

"This is right where a young man found ol' Tyler Macomb in 1998. Tyler was a local teenager that liked to disappear off into the woods for hours. No one ever really knew what he was getting up to. Everyone in town figured that Tyler came out here so much, he could handle himself. That was, until the young man found him—dead."

Tom was nodding along; he already knew every word of this story, she was sure. But he still had sparkles of glee in his eyes.

"The man searched for a wound. Some evidence of what happened to poor Tyler. But there was nothing. Well, not at first, anyway." This story was about to take a dark turn. Seeking comfort, she reminded herself none of this really happened. Tyler Macomb was as real as the tooth fairy. "Then, the young man rolled the highschooler over and saw his eyes were stained red like they had popped, then frozen solid." Disgusting visual, but okay, and… "and his brain had exploded out the back of his head. Folks in town reckoned someone had stuck a shotgun in his mouth and pulled the trigger."

Jesus Christ. That's horrible.

It didn't happen. It didn't happen, the voice in her mind soothed.

"Then as the legend goes, the HO-HO appeared right over there." He pointed toward a small hill of boulders that looked like it might have a cave or, at the very least, hidden shelter beneath. "The creature stepped out, looked straight at the young man, and then bellowed." *Really?* She'd been expecting a roar or a scream. "It was slow, like a funeral dirge." Extending his arm out, Jesse traced an arc from the cave to the clearing, then off into the gulch below, dimming to purple and pink under the sunset. "And then the HO-HO took flight across the valley."

Jesse moved close to them. Making sure he had their undivided attention. "I know all this because that young man was me."

If she could've stopped, she would have. But she had reached her breaking point. She was tired, hungry, and fed-up with Mr. Hillbilly's bullshit.

She laughed. Long. And hard.

"Once again, ol' Miss Hannah is a doubter."

With that Miss shit again. What was it with this guy? "Yes, you got me," she said, then put her hands up as if to say, *Officer, don't shoot.* "I'm not a believer. But I'll give you this Jesse, it's a helluva story."

"It's not a story." His eyes had gone cold. "It happened."

"Sure, sure." She nodded. "Not something you just tell people to get warm bodies up here."

"Hannah, take it easy," Tom, right next to her, whispered. "He's just trying to be a good guide."

With a devil-may-care grin, Jesse shrugged. "Ahh, no worries, Tom. It's usually the women that don't have enough imagination to get it. I understand. They just need to feel safe." He snickered; granola-girl chimed in with him.

Maybe on another day, she might have let it go. But she saw right through this man. Sure, he was full of bonhomie and back slaps when he wanted to take your money. But, at heart, he was like all the other country-fed, hill-dwellers: He didn't like women. Thought they should be quiet. Nod and fall in line. Smile and be okay when he called them diminutive things like *Miss* and told them their imagination couldn't match the breadth of a man's. Probably had some poor cowering wife back at home afraid of her own shadow after years of manipulation and abuse.

Screw this guy.

"Oh, I can imagine it alright, because it isn't hard to figure out." She stepped forward, staring him and his underling down. "After what happened in Point Pleasant with the Mothman, your family saw an opportunity to make money. A way to get tourists to come here and dump money into this place that otherwise has no reason to exist. So they cooked up a bunch of stories and thought up a creature, that I'm sorry, seems a whole lot like, I don't know, the fucking Mothman!" she yelled. Then, lowering her voice, she delivered the death knell: "It's a con, Jesse." She lunged forward and stuck her finger in his face. "And stop calling me Miss."

He didn't respond. Rather, he just stared at her. Slowly, bit by bit, his face hardened into stone; he looked as if he wanted to filet her skin. Watch her squirm while he cut her apart.

It silenced her.

They were out in the woods. Isolated. No cell service.

And what she saw in his eyes was hungry, feral, primitive. Desperate to feed.

Suddenly, out of left field, Jesse shattered the tension by laughing. It was loud, over-the-top, forced. His underling laughed just as hard. "Shwwooo, can't fool you, Hannah." They kept on, doubling over. "I can't believe we've done all these tours and you're the only one that had the balls to call us out," he said, still cackling.

They walked over to her, collecting themselves. It seemed all was forgiven.

"You got our number." Close to them now, he whispered: "But please keep that to yourself. We rely on this money." He put his hands on their shoulders and turned them around.

The feel of his hand turned her stomach.

Pointing at the collection of boulders, he said, "Last stop, straight ahead," and chuckled.

As they started walking, she realized the sun was gone.

CR&SO

"Hey, isn't it about time to head back?" Tom asked.

Jesse had already given them the history of the creature's lair. The collection of rocks they'd walked over to—about an hour ago—was actually an entrance to a small cave. He'd let them peek inside, but it was too dark to go in; he'd offered, but both she and Tom declined. Which had surprised her; she thought her husband would want to take the flashlights their guides offered and explore. But things had been off ever since her outburst. Jesse's hard stare and over-the-top laugh had unsettled her husband just as much as her. It was pitch dark out and they were ready to go.

"We're about to head back, hoss, don't you worry," Jesse replied. He and Brenda had been standing off by the trail they had walked in on. As if they were waiting for something. Without any explanation, they had asked that she and her husband wait over here.

"What do you think they're doing?" Tom asked, keeping his voice down.

"Who knows, maybe praying that the HO-HO will make another appearance," she responded, laying on the sarcasm, trying to lighten the mood, but failing.

Something wasn't right. They should've walked back before sunset. A well-funded theme park would have had lights bordering the trail, guiding their way back to the cabin. Out here, there wasn't a light for miles, save the two flashlights their guides had and the small cheapo ones they'd offered to her and Tom to explore the Holler Owl's den.

"We need to get the hell out of here," she said. "Let's just start walking back. It's the same trail all the way back in. If they don't want to come, then screw 'em. We already paid. What are they going to do?"

Tom nodded. "Let's do it."

They walked over. To keep the peace, she let Tom address them. Based on recent events, that was the better play.

"We're going to head back, y'all. We really appreciate all you've shown us. But we're exhausted and want to get an early start tomorrow."

"But you haven't even seen the best part," Brenda said, giggling, as if teasing them.

"She's right, y'all. Why come all this way and then leave right before you've seen it?"

Okay, enough with this shit. "Look, we're headed back," Hannah declared.

She put her hand on Tom's lower back, pushing him along. They started walking away; she felt her anxiety wane with each step.

"Can't let you leave," Jesse shouted behind them.

The two men she'd seen earlier milling around the cars, then disappearing into the woods, appeared on the trail, blocking their path, each holding something long and black: shotguns.

"Y'all come on back over here. No sense in fightin' it or trying to run. We all know these woods through and through. We'd find you quick."

The men started closing on them, forcing them to backtrack toward the cave.

There was still enough distance between them that she and Tom would have a running start, but their deranged guide was right: They wouldn't stand a chance in these woods. They weren't hikers or campers. They were city folk. Pampered. Spent their Saturdays drinking bottomless mimosas and shopping in stores downtown. She couldn't remember the last time they'd stepped foot in the woods.

As panic and anxiety started to sink their hooks in, she heard a buzz in Tom's pocket. Did he have service?

"Tom, your phone." She looked at his thigh.

He pulled it out, trying to keep it low, out of sight. Hope bloomed in his eyes. "It's got one bar. Enough to try."

No need to talk about which number to call.

She saw his fingers subtly tapping away. "What are you doing?"

They were backing up, leaving the trail for the cover of the trees; she was in front of him, attempting to create a shield.

"Text to voice," he replied. He didn't have to explain: He types and the person on the other end hears a computer-generated voice. Brilliant. It pays to be with a nerd.

"It connected."

Hope shot through her, then died off fast—a quick, cheap bottle rocket that popped, then disappeared. This was a fool's errand. The Sheriffs would never make it in time.

A grim thought occurred to her: It could lead deputies to them if they were held captive. Or grimmer: It was a way for law enforcement to return their bodies to their parents.

The dull tap of Tom's fingers continued.

"Why y'all taking a detour? Told you to come this way. Quit wasting time," Jesse yelled. Then: "Sam, get em'."

Two shadows started running toward them.

She turned to Tom, looking down at the phone. Tom had it set where the dispatcher's responses were being transcribed in real time. They couldn't pinpoint them based on the description of the cave. Too many cave systems in that area. The instructions were straightforward: Keep the phone on as long as you can so they can ping it off a tower and create a search area. She told them to kill the call and put the phone in low-power mode to preserve the battery.

The two men were almost there. Close.

But, a few feet away, she heard the abrupt grind of gravel and cracking sticks. For some reason, they'd stopped.

She turned to see where they were, then turned back to say they should surrender and take their chances the deputies could find them.

Without warning, in a handful of tiny seconds, her world shattered.

A thunderclap boomed, blotting out her hearing, leaving a steady high-pitched whir.

With a trembling hand, she felt her face; it was wet. Misted with her husband's blood. The same with her flannel shirt: soaked through, pieces of Tom stuck to her clothes like food crumbs.

He'd been blown clear back, like he'd been struck by a high speed car.

Void of thought and speech and sanity, she hadn't the will or the control to move. She shook and descended into shock, firmly shackled to the backwoods nightmare that had become her new reality.

ᙣᙢ

Dazed, she stumbled along as they led her back to the rock formation. Faintly, as if coming through a radio broadcast at low volume, she heard them discussing why Sam took the shot. *Phone. The guy had a working phone, Jesse.* She didn't see it happen but she figured they had immediately destroyed the phone, simultaneously destroying any chance of her being found.

How could a road trip so stupid and harmless—a trip to see a make-believe creature—have come to this? How?

They sat her down near the rocks while they got a fire going. Once the flame was good and roaring, they took their seats around the campfire and waited. They didn't speak. Didn't move. Just looked at the tongues of flame with dumb glee; it was the same look she saw earlier in the museum, when they were beholding the statue of their beloved HO-HO.

Slowly but surely, acceptance set in. They were going to kill her. It wasn't a question of if, merely, when. There was nothing left to fear. And there was nothing left to lose.

"Y'all actually believe in this shit?" Her tone was cynical, resigned, but still laced with poison. "You really think a giant winged creature is about to show up and show you the future, huh? Well, let me tell you, if that's what you believe then you're a whole lot dumber than you look. And that's saying something."

Unexpectedly, Jesse laughed. Subdued. Subtle. Not like earlier when he was acting. "Still don't believe, do you, Miss Hannah."

"If you don't stop with that Miss shit I'm going—"

"You're gonna what?" he stopped her. "You're trapped. Accept it."

You killed my husband! You blew a hole through my best friend! her mind screamed, but she didn't say it out loud. And she wasn't done prodding them. Not by a long shot. "So what made you lose your minds? Meth? Moonshine? Too many rolls in the hay with your cousin?"

Brenda laughed. "I like her, Jesse. She's funny. She's gonna fit right in," she said, bright and animated. Totally unlike the scowling mute from earlier. "We've needed another woman around here."

Were they planning to keep her?

All things remaining equal, she'd much rather die than live with these freaks.

Sam and his second (*Maybe he was Will*, she thought) were sitting by idly, saying nothing. Hannah wasn't convinced they could speak. She saw intelligence in Sam's eyes—not the sharp light of brilliance by any stretch, but a steady glow of wherewithal. The other man, the larger one, had dead eyes. Man had likely never lived in the present his whole life, imprisoned by a malfunctioning brain.

Without preface, a low moan washed away the night's silence. Starting soft, then growing into a dense bellow, almost like the sad moan of a whale, but lower-toned. Lower than anything she had ever heard, in fact.

Everyone around the fire spun their heads toward the rocks—totally enrapt, nothing else existed to them, nothing but that mournful sound.

It grew louder and louder. A dome rising up and forming, then descending and cordoning them off from the rest of the world.

In the firelight, an impossibly large shadow appeared on the rocks.

Jesus Christ. This isn't possible.

It emerged and stood tall. In a strange way, the creature felt familiar. The explanation was simple: she'd already seen its likeness back at the cabin. Jesse's father's rendering had been pitch-perfect. Not a detail lacking. Its limbs were wiry, barely held together by meager strands of flesh. But there was strength there, she could sense it. Like the thing could scale a mountainside in an instant, its long limbs pulling its light frame up to the top with ease. Drooping skin, as if melting, lay below two gleaming yellow spheres—four times the size of an owl's, possessing four times the knowledge.

Thunderstruck, she stared at it.

The others were on their knees, genuflecting, paying homage to their God. Then, without a word, Jesse pointed down the trail toward Tom's body.

The creature bent down, then jumped higher than any human could ever dream of. He landed near Tom, light on his feet, not making so much as a sound.

Many sounds followed though. Horrible ones. The wet sucking of flesh and gristle through teeth and the crack and crunch of jaws biting clean through bone.

In death, Tom became a meal. Devoured by one of his favorite cryptids. It'd be funny if it wasn't so disgusting and sad.

This was her chance. She could try to run. Her captors were absolutely hypnotized by their God fallen to earth. She might not make it, but at least she'd die fighting.

Truth was, though, she didn't feel like moving because deep down, she could feel herself being drawn by the creature. Reeled in like a fresh catch. It had a magnetism, a force that at once put her at ease and made her body and thoughts feel light as a feather. Like she was stretched out relaxing on a cloud.

Within seconds, the Holler Owl returned and landed in front of her. Its disciples gathered around and got back down on their knees.

Backlit by the fire, the creature consumed her field of vision. He'd become her entire reality. Its low, whale-like moan soared, as it stretched its mouth open wide as a garage door. Inside, she saw everything. All of it. Every scenario. Every path. Every divergence. Her entire existence—and all of it yet to come—playing out like a film in its giant maw, projected off spherical walls. Her life's movie in a globe:

Run and die.

Submit, live among them, then escape, only to be committed by her parents.

Live with them, escape, and die.

On and on…

Or live with them, worship this creature, live to a ripe old age and be a part of something that actually mattered. Something of cosmic significance. Of true greatness. Well beyond the humanly matters of Earth.

In the movie, she'd seen the Holler Owl right alongside her, watching over her, protecting her, ensuring that not a single ounce of harm would befall her. In exchange, it asked for complete obedience, and in due time, if the owl saw fit, it would tell her the hows and the whys. But now, the time had come for her to decide.

She didn't think much on it. The path forward was clear.

It was a chance to sit side by side with a God.

Who turns that down?

✿

Before it retired to the dark, they'd said a prayer to the creature. She didn't know the words yet, but she followed along, starting the process of memorizing it. The boys had decided to stay behind and camp; Brenda said they frequently did that after the feedings.

Walking back, Brenda said she was sorry about Tom. But they couldn't risk outsiders finding out. There was too much at stake.

Hannah said she understood. Her old self would've been disgusted. Crying and heaving and grieving her late husband. But she had a new love. A new purpose.

The Holler Owl had looked deep into her soul and she'd given herself over to it mind, body, and spirit.

Tom was dead and gone. A sacrifice ensuring her God could live on.

"Come on, let's get back to the cabin," Brenda said.

"Is that where y'all sleep?"

Brenda shook her head. "We've got an old farmhouse a couple miles from the cabin. Pretty big, actually. The boys are always working on it, fixing it up." They were walking side by side, holding hands. Newly-minted sisters of the faith. "They'll build you your own space. For now, you can bunk up with me."

- THE END -
ENJOYED THIS? CHECK OUT:
BLACK ECHOES
BY J.B. McLAURIN

MY VALUABLE HUNTING KNIFE

MAX PALERMO

A full tang of high-carbon steel, a smooth guard, diamond-like facets, and a stag antler handle. Sharp as a razor, strong as an axe. A veritable jewel of cutlery; a knife you could trust. The Puma Hunter wasn't worth a ton, but it meant a ton to Rob, the only object in his possession that belonged to his father Mick.

In the late seventies, Mick worked the Everglades—airboat tours, swamp buggy rides, alligator shows—and some mornings, before dawn, he and his buddies would load a dinghy with Coors Light and hunt the mangroves. He'd come home drunk with gators to skin and filet. Rob was a kid and thought it was the neatest thing. He'd help his dad wash the gators with soap and water, then disinfect them with bleach, all of which had to be done before Mick could skin his catch, removing thick scutes from the critter's back and saving the hide for the tanners. Then he'd flip the skinned carcass belly-up and start carving the swamp meat with his stag hunter. The tail fin, the jowls, the tenderloin and legs, careful not to pierce the stomach, which was full of bacteria that could infect the harvest. Rob loved his dad's deep-fried gator fingers, and most of all, his signature Key Lime dipping sauce.

Years later, in the mid-eighties, Rob and his mom, Nina, left Indiantown and moved closer to the coast. They'd left Mick behind too, who'd become a good-for-nothing drunkard, spending most of his days with his ass parked on a stool at the Tipsy Tiki. Everglades work was dirty work. Long hours slogging through the swamp under the blistering hot sun, ninety-eight percent humidity, and enough mosquitoes to make a man pray for the West Nile virus. With all the years of drinking and smoking, Mick's body couldn't do it anymore, and when Nina had had enough with his drinking and his smoking and all his self-loathing, she packed her bags, threw Rob in her Chrysler LeBaron, and moved out to her mother's condo near Tequesta. The day they left, Mick took Rob aside and handed him the Puma Hunter in an alligator skin sheath.

"This is yours now kid. Guard it with your life."

That was the last time Rob saw his dad alive.

⌘

Rob met Pauline outside a Metallica concert at the Miami Orange Bowl. By the late nineties, Metallica's merch had become so expensive that it spawned an entire cottage industry for unauthorized memorabilia and apparel. The day of the concert, the last stretch of road into the Orange Bowl had transformed into an impromptu bazaar, humming with tents and gazebos where glassy-eyed, tattooed vendors hawked t-shirts, stickers, patches, lighters, and all the assorted knick-knacks of the metal world.

Pauline saw Rob waiting to buy a shirt and was instantly attracted to his shaggy hair and strong jawline. He had grown into a handsome young man, taking after his father, spending much time outdoors, boating and hunting in the Turtle Creek Wetlands. He wore a John Deer hat and a faded Alice in Chains shirt, a wallet chain draped over his ratty blue jeans.

Rob grew up with Mick's Def Leppard and Iron Maiden records around the house, and then he graduated to Metallica, Exodus, Pantera, and so on. Heavy music made the young man feel connected to his father, whose absence and death were gaping stab wounds in the body of his life.

Pauline was from nearby Jupiter, a country bumpkin at heart but with a hard rock flair. She listened to Korn and Limp Bizkit when they first met, radio rock essentially, and she was taken by Rob's darker tastes in heavy metal. She had an innocent quality to her, the likes of someone who had never truly suffered loss, and her bright, curious disposition was very much complementary to Rob, who had a tendency to be stern, even sour at times. The two grew close, driving around Tequesta in Rob's Ford Bronco, smoking joints as one song bled into the next.

Rob was able to be open about his father with unassuming Pauline, about the airboat rides, the fishing trips, the gator fingers, all the good times, and then his sad decline. He told her all about the boozing and yelling, the holes in the wall, and finally, how the game warden had found him floating in the swamps near Indiantown one morning. Ivory white and bloated like a puffer fish, with gator bites covering his stomach, his neck, and worst of all, his face, which had been gravely disfigured, left looking like a tattered plastic bag of soggy chicken livers. The police assumed his death was an accidental drowning, since everyone in town knew Mick to be a drunkard, but the coroner's report indicated the cause of death to be blood loss sustained from alligator bites. Mick's death was ruled accidental, yet the irony wasn't lost on anyone:

"All them gator fingers finally caught up with him," the warden said to his deputy, "and I ain't talking high cholesterol."

Pauline listened generously and was a source of consultation for the young man. She had a simple way of disarming Rob with innocuous, cunicular remarks like,

"Well, honey, I ain't never tried gator before, maybe you can take me out and show me what all the fuss is about?"

The whole situation disturbed Pauline, frightened her even, but she put on a kind face, since she was head over heels for Rob, whose melancholic, often brooding disposition she found nearly irresistible. So, one night, Rob finally threw on a white polo, pulled his wild hair back into a ponytail, and took Pauline to a nice Old Florida restaurant on the beach—Casablanca—where Pauline tried gator for the first time. It wasn't the fresh-caught alligator and Key Lime dipping sauce Mick would make; it was an appetizer of gator bites, but they were deep-fried, seasoned well, and made muster for the night. Pauline loved the dish to her surprise, and she held dear that Rob had made a special effort to take her out for this particular meal. After dinner, the two sat on the sand to listen to the crashing of the waves as young lovers often do. Rob drew the Puma Hunter from its sheath and displayed it to Pauline as pearls of moonlight bounced along its contoured edges.

"Rob, what are you doing with that big knife?" Pauline asked, a tremble in her voice.

"Are you scared? Don't be crazy, Pauline, I ain't gonna hurt you. This was my dad's hunting knife. Really the only thing he ever gave me—it means a lot to me is all, and I just wanted to show it to you since we came out here to get you some gator after we talked about my dad and you told me you ain't never had none."

"Really, this was his knife? You had me worried there for a minute," Pauline said, taking the Puma into her hands. "I see how much your dad meant to you and how much his being gone hurts, and I think it's kinda sweet that you brought it out tonight. I think he must have loved you a lot to give you his knife, huh?"

"Maybe, something like that," Rob replied, "but it's mine now anyhow and as long as I have it, there's a part of him with me. I ain't never getting rid of it. It'll be with me til I die or give it to my own son."

"Well then, honey, you better get a move on if you want a son to give it to," Pauline said with a wink as they began to kiss on the sandy shore.

They spent the night making love on a beach towel with the Puma Hunter resting in its sheath just above their heads.

∽

Some years went by, and they stuck together, Rob and Pauline. Rented their own place in Tequesta—an Old Florida ranch, flat roof, seafoam green stucco, and a wide three-panel window that let plenty of natural light into the living room. Cute place. Pauline started working full-time at the Home Depot, and Rob got a decent job as a groundskeeper at Jonathan Dickinson State Park through Mr. Tobin, one of his father's old buddies from the Everglades. The couple spent their free time together at the beach, or going to concerts, watching movies, cooking. They smoked a little weed here and there, had a couple drinks too, but it was a quiet life, and a good life together. Nina would always pester Rob about getting married and cranking out a couple rugrats. She got along with Pauline well, and she thought Pauline was great for Rob. But Rob wasn't ready to marry, let alone have a family. He liked his life as it was, with few attachments, few entanglements outside Pauline, and he wasn't willing to decide on any big changes.

But as more time passed, something started to fester beneath the surface. In long-term relationships, there's often one party who pursues the other; in other words, one person loves the other more intensely, more passionately. It seems a rather natural phenomenon, but if that dynamic becomes too one-sided, too unequal and imbalanced, the fabric of the relationship will begin to fray. And Pauline was beginning to see the strands unravel, as if it were a given that she love Rob unconditionally, despite his unwillingness to take their relationship to the next level. Pauline wanted marriage, a family, and she wanted those things with Rob. But the man had become a little distant, and it had become difficult for Pauline to express those feelings to her partner. She felt as if she had to protect Rob somehow, since he had suffered and she hadn't; she felt it was her role to keep him content, to keep him stable. Their sex life suffered, their social life suffered, and most nights, Rob would finish dinner, go to his game room to play *Call of Duty* or sit on his phone with drone metal blasting in his earbuds—essentially dead to the outside world.

Pauline was becoming increasingly insecure, a little paranoid, asking herself, *well if he ain't even fucking me, is something else going on?* So, she looked through his phone one night when he'd passed out early, and not only did she see dozens of porn links in his search history, but she discovered he'd been paying cam girls on the regular, which stung bad. She tried to let it go but couldn't help but confront him, and when she did, Rob was embarrassed and apologetic. He'd been feeling the drag again, thinking about his dad, and he'd been retreating into himself. He promised the cam girls were "just a computer thing," a way to let off steam, and that he'd do better by her. Pauline forgave him, of course, because that was her nature, and things were good for a little while, but before long, the distance came back onto the horizon like that stretch of highway on the Seven Mile Bridge.

Rob started working longer hours at the park with the excuse that the rainy season called for more maintenance, since the rainstorms had flooded certain areas and knocked cypress trees onto the boardwalk that crossed into the swamps. Pauline hardly saw him for a couple of weeks, and she had a bad feeling the relationship was on its last legs. It was the weekend of the Fourth of July when things came to a head. Rob texted that he wasn't interested in going out to see the fireworks when she got home; instead, he told her they needed to have a serious talk. He was sitting on the bed when Pauline came through the door.

"Look, I know it ain't been right between us for a while, and I've been thinking a lot lately, so we need to talk," Rob said.

"OK, well let's talk then," Pauline responded.

"I just ain't been feeling good, Pauline—I've been thinking about my dad a lot again, feeling like a goddamn zombie at work, and it just ain't something I think I can fix right now—not now, not here."

"So, what are you saying?"

"I'm saying that I want to start a new life. Somewhere far away from here, somewhere I don't have to think about my dad every time I drive to work, every time I see a cattail, every time I see a goddamn gator in the swamp. Somewhere cold, maybe work on a fishing boat in Alaska or Greenland or somewhere—I just gotta get the fuck out of Florida, leave this shit behind."

"And where's that leave us?" Pauline said with a frog in her throat.

"Pauline, you know I care about you, but it ain't been right between us for a while, and I can't give you what you want. I ain't ready to get married, be a father—I got my own demons to handle. I got to figure out this whole thing with my dad, and I think I gotta do it alone."

She had heard enough and reached her breaking point, yelling, "You selfish little boy! I been there to hold your hand, while you bitch and whine about your daddy! For years! Get over it! Your daddy's dead, Rob, but I'm here! I been here! And what about me? You ever stop to think about me? Everything I done for you, waiting for you to wake up and see what's right in front of you? I can't..."

Pauline started to sweat. She could feel the goosebumps forming on her arms, and the blood pulsing through her arteries, the nerve endings bristling all the way down to her toes. Something strong had come over her, a surging energy she'd never felt on her body. She leaped to his dresser, grabbed the Puma, and stabbed it into the mattress as hard as she possibly could, burying the knife down to the hilt, a few inches from his toes. She looked up at him, and her eyes were frigid and reptilian, devoid of love and any sign of human warmth.

"This is your bride, huh? Your daddy's knife? Your pride and joy? Then go on, take it with you 'til you die,' just like you told me, til you die alone, somewhere cold."

⊗⊗

Stupid fucking knife. All he cares about is that stupid fucking hunting knife. And I know he was fucking that little skank Lora at the park. Rainy season bullshit, yeah right, he was fucking her all that time. I loved him, I actually loved him, I can't believe I wasted all that time on this loser. And now what? What the fuck do I do? Did he even consider that? He ain't never really asked me nothing about me, about what I wanted. It was always me, me, me. Real piece of work like his daddy.

Pauline grumbled angrily in a hazy state of hypnagogia. As she opened her eyes and came fully into consciousness, she was surprised to be sitting in her Jeep Grand Cherokee, off the shoulder of what looked like an interstate. A road sign up ahead read: Ten Miles to Tequesta. She had no memory of how she got there. The last thing she remembered was slamming Rob's bedroom door. She opened the glovebox, reached for a pack of Marlboro Silvers and a lighter. Lit a smoke and took a deep drag—she had quit six months previous but hadn't had the strength to throw away her last pack, keeping cigs in her glovebox in case of an emergency. She turned on her car, merged onto the interstate, and began to drive home.

It was late morning when Pauline got back to the house, and she was a little anxious to see Rob's Bronco still parked in the driveway. She knew he had to be at work that morning and assumed he must have called out because of the previous night's blow-up. She was worried it was going to be round two, thinking to herself, *here we go again.* When she walked in, the house was quiet. She didn't immediately see Rob, not in the kitchen nor on the living room sofa. She walked to his bedroom, knocked gently on his door, and then opened it. There he was, lying on the bed, a look of serenity on his face. His body sat atop a wet satin sheet of cruor; he had been utterly gored to death.

The wall was like a monochrome Jackson Pollock mural. Multidirectional lines of textured splatter covered the room in tiny bubbles of sanguine red from floor to ceiling. He had been stripped to his boxers, and his torso, arms, and legs were ridden with countless wounds of varying size and shape: from little nips to profound ovular gashes still pulsing with blood. The remains of his stomach, which had been mangled from repeated heavy prodding, were a soupy pulp of entrails and viscera through which his organs jutted like chunky hunks of meat in a vat of chili con carne. The Puma Hunter was stuck into the mattress, right as Pauline had left it the night before. Its stag antler handle, pristine, untarnished by a single drop of blood.

Pauline was in total shock—a mix of repulsion, dread, confusion, and sorrow. She went to the kitchen, dialed nine-one-one, and left the phone off the hook as she ran to her Jeep and drove off. When the police discovered Rob's body, they instantly suspected foul play and considered Pauline to be a prime suspect. The position of the body, the nature of the wounds, the splatter patterns, all ruled out the possibility of suicide. No one, the police reasoned, would be capable of inflicting such damage on themselves.

The hunting knife, however, confounded investigators. *Why would she leave behind the murder weapon? And how had she managed to keep it so clean?* DNA analysis detected no trace of Rob's blood on the blade. Forensic experts are aware of methods for removing DNA from a weapon through precise chemical means, but given the passionate nature of the crime, police found it highly improbable that a woman like Pauline, with no prior criminal record or history of violence, could commit the crime and clean the weapon in the time elapsed between Rob's death and the discovery of his body by authorities. Nina, Rob's mom, even defended Pauline, telling police that she was a good person, that she loved her son, and that she could not imagine the girl committing such a heinous act of violence. Still, police found it extremely incriminating that Pauline had chosen to flee the scene. In the end, Rob's death was deemed a homicide; the case however remained unsolved with Pauline at large and no other persons of interest under investigation.

Pauline was last spotted eight weeks after the murder, buying cigarettes at a gas station in Dayton, Ohio. Police were unable to apprehend her and believed she was headed toward the Canadian border. The suspected murder weapon, the Puma Hunter, was locked away in the evidence room at the Tequesta Police Station in the event that Pauline ever decided to come forward for questioning.

– THE END –
ENJOYED THIS? CHECK OUT:
PERSEPHONE'S ESCALATOR
BY JOE TAYLOR

THIS POEM (EDITED BY SLEY HOUSE'S NEWEST EMPLOYEE AMELIA HIRSCH), IS A HORRIFYING LYRICAL PEAK INTO THE INSATIABLE WALKING DEAD. TAKE A QUICK BITE OF THE TERRIFYING STANZAS OF . . .

UNWANTED ADVANCES

KC GRIFANT

The day is like any other:
the moaning Undead strain
against the fence.
She fights the urge
to run, forces herself
to walk, to not
Overexcite.

They are sensitive,
prone to distraction,
the sight of moving flesh
sets them on edge.
The zombies hurl offerings,
things she does not want:
Dried chunks of muscle, flaps of skin, a broken tooth.

Feting her, their inevitable
feast.
The fence wavers,

always on the verge
of bursting,
of showering her
with their wanton needs.

She has long cultivated carefulness
but the sun smolders the sky,
smug as a golden-toothed grin,
when the fence finally falls.

Steel wire warps and breaks:
an endlessly widening metal smile.

Her pistol pops while the masses swarm her;
the kickoff to a banquet, jubilant.

Dozens of rotten heads exude eau de toilette
of degraded leather and roadkill.

Fingers tipped with maggots snatch what they can,
consuming and consummating, never satiated.

Fingernails peel her skin, eager as a bereft housewife
tearing into Tiffany-blue wrapping.

One Undead lifts his head
with a ruby beard made from her innards.

The bliss of frenzied frenetic eating
transforms to rage on its half-formed face.

It is her failure to fully quell his hunger,
its eyes say.

She took every precaution.
to stave off their starvation.

But now her scream unspools,
succumbs to their enraged embrace.

– THE END –
ENJOYED THIS? CHECK OUT:
MELPOMENE'S GARDEN
BY CURTIS HARRELL

GREETINGS GHOSTS AND GHOULS, GET YOUR SUNSCREEN AND HATS ON BECAUSE TODAY WE GO ON VACATION. TERRORIZING HUMANS IS HARD WORK AND YOU ALL DESERVE A BREAK TOO. BUT DON'T GET TOO COMFORTABLE IN THE SAND, YOU NEVER KNOW WHEN SOMETHING UNEXPECTED MIGHT CRASH THE PICNIC AND TURN A DULL OUTING INTO A NIGHTMARE.

WHAT REMAINS

SHELLEY LAVIGNE

Catalog of the Museum of the First Age Collection – Remnants of pre-contact civilization,

Sub collection: firsthand accounts of contact (non-military)

Objects from Collection #CG45 (Tobrouk Beach, Crete, destroyed settlement)

Note: The following items were found tied together with a rubber band, assumed to belong to the same individual

Item #CG45.1 – Canadian passport for Emmanuelle Watts, expiry date 07/05/2027

Item #CG45.2 – Diary (likely belonging to Timothy Watts)

[Transcript follows]

June 5th

I get to skip the last month of 5th grade because Mom wanted to take me on vacation and she said it's too hot in Greece during July and August to go then. My classmates are so jealous of me. Most of them haven't travelled outside Canada before.

I have to write ten sentences per day because mom says it's a good "souvenir". So much for vacation, if I have homework that's school.

Mom said she'll buy me a phone as a reward if I do it.

I flew on a plane for the first time. It was cool but also super noisy. Planes are never that noisy on TV. Dad let me borrow his big headphones so that was nice, but mom kept taking pictures of me wearing them. It was kind of embarrassing.

Oops, I wrote too much.

Timothy

Dear Mittens,

Your first plane ride! You did so great! You're my brave boy! You looked so silly wearing your dad's headphones. They were as big as your face! Aren't you so excited to be in a whole other country?

XO

Mom

June 6th

Apparently, mom is reading and writing in here too. Not sure why she can't get her own journal instead of stealing mine.

We got here very early this morning. I don't really like planes. My tummy was full of gas and it didn't help.

This house is small, way smaller than mine. It's white on the outside and it has blue shutters. It smells a little weird.

My friends would be jealous though, cause it would be great if we got attacked by zombies. You could just close the shutters to protect yourself and there's a little enclosed backyard so you could grow food.

See mom, I can be positive.

I wrote too much again.

Timothy

Because the pressure of the air is lower when you are high up in the air, gas in your body expands and needs to be let out. So, you end up farting more. Fun fact: Broccoli can make you fart so I guess you have an excuse not to eat broccoli when you're on a plane!

Dad

June 7th

Mom took me to see some old castle, Knossos (but you don't say the K). I thought it was going to be a normal castle but there's not much there, just some columns and a bunch of smashed pottery on the ground. It wasn't that impressive. Mom kept telling me how old it is (as if I couldn't tell). It's all smashed up. It's gotta be old.

Mom's Greek is bad. And she says she didn't have enough time for lessons before we left. I think it's more cause she knows that school sucks and didn't want to do special school as an adult.

Some old ladies taught me how to say hello: Geia. Soon, I'm gonna be better at Greek than mom.

Timothy

Dear Mittens,

I'm so glad I got to spend some quality time with my big boy. I know the castle was not what you expected but hopefully you still had fun.

Love you lots,

Mom

Mom, please stop calling me by that kiddie nickname. I'm eleven.

Timothy

June 7ᵗʰ Extra bonus night-time entry:

The coolest thing happened!

I saw a shooting star tonight. I was sitting on the little balcony with dad. He let me stay up a bit later cause I'm on vacation (mom thinks I should be going to bed early so I won't be too tired to do activities. Mom is no fun sometimes. Mom you are no fun sometimes.

We watched the stars and talked about man things and then… I saw a shooting star! I bet Jamie would have LOST IT!

I NEVER saw one before! It goes really fast! I know it's a kiddie thing to do but I made a wish. I can't say for what because then it won't come true.

Tim

June 8ᵗʰ

There were pictures of the meteor (that's what scientists call shooting stars) all over the news. The news people were all pretty excited except for one guy who seemed scared.

It looks like it landed in Italy (it looks like a boot). I wish it would have fallen here, that would have been so cool! Italy is super close to Greece, so we were so close!

Better luck next time.

We tried to go for a car ride after ice cream but I just ended up getting sick so we had to come back home.

June 9ᵗʰ

The meteor was in the news again. On TV, I saw some guys getting out of a van wearing yellow suits. When they got close there was a bunch of smoke and then this loud metal noise started and I think I saw a black thing in the smoke. I think it's maybe aliens! They're so close by! The kids at school are going to be so jealous that I was so close to REAL LIFE ALIENS.

Maybe someone will study my journal someday and it will be super important to history!

Anyways, Dad unplugged the TV in the living room and brought it up to his bedroom and that SUCKS! Even if it's an old TV and I can't understand Greek.

This is why I need a phone.

We went to the beach today and it was almost empty.

It's kind of lonely here. I wish Jamie was here too. I miss him, even if dad says he's not a good person to be friends with.

Mom, please don't show this to dad.

Dearest woolen mittens,

I'm sorry that you're lonely. You're just a little homesick. Maybe next time we go to the beach you can make some friends!

Your dad loves you very much. He just knows that kids tend to bully people who are different, like Jamie. He wants you to be happy and safe.

XOX Mom

June 10th

The old guy next door was hammering early and it woke me up. When we left the house to go get groceries, I saw his windows were all boarded up. A lot of the houses are boarded up, folks even put boards over the shutters.

The grocery store was kind of empty and the stuff that was there was different than the stuff in stores back home. The person at the cash register wasn't very nice to mom. He was shouting in Greek. He kept saying something about Euros. Mom ended up having to get money out of her money belt to pay even though she always says never to show our money belt to other people.

In the streets, dad kept talking about how we got "ripped off" and how he was "going to give that crook a piece of my mind".

We didn't go to the beach today. Mom made me do some of my school exercises.

June 11ᵗʰ

Mom and dad were fighting this morning. I guess my shooting star wish didn't come true.

I tried to listen at their door but dad caught me. I don't know where the creaky spots are in this house. It sucks that I can't sneak around like back home.

It is really hot but mom said we have to keep the windows closed even during the day.

I didn't get to go to the beach again today. Mom made me do school work. When does real vacation start?

June 12ᵗʰ

Last night, there was noise outside. It sounded like the whistle before fireworks. I couldn't get my windows unlatched to see what it was.

I know that I'm getting pretty old, so I shouldn't be scared but I was. And I think my parents are too.

They're fighting again. I heard mom say "We're lucky. They haven't crossed over onto any of the islands. We'll be okay." I think they're talking about the aliens. I guess they think the aliens are bad or something cause they usually are in stories and TV and stuff. But it's not like we've seen them being bad. Mom always says just because something is bad on TV that doesn't mean it's bad in real life. She says that's prejudice.

They try not to fight in front of me but I can tell when they do because they talk quietly and pretend to smile but it doesn't look right.

I asked to go to the beach and dad told me to "act like a man". Mom said "I'm just a kid".

I don't know which one is better. I don't like when adults call me a kid but dad has been saying that I should act like a man a lot lately. Ever since what happened with Jamie. And he said it again when I cried after he told me we couldn't be friends. "A man doesn't act like this."

Is it because grown-ups don't have friends?

June 13th

WE WENT TO THE BEACH TODAY!

There were still some people but not very many. The adults were drinking some ooze-o (mom says it tastes like black licorice which is gross) and beers and wine. The soldiers with really big guns asked them to calm down. The soldiers also came to talk to us and one could speak a bit of English, so he and dad went away to talk.

Dad said the soldier thinks we should turn off the lights after it's dark now. I wanted to ask why but dad gave me his "no more questions" face. Besides, I know why.

June 14th

Dad went out early this morning and came back with groceries. He mostly bought weird canned fish. It's not like tuna back home.

The fish still had their heads and tails attached. I chewed a lot so they would not come back to life in my tummy in case they became zombies or something.

Dad also bought newspapers but he hid them in his room. It's not like I can read them or anything.

They aren't really reading my journal anymore so I guess I could stop writing in it but I kinda like it now. It's like I'm talking to someone.

I did some school stuff today cause I got bored. Only nerds do school for fun on a vacation.

June 15th

Dad's gone to church although mom pointed out how silly that was because he won't understand anything. Mom is napping on the couch so I'm going to try to see if I can find the newspapers.

. . .

The pictures weren't even clear. I mean it looks like there's some kind of creature or thing coming out of the meteor but it's so blurry. It reminded me of that video Will showed us to prove that bigfoot is real. I can't tell why my parents are hiding this from me.

The date of the newspapers was the 10th. If I had a phone, I bet I could find dad much better and more recent pictures.

June 16th

We tried to go to the beach again today but the army has set up barricades and tents. We saw a whole bunch of boats in the water and there were groups of people standing around near the tents. I asked mom what was going on. She ignored me and made us go back home.

It looked like people were coming into the island, not leaving.

Dad started boarding up the windows downstairs. I asked him if he had permission to do that but he also ignored me. It's like I'm a ghost now.

I heard mom say "We're safe here, they don't go on the water" and dad said "I'm not worried about the aliens."

Dad is brave.

June 17th

It was noisy last night. I couldn't sleep.

I'm not sure what we're going to do today. Mom got me to pack all my stuff "just in case".

I found a box of colour pencils so I've started drawing on the walls in my closet. I'm drawing a castle where I'm the king and I can protect everyone from the monsters.

. . .

I got woken up by a loud crash in the middle of the night. Dad ran in my room and told me to stay there and then ran back out. There was crashing and banging on the stairs and mom ran in and grabbed me and held me hard against her and we hid in the closet. She held me so hard it hurt.

There was a whole bunch of crashing and banging and screaming. It sounded like dad and someone else too. Then after a bit the noises got quieter and stopped. I wanted to go see but mom wouldn't let me go. When the closet door opened, she screamed so I screamed too.

It was just dad.

He was covered in blood there was blood on his hands but also his chest and his face. It dripped from his knuckles on the floor. The house was silent, so was the street. I could hear it, like the water dripping from a leaky faucet.

Mom shouted at him for not cleaning himself up before coming in. He said he figured she would rather know he was alive than tidy. Then he stomped out.

Mom kept hugging me and crying until the sun rose.

June 18th

I can't stop staring at the bruises and cuts on dad's knuckles.

There's also a body in the backyard. Dad covered him with a yellow sheet with daisies on it like the one on my bed. There are some blood stains on the sheet. Mom says the glass coffee table is smashed so I'm not allowed in the living room. I think it's probably because there's blood everywhere.

I keep hearing mom and dad whisper talk about airplanes. At least they're fighting over important stuff now.

. . .

Mom came in my room all frantic this afternoon, she thought someone broke in and stole me but she found me in the closet with my drawing. I told her what it was. She was crying a lot and at first, I thought it was because she was upset that I had done something so childish and silly like drawing on the walls but then she told me that it was because she also wishes she could build a castle with walls as high as the sky and keep me safe.

I reminded her that the meteor fell from the sky so even that wouldn't help.

Dad yelled at me later for making mom even more sad.

June 19ᵗʰ

The sky was all bright again and there were loud bangs. I managed to sneak and listen at my parents' door. They said they aren't sure if it was aliens or missiles.

The power is out now. The light switches don't work and the fridge wasn't cold this morning.

We packed food and some clothes and filled some big jugs with water. Dad says we're going on a hike for fun. He tried to sound cheery but it was so fake.

Mom says there's an army base not that far away, that they'll have guns and generators and stuff. At least she's telling me the truth. Dad thinks he's protecting me by lying even if he wants me to be a man.

The sheet had blown off the dead man in the backyard when I went out to check. His chest was kind of puffy and his face was a mess. He didn't look like he was sleeping like when folks die on TV, he looked really dead and it made me feel dizzy. There were flies all over him and he smelled super bad so I'm not sure why the bugs went in so close. The smell almost made me throw up. I got worried that it made me stink but mom or dad didn't say anything.

I keep hearing the flies still buzz even now that I'm inside.

I packed some clothes and this book. I closed the closet door on my kingdom.

Dad says we're leaving tomorrow morning.

June 20ᵗʰ

We're sitting in a grove of orange trees.

My feet hurt. But the oranges taste really good.

There were some noises like on the TV last night. I think maybe some aliens landed here too.

I know my parents are scared but I still think it might be cool to see an alien from outer space! I wonder what their planet looks like.

June 22nd

I don't want to see another alien. I didn't see much before mom covered my eyes. It looked dark, it had a lot of arms or what looked like arms but they were much longer and bent in a bunch of places. Like a spider and a squid had a baby.

It was chasing after a family that was running on the street. Mom and Dad lay over me and hid us in the grass next to the road. I could hear the noise it made, it sounded like metal screeching. The family screamed a lot and then they stopped screaming.

We didn't move for so long, even way after it got quiet. When my parents let me go, the sky was dark.

Dad says we'll be at the base tomorrow.

I don't want to walk anymore.

June 23rd

It's my fault.

I was asking for food and dad was telling me to wait and the aliens must have heard me complaining and so they came and they got him and mom grabbed me and pulled me away and I didn't even get to say sorry and mom wouldn't tell me if they bit him or swallowed him whole. I tried to tell her that if they swallowed him whole then maybe he can fight his way out because Will says if you swallow a bee whole it can sting you on the inside so maybe he's okay.

But then the soldiers showed up. They were in a big truck. I told them not to shoot, that dad might be alive in there and if they shoot the alien, they might kill my dad but they didn't listen. Maybe they didn't understand me.

And mom just kept telling me to hush but I couldn't and I just kept screaming. I tried to stop but I couldn't.

And then it went black.

Now my head and my tummy hurt. It feels worse than when I was on the plane and I know dad would be able to explain why but he won't be able to anymore cause the army shot him full of holes.

.

. . .

.

. . . .

June 24th

We're still with the army. They took us in for a bit although mom has been arguing a lot with one of the guys who speaks a little English. I know they're talking about me.

I tried to go see if I could find dad but the soldiers found me sneaking away and dragged me back.

Mom was really worried and gave me a dad-level scolding. Mom says the soldiers won't take us to safety if we don't behave ourselves.

June 25th

The soldiers have a boat. Mom says it's going to bring people from the island back to the mainland where there are more soldiers and military bases to keep us safe. The boat is apparently full but mom says she got us a spot.

Mom gave me the money belt and my passport and her ring and she'll hold onto my journal. She says it's cause I'm better at keeping the important stuff safe but I'm not a dummy I know what this means.

Mom, please don't leave me. I'd rather be with you then with some soldiers. Dad's already gone please don't leave me too! I love you mom!

Days since I last saw Mittens (57 tally marks)

Dearest Mittens,

I've been trying to build a boat but it's a lot harder than it seems to find supplies. There are other boats are being guarded by gangs that have pretty much taken over now that the military is gone.

I'm sorry I couldn't go in with you but they didn't even want to take us in since we aren't citizens.

At least they ended up taking you. At least you might be okay. I hope you're okay. It's definitely safer on the mainland with the soldiers keeping you safe than here.

When I read your journal it's like you're still here with me. I'm sorry you saw us fighting; I'm sorry we took you on this vacation. I love you so much even if I'm not always perfect.

I'll find you once this is all over.

– THE END –
ENJOYED THIS? CHECK OUT:
THE CARTOGRAPHY DOOR
BY SEAN EDWARD

ALLURING

CASSANDRA DAUCUS

Dead leaves squelched under Sue's feet, their crunching days long behind them. She breathed deeply, her lungs filling with fresh air, heavy with the scent of pleasant decay and only slightly tinged with salt. Her hands clutched on the nothing in her pockets, and she wished that Fred had brought her Walkman along with her jacket when he'd swept her out of the house. As they walked the half-mile down the road she distracted herself from the hollow feeling in her chest by focusing on her senses. The chill of the air against her cheeks, the soft illumination of the sky through the trees, the tang of the ocean as they left the woods and picked their way down the slope to the craggy expanse of the tide pools.

Sue followed Fred, stepping carefully to keep from slipping on the worn soles of her rain boots. She squinted across the rocky plain, which was located at the awkward convergence of the woods, a small cliff, the beach, and the ocean. At high tide the plain would flood, but at low tide the water receded, leaving behind indentions filled with brine and all the creatures who thrive in it.

As she took her first steps onto the rock, she had the sense that something was wrong; even more wrong than usual. There weren't any seagulls feeding at the pools today, although Sue could hear them screeching down the beach. Their absence seemed ominous, and made her feel strange. Like she was haunted by nothing. It didn't stink quite as much as it had the last time they'd had to go to the pools, either, just a few weeks before. Although Sue didn't much like going to the pools she'd never minded the smell. It was a secret smell. Like whatever was revealed when the tide went out wasn't meant to be perceived by humans and was rebelling at their intrusion. She wondered if it smelled stronger down where the seagulls screamed, and wished she could join them.

The tide was on its way back in, but despite the hours it had been uncovered, the ground was slick, thanks to the seaweed blanket and intermittent rain. Fred wandered slowly, not pausing to glance into the pools but instead staring out towards the gray horizon. Sue padded along beside him, peering into each pool as they passed.

After a few minutes Fred paused and pulled a battered pack of cigarettes out of his jacket pocket. The wind was strong, but he managed to light his smoke with a cardboard match after a couple of tries. He carefully wrapped the failed matches in a tissue before tucking it all back in his pocket. Sue stood next to him, shivering in the chilly breeze and taking what warmth she could from breathing in the acrid smoke.

"I'm sorry. I know you don't like coming here." He sighed, puffs of white blowing out his nose like he was a dragon that had given up on making fire and was accepting whatever it could get. "I just… I like remembering her, you know?"

Sue shuffled, her gut clenching in an uncomfortable knot, and remained silent.

"I wish, I wish…" He glanced down, caught her eye, and gave her a sad smile. "I wish things could be different."

Sue stomped a foot into a pile of seaweed, which squished pleasingly, releasing a nice gush. "I wish Mom and Dad would stop fighting."

Fred scoffed, then lifted his foot so he could stub out the cigarette on the sole of his boot. "They're not fighting, Sue. I need you to understand that. He's beating her up. He's a fucking bully who gets off on hurting his family." He wrapped the butt in the tissue with the matches. She admired his profile. His nose was crooked since the summer before, when Dad had one of his whiskey nights. He didn't like to look at himself in the mirror now, but she thought it looked nice.

"If Chelle—" Sue started, but he cut her off with a glare.

"If Chelle was here he'd still be doing it. Hell, maybe he'd be even worse. You were so little you don't remember, but he was like this before she died. Maybe not as bad, but he was. Her being alive wouldn't change him." He rubbed a hand across his face, his expression pained. "Mom deserves better, and so do you. Please promise me you'll never let someone treat you the way he treats her, no matter how much they say they love you."

Fred looked down at Sue so earnestly, but it took her a moment for her to reply. Some of her friends had started having crushes; they put up posters of actors and singers they pulled out of Teen Beat, and talked about the cute boys in the upper grades. Jennifer, who just turned fourteen, even had a boyfriend in high school—a senior, like Fred. But Sue wasn't there yet. She just wanted to hang out with her friends; she barely even noticed boys in the way that it seemed her friends did, the way that they expected her to. But even so, it wasn't a hard promise to make. Sue wouldn't want to be treated the way Dad treated Mom, by anybody at all.

"I promise."

He nodded, satisfied, and patted her on the shoulder before wandering towards the larger pools, closer to the cliff.

Sue followed him slowly, trying not to think too hard about the sister-shaped hole between them.

She concentrated on the pools. She moved from one to the next, cataloging the little animals in each. Fewer than the last time, she was sure. There'd been an oil spill up in Alaska; one of the reasons Dad was so angry now was that the spill was affecting the catches down here. Fewer fish, less money. Less money, angry Dad. Angry Dad… Well.

That could be why the pools were so empty. Maybe instead of coming in to visit, the critters were dying out in the ocean. It didn't make her happy, but it explained things.

She was pleased to find that there were still some treasures to be found. One pool contained a couple of orange starfish and a handful of limpets, another a larger gray starfish and a few tiny silver fish darting from edge to edge. One was lined with purple anemone. Sue carefully reached out and touched one tiny anemone tentacle, as gently as she could. The barbs were too small for her to really feel; they weren't painful, yet they still held her skin when she tried to pull away. She tugged harder, freeing herself, and the anemone curled in on itself as though giving itself a little hug, like it was lonely, too, and sad to see her go.

Every pool was another little world, existing alongside but wholly independent from the one next to it. Until the tide would rise, mixing everything up, only to recede again, making new communities in the same little pools. Sue wondered what it would be like to get out of her little pool, here on the coast. To move to Seattle, or maybe even Los Angeles. Out of the pool, into the ocean. Maybe things would be better there.

Sue was rocked out of her reverie when Fred started yelling. He stood under the cliff, bent over with his hands on his knees. It reminded her of how he'd yelled when Chelle'd fallen in, and the thought made her gorge rise. She ran over as quickly as she dared, avoiding the larger patches of seaweed and jumping over smaller pools. He didn't seem to realize she was close until she was almost there. "Sue, no!" He attempted to block her view of the pool he was standing beside, but it didn't work.

A body was lying in the pool. It was small, smaller than Sue, and floating on its back. Masses of red hair drifted out from the head like a ginger halo, and the green corduroy skirt formed a bubble on the surface, not quite yet soaked enough to sink.

Sue's heart froze. "Chelle?" How could it be Chelle? She'd been dead for seven years.

Fred grabbed her into a bear hug, turning her head away and holding it close to his chest. His voice shook as he scolded her. "What the hell? That's not Chelle. Why would you say that?"

Sue couldn't remember the last time Fred hugged her that way. Years and years, probably. Before Chelle died, maybe. She gave herself a moment to relax into it, to enjoy the warmth and strength of her brother's arms, before twisting so she could turn her head.

"Sue…" His voice contained a warning, but he didn't stop her.

Sue looked into the pool again, and released a long sigh. It wasn't Chelle in the pool. There was a body, but it looked nothing like Chelle and Sue wasn't sure what her brain did to make her think it was her sister. This was a woman's body—not as old as Mom, but older than Miss Gibbons, who was Sue's student teacher for math in seventh grade. Miss Gibbons had golden hair, and she wore makeup that made her eyes sparkle. She smelled like oranges. Sue had an A in math but she'd done some after-school tutoring with Miss Gibbons, just so she could be close to her.

The woman was lying face up. She had long hair that would probably shine gold in the sun, like Miss Gibbons's, but wet and with the overcast sky, it looked much darker. Her face was nice, with a small nose and wide blue eyes and a mouth that was red and reminded Sue of a rosebud.

Sue catalogued all these things, but the very first thing that Sue noticed was that the woman was naked. Totally naked, with smooth pale skin, dark nipples, and clutches of dark hair between her legs and barely visible where her arms met her shoulders.

She was also, without a doubt, very dead.

"She's dead," Sue said, her voice muffled by Fred's coat.

"I know."

"Do you know her?"

Fred shook his head. "I've never seen her before in my life."

"She's naked."

"I *know*. Dammit, Sue." He was still shaking, but he slowly released her. He patted his pockets, rocked from foot to foot, ran his hands through his long brown curls. Their dad said Fred's hair made him look like a pussy but Sue thought it was pretty.

"Should we go get—"

"Fuck!" Fred yelled, stomping, his voice echoing around the plain. "FUCK! *Fuck!*"

Sue took a step back, stricken. She couldn't remember the last time Fred had yelled at her.

"I'm sorry." He rebounded quickly, using his usual quiet voice but she could tell he was working hard to keep it that way. He rested trembling hands on her shoulders and turned her to face him. "You're right, you need to go get someone."

"I…" His wording struck her, and she looked back at the path where they came in, yards and yards away, over at the edge of the woods. The sky responded to her glance by ticking one shade of gray darker, and a gust of wind blew in from the water. "Me? No, you come with me." She didn't want to go alone. Not across the plain, not through the woods, and not home. *Definitely* not home. The corners of her eyes pricked. "I can't—"

Fred leaned down into her face, his brown eyes wide and serious. "You can, Susie. Go to the Johnsons' house. You can almost see it from here." She glanced back, and although she was sure their neighbor's house—the one at the end of the road, and closest to the water—was too far in the woods to see, she could imagine that she did see the white edge of their slanted roof.

"But I don't want to go alone." The pricking turned to tears, wet tracks that almost felt good against her cheeks before Fred's fingers smeared them around and just made her colder.

"Susie, I can't… I can't leave her alone."

Sue swallowed around the lump in her throat and gazed into her brother's face, imagining that he was reliving the same memory she was. Chelle, floating face-down in a tide pool, a smear of blood along its lip, the shallow water slowly turning pink. Her laugh and the crack of her skull had still echoed over the cries of the seagulls and the far-off pulse of the waves working their way up the beach.

Fred had wanted to pull Chelle out, but Sue was crying, hysterical—she remembered this, being confused and sad and not understanding, but knowing that something terrible had happened to her sister. Fred had made the decision to leave Chelle there and go get help, instead of waiting for someone else to come to them, which he knew could have taken hours.

When they'd returned, the tide was high, and Chelle was gone. She'd washed out to sea; her body had never been found.

"Would that be so bad?" Sue whispered. "If we left her alone and she wasn't here when we came back? We could forget this ever happened."

She prayed silently for him to see reason, and there was a moment when his face cleared and she thought he was going to say yes. But then he looked in her eyes again, and shook his head.

"No. If it was you, I wouldn't want you to be left alone. So I'm not going to leave her alone."

"Fred—"

"I'm *not*."

"Okay."

A gust of wind ruffled her hair like frigid fingers, and Sue shivered, wishing Fred had picked up her heavier coat.

"You can do it, Sue. It's just right across the pools. The Johnsons'll let you use their phone. Call 911, then come back. It'll take ten minutes, maybe fifteen. Okay? And I'll be right here."

Sue steeled herself. "Okay."

Don't try to pull her out, she didn't say. She knew that's what he regretted the most, that he didn't pull Chelle out of the water; that he left her alone. Later, she'll wonder if things might have been different, if she'd said it out loud.

One last glance at the body, and one final feeble smile for Fred, and Sue set off across the rocky plain. She breathed carefully, forcing calmness through her veins when all she wanted to do was run back and hold onto her brother as tightly as she could. But he needed this, she understood that. Maybe doing this would help him, and the best thing she could do was to let it happen.

Sue walked quickly but as carefully as always, stepping around the piles of seaweed and not pausing to examine any of the pools. When she was almost to the slope she glanced back. Fred looked so small and far away, under the shelter of the cliff. He was crouching next to the pool, staring into it and smoking a cigarette. The clouds were beginning to churn, the ocean becoming angry, and Sue knew she needed to be quick. But she couldn't help but take a moment to watch him. Just a few seconds. Then she waved, even though he wasn't looking at her. She turned back, took one step, and was halted by the sound of a splash behind her. Annoyance bubbled in her chest.

"Fred!" She yelled, swinging around. "What—" But whatever she was going to say died on her lips.

Fred wasn't there.

Breathless, Sue ran back to the tide pool, not caring about the seaweed sliding under her feet. When she peered in, only the dead woman stared up at her. A gust of wind played across the water, making the woman's hair sway slightly. She looked the same, Sue thought. Maybe… maybe her foot was at a different angle? But Sue hadn't paid a great deal of attention to her feet when she'd looked at her earlier. Sue also thought her lips were too red. Shouldn't they be blue? Isn't that what happens when you drown? But maybe she only fell in a few minutes before they arrived. Anyway, he obviously wasn't in there with her, and the dead woman wasn't going to help Sue figure out what had happened to her brother.

She glanced at the nearby pools, but although they all contained a bit of life, none of them contained her brother's radiance. Something tickled the hair at the back of Sue's neck, and she glanced around, first at the cliff, then towards the beach, as though Fred might jump out from some hidden place with a shout of "Surprise!" Like it was all some great joke.

But that wasn't something he would do, and there was no Fred. It was just Sue, the dead woman, and the tide pools. The lingering odor of cigarette smoke tickled her nose.

"Fred!" she yelled, her voice echoing as his had just minutes before. "Fred! FRED!" The only answer was the rumble of the waves, louder than they'd been a moment before, and the distant shriek of seagulls.

"Fuck." Sue was frozen with terror. Fred had been there, then he was gone. But there was nowhere for him to go. What the hell was she supposed to do?

She should leave, certainly. Do what Fred told her to do: Go to the Johnsons. Call an ambulance. The police. Get some grown-ups here to search for him.

But Fred hadn't wanted to leave the dead woman. He'd insisted she not be left alone. "If it was you, I wouldn't want you to be left alone." That's what he'd said.

Sue looked back at the dead woman, really looked at her. Did Fred see a reflection of his sister in this dead, naked woman? Both his sisters? It was an odd thought, and Sue didn't like it. Sue didn't particularly like the feelings the woman dredged up in her, either. Sue thought the dead woman was pretty, and she knew that was wrong. Wrong because she was dead, and wrong because she was a woman. Wrong, wrong, wrong. Dad would say that her looking at a naked woman was wrong, even though she'd seen the magazines he had tucked under his side of the mattress in the bedroom he shared with Mom.

Sue looked at the woman and thought about her friends— Jennifer, who was the first to wear a bra; Karen, who sometimes let Sue use her lip gloss; and Laura, who always showered after gym class. Sue wasn't brave enough to shower at school, but she would change into her school clothes in the corner nearest the showers and would occasionally catch glimpses of Laura, glistening under the spray. She knew that was wrong, too, but she didn't want to stop.

A soft rumble of thunder rolled in from just off shore, and Sue tore her gaze away. It was time to go. But only a moment later, her brain caught up with her eyes and she snapped back, certain she'd seen something odd.

And there it was: The dead woman's left eye was gone. Not closed, and not an open socket with no eyeball. It was like skin had grown over it when Sue had been distracted. There was no sign an eye had ever been there, no eyelashes or even an eyebrow.

A crash came from the direction of the ocean, and it was so shocking that Sue, long inured to sudden noises, jumped and screamed. The weather had shifted in the time she'd been standing there, lost in thought. The plain was growing darker by the moment, clouds billowing like black smoke as they rolled towards the land; the storm had nearly arrived. Waves lashed at the edge of the rock. It would soon be flooded, and when it did it would carry everything away, including her.

Sue looked back down at the woman, and her heart stuttered. This was no longer a woman, this was… some *thing*. Not only its eye, but its whole face had melted away. Its limbs, too, were losing definition, fingers and toes melding together so quickly that Sue could see it happen. It was sickening, and wrong. The legs began to fuse, starting at their apex, where the thatch of hair turned pink and thick before being sucked into the body, wriggling like a handful of earthworms.

Sue thought she might throw up. She wanted to run, was *desperate* to, but something about whatever was floating in the water wouldn't let her go. It was only when a line of ocean froth rolled over the toes of her boots and into the tide pool that she was knocked out of her thrall. When the seawater touched the still water of the pool, the thing *lunged*, switching color from pink to a luminescent black that made Sue's eyes hurt to look at. It whipped up as though to grab whatever it was that had touched the surface and whacked heavily against the rock next to her.

She ran. The ground was slick from the oncoming waves, and it was starting to rain, too. She tried so hard to avoid the seaweed, and to keep from falling into any of the pools; to ignore the slapping of the thing against the rock behind her. She pounded through the water, tears and raindrops filling her eyes, her mind focused on her poor, poor brother. What he must have seen, just before he died.

She somehow scrambled up the slope and reached the trees without falling, and only then did she turn around to look.

The creature was searching for her, but without her footsteps in the water it flailed. It wriggled and writhed and smacked the water with each incoming wave, but eventually it seemed to grow complacent, and lowered itself back down, disappearing under the surface.

Sue huddled shivering under a bush for hours while the rain fell and watched the tide come in, and watched it start to go out again. She had so many questions. The creature lived under the tide pools. How deep did it rest? How far was its reach, under the ground? Had it come here from out of the depths? Had it brought the foulness of the oil spill with it?

She thought about poor Chelle, who'd been left behind, and Fred who only wanted to do what was right and had apparently paid for it with his life. And her thoughts turned to Mom, how devastated she'd been when Chelle had gone. Fred was her only son; she'd have only Sue and Dad to console her. Sue wasn't much, but Dad was worse than nothing.

The storm had long since passed, and the moon rose. Sue rose, too, and made her way slowly towards home. She'd be back, though.

Mom would be sleeping. Dad was probably drunk, but Sue was hoping she could get him to help her look for Fred.

Right now.

Down at the tide pools.

- THE END -
ENJOYED THIS? CHECK OUT:
ATACAMA
BY JENDIA GAMMON

DEEP IN A CAVE IN THE MIDDLE OF THE WOODS, YOU MIGHT DISCOVER SOME BEAUTIFUL WOMEN IN NEED. BUT WHAT DO THEY NEED? THAT'S FOR YOU TO FIND OUT . . . IF YOU DARE. "TO SCORN THE POWER OF MAN" TORTURES US MERE HUMANS WITH NATURE'S EXQUISITE ALLURE. SHAKESPEARE HIMSELF WOULD BE QUAKING IN HIS CODPIECE IF HE KNEW WHAT THE WEIRD SISTERS FROM MACBETH INSPIRED!

TO SCORN THE POWER OF MAN

AMANDA NEVADA DeMEL

There's a sense of innocence in nature that I've always been drawn to. My friends feel it too, but their lust for it isn't as strong as mine is.

As the day ends, we make our way out of the cave, though I don't want to leave. When we're nearly out of the alcove, I get the feeling that we forgot something. I turn around to face the room again, taking in the stalactites and the stalagmites that frame the darkness of the gigantic, motionless pool of water. I bask in the general calm of the scene. It feels like I'm walking in space, surrounded by nothing, all sense of distance skewed. Yet a sense of peace wraps around me. I feel at home, like all of this is mine. It is as if I have always been in the cave.

Even with my headlamp on, I can't see very far. Only a few yards ahead of me are illuminated. The rest of the massive space is submerged in thick darkness. But I know we must have left something behind. I'll just take one last look. My friends are busy talking and following the markers back to the main chamber. Now is my chance to sneak away. The loud sounds of my boots stomping on the ground would surely raise alarm, so I take my time walking back to the water.

Gazing upon the perfect lake, I am mesmerized. My hand clutches the cool, jagged wall to hold me up. In front of one of the large tufa towers breaking the surface of the muddy water, a wide mass emerges from the pool inch by inch. It isn't simply rising out of the depths; it is also breaking apart and sculpting itself into three distinct structures. My headlamp shines a dim light on new bulges and hollows as they form. Slowly, so slowly, I start to recognize shapes. There's an arm, there's a shoulder, there are breasts, and then there are three heads with long hair in mud-clad tendrils. They look like ancient Greek statues, with soft curves and full, natural figures. Their distinct features, though caked with dirt, entice me into their realm of raw charm. To me, these women are truly goddesses. I never want to leave them, to desert them, to blaspheme. The middle one's arms are around her sisters, and all three bend their heads to gaze forlornly into the pool. I hold my breath, not wanting to disrupt their sacred beauty with my human exhalations. I feel filthy and intrusive when I have to let out a breath. I feel greedy when I have to take in more air.

From somewhere in the distance I hear my name. It echoes off the cave walls, wrapping around me. The voices sound too deep to be coming from the women, but I can't imagine where else the sound could originate. Now heavy boots are pounding on the rock floor. Noises attack me from all angles, compelling me to flee, but I can't bear to leave the gorgeous sisters.

A hand clamps down on my shoulder and forces me to turn around. Instead of an elegant woman, I see the bulky shape of my partner Brian.

"Michael, are you alright?" he asks with worried brows. My shaken expression and disappointment must be obvious.

"Yeah," I whisper, "but are they?"

"Who?"

I turn back to the water. The sisters are gone.

"I think you need some air, dude."

"No! Three girls were in the lake, I promise. I saw them a second ago."

"Come on," Brian says, taking my arm and leading me away. "It's okay, you're just a little disoriented."

I try to shake him off, but something about his touch always soothes me. This time is no different, though I do give in with reluctance. I heave a great sigh and we head out of the cave. I check behind me several times. The sisters aren't following us. My discontent grows.

It doesn't take too long to get to the mouth. We want to see how far we can go in the coming days, so we'll probably need to sleep in the cave. Tonight, though, the four of us set up camp outside. Before we are too far from the mouth, each of us slows to a stop. We look at each other and simply know that we should set up camp here. There's a physical ache, as if we can't bear to stray too far from the cave. Without a word, we get to work. We build our tents as close to the flat sheets of limestone as possible, forgoing the comfort of a softer, more vegetated landscape. The compact dirt, the hard rocks, and the air around us all hold the chill of autumn. Every gust of wind shakes our tents. The brisk atmosphere is not preferable for a night in the wild, but it is invigorating.

We light a fire before the night gets too dark. Soon enough, the flames become our main source of light. The details of our faces fade in and out of the night. Brian always looks so rugged, so handsome in the glow of a fire.

John and Rahul are blathering on about their day jobs. I couldn't be less interested. Why do they choose to focus on day-to-day life when we're in the midst of true, palpable grandeur?

"Hey," Brian says, plopping down next to me. He's already prepared to sleep, wearing only his long johns and socks.

I stare into the fire and grunt in response.

"Everything alright? You still shaken up from this afternoon?"

"I'm fine, I'm fine," I say, waving away his question and his worry.

"Whatever," he says with a shrug. "You just don't look fine, that's all. You look the same as you did when I had to drag you away earlier."

I turn to look at him directly, take his rough hand in mine, and reassure him that everything is okay. If he sees the hurricane of thoughts behind my eyes, he won't let me be. But then he shrugs again and looks over to the others.

"The kids in my class are driving me nuts," Brian exclaims, inserting himself into the conversation. "It's barely been a month and I'm already counting down to winter break."

They laugh at his exaggerated misery. Although I see their shoulders bounce, their faces scrunch up in mirth, I don't hear the accompanying sounds. I remain silent, distanced. The tones of their conversation echo around me, but they don't quite hit. It feels like I'm still in the cave, still cradled in the dampened noise. Morning cannot come soon enough.

While my friends fall asleep, I toss and turn in my sleeping bag. Some force pulls me back to the cave. There is no way that I will abandon my discovery. I need to see them again, with or without the others. One single glimpse of them would be worth any injury that my lone mission might get me. Images of the sisters, half hidden in shadow and half illuminated by my headlamp, have been my only focus for hours. My mind has wandered, of course, prompting me to question what these women are, how they formed, and why they had such somber expressions. I will see them again, even if I can't remember exactly where to go. If I pop into the cave for a few minutes, I can at least eliminate some of the passages without water.

Though I know nothing about the women for certain, I have my theories. They are clearly preternatural, and possibly ethereal. No one else could see them, which makes me think that they chose me. It would be an imposition to bring my friends. Perhaps they appeared only to me in order to tell me something. But what? And why were they so despondent? I must know.

Keeping as quiet as possible, I unzip the tent I share with Brian to gather the basic supplies I need. He rolls over as soon as I step outside, but he starts snoring again not twenty seconds later. It's a cloudless night, with the stars and moon shining at full force, so it's not difficult to see my surroundings. The light from the sky seems brighter than usual, even considering the unobstructed view. As I collect supplies, I cement my resolve to see the sisters tonight. It isn't enough to just explore the cave again. Equipped in my coveralls and hardhat, a water bottle, flashlight, and extra batteries stuffed into my backpack, I am ready to go. The glowing digits on my watch tell me that it is just after one o'clock. I can explore for 45 minutes and return to camp without anyone suspecting a thing. My friends should all be asleep until sunrise, which is still at least six hours away. I can, and will, find those women before my 45 minutes are up. If something were to go wrong, those extra hours will keep my secret safe. Excitement flows through my veins and fills my thoughts.

When I get to the mouth of the cave, my heart thunders and my lips spread wide in an indomitable grin. I am absolutely giddy. A few boulders at the entrance wear thin coats of moss. I peel off a glove and, running my hand over one, hum at the soothing sensation.

Waving my flashlight around the area, I once again revel in the sheer beauty of the miraculous structure. The ceiling is covered with scores of stalactites of various sizes, which cast long shadows when my light passes over them. A colony of bats flutters and squeaks about the cave. I inhale the strong aromas of slightly moist dirt and stagnant air. They are welcome and comforting, and precisely what I need to refocus.

I try to picture the path I took earlier, but I can't. Of course, with the nature of caves, there are so many directions I could take, and nothing looks the same as it did when we first entered. The enormous main chamber stretches on for thousands of feet and there are passages at all angles. Some rocks look like they are dripping down the walls. Other specimens offer massive geodes that look like they have been crafted by an entity too perfect for this world. One group of boulders seems to form a flight of stairs that leads up to another level of the cave. I don't remember these steps at all. I've never seen a natural formation like this. Were they placed here by the sisters? Were they placed here for me? My legs walk me onto the first step. A hot gust of wind blows in my face. It feels like a huff of breath, only from some enormous, inhuman lungs. The ground on these stairs is strangely moist and it gives slightly under my weight. The steps lure me upward. I wonder where they lead, and if the breath came from their summit, but then my brain shuts down any further action. I need to stay on task.

My eye catches one of our markers near the first passage to the left of the mouth. That will be as good a start as any. It's not long before a smile takes hold of my face. There it is: the dark plane of water with several tufa towers protruding from its level surface. Fortune must be guiding me, smiling on me. I dip my hand into the lake and swirl it around, trying to stir up some movement, anything at all. The water is cool as it seeps through my glove. It grounds me in the present.

"Hello?" I shout, my voice ricocheting off the cave walls. One of those echoes doesn't sound like my voice—in fact sounds more feminine—but it's gone before I can think about it too much.

Other than the strange echoes, the only reply I get is the screech of some bats. I wait a couple minutes longer, but when I look at my watch, I see that my time is ticking down from fifteen minutes. I start to head out, lamenting my failure as I go along with slumped shoulders. Before I'm too far away, I turn around, checking the scene a final time. There is nothing new to see…until a dark silhouette rises out of the water.

My boots crunch the little rocks on the ground with each sprinting step I take back to the lake. The sounds assault my ears, and I fear that they will scare away the sisters, but they look unfazed. When I stop this time, the woman in the middle looks up. We make eye contact. Her gaze fixes me to the spot. She tightens her arms around her sisters, nudging them to look at me, their visitor. Their eyes twinkle with tears, though their faces remain unmarred by wrinkles of worry. Their lips, however, tremble with what must be the struggle of restraining their sorrow. I'm so struck with awe that I can't find my voice. I simply blink and swallow hard.

"The battle's lost already," the sister on the right says. Her voice caresses me.

Finally able to speak, I say, "Who are you?"

"We'll meet again soon," the sister on the opposite side promises.

At that, they start to sink back into the water.

"Wait!" I cry.

The middle sister lays her finger on her full lips as their bodies continue to gradually disappear. For some reason, the gesture works and I don't yell any more, though my curiosity is only piqued further.

I don't know where they are going, but I can't reject the invitation to follow them. I am guided by my goddesses. I stand at the edge of the lake for a moment longer, and then I step forward. Water engulfs my boot, though I am only aware of the discomfort for a second. I ache to be fully submerged. The ground doesn't hold steady under my shoes. It seems to grab my feet and pull me onward. I continue wading into the pool until the murky water is up to my neck. I stop and take a breath. The women look at me, their faces the only recognizable feature left, and that's all I need. This cave is where I belong.

⚜

Brian woke up to find that Michael was not in the tent. He must have gone out to pee, Brian thought. The morning was cold and silent. He dressed himself and went out, smelling beans cooking over the fire. He searched for his partner but found the other two men instead.

"Hey, have you seen Michael?"

"Nope," Rahul said, stirring their breakfast. "We thought he was with you."

"Hmm. I thought he was taking a piss when I woke up, but that was, like, ten minutes ago. I'm gonna look around for a bit. Be back in a few."

Brian walked away from camp and into the woods. He called out for Michael a few times, but he didn't get a human response, only a flock of birds flying away with squawks. With a sudden idea in mind, he rushed back.

"What's wrong, man?" Rahul said.

"Remember how impatient he was to get started on our last trip? Maybe he went in already. He's probably not far, but still, he might have started."

"He knows better than to go in alone, doesn't he?" John asked.

"I mean, he should, but we all know how impulsive he can be," Brian reasoned. "Think about it. He walked away from the group yesterday, like he forgot everything he's learned. What if he went back and got hurt?"

"Okay," Rahul said around a mouthful of beans. "We'll go in a few minutes. We still have to pack up."

Brian groaned with impatience and frustration but agreed. Rahul and John believed that he was overreacting, as he was wont to do. After scarfing down a bowl of breakfast, Brian quickly gathered his supplies and waited for the others. He noticed that Michael's supplies were missing and cursed his friend for his damned stupidity. He was tempted to yell at the others to speed up but knew it would do nothing to help. They weren't dawdling by any means, but they weren't rushing with panic as Brian was. Rahul and John packed with nonchalance, while Brian paced back and forth with mounting unease. He settled on collecting their trash until they were at last prepared, then tied the bag to a tree to retrieve later. Brian walked ahead of his fellow spelunkers, and he was the first to go into the cave. He stopped barely thirty yards in, his chest tightening, overcome with the multitude of routes that Michael could have taken. The possibilities would usually have inspired him, exhilarated him, but the weight of the situation robbed him of all joy. The other men began to feel a niggling anxiety at the napes of their necks. No one noticed that all their markers from the previous day were gone.

"Let's start here," Rahul suggested, heading to the first passage on the left. He didn't know why, but that passage felt right.

They turned on their flashlights. The sounds of their boots stomping on the cave floor echoed around them, making it seem like more people were present.

Images of Michael alone in some deep crevice of the cave came into Brian's mind. He saw Michael on the ground, his foot bent the wrong way, his knees and elbows bleeding. He envisioned Michael sprawled out, his helmet rolling away, his head lolling to the side, his eyes closed. He wouldn't let that happen again, couldn't bear the sight of a bloody, unconscious Michael once more. A shudder pulsed through Brian and he moved a little faster.

"Guess it's not this one," John said of the room, nodding at the lake that prevented them from going any farther.

Brian punched the rugged wall, a grunt bursting out of his mouth. His friends whipped their heads around to stare at him with raised eyebrows. They knew how much Brian loved Michael, but they still had hope, which Brian seemed to have lost. He stood still, save for his heaving shoulders, and cradled his throbbing hand.

"We'll find him," Rahul said in a soothing voice. "Just try to stay calm."

"Michael!" Brian called.

"Come on, let's go. He's clearly not here."

"Michael!"

Rahul put his hand on Brian's shoulder, trying to guide him back to the main room. Brian shoved him off.

"Michael!" Brian screamed again.

John wrapped his arm around Brian's shoulders and forced him to turn away from the water. After struggling for a minute, he gave in with a groan. He tried to quell his mounting frustration and panic with deep breaths, but he felt like the oxygen in the room was running low.

As they walked back to the central chamber, there was an irksome feeling like something was staring at him. They were almost back to the large cavern when Brian looked back.

"Woah, did you see that?"

His friends turned around too. Their headlamps couldn't reach all the way back to the lake, but they were certain that Brian was seeing things with his wishful, willful thoughts.

"What? There's nothing there."

Brian ran back to the lake before the others could stop him.

"Come back here," Rahul said, clearly exasperated, as he and John walked toward their desperate friend. "Nothing's there, man."

"Yes there is!" Brian shouted. He pointed to the three sisters who were looking at him with inviting, knowing smiles.

John glanced at Rahul with a furrow in his brow and said, "You're freaking out. Michael's somewhere else, and we need to find him. Come back here."

Brian ignored John's demand. He stepped into the water.

"Dude, what are you doing?" Rahul yelled, running to pull Brian out of the lake. By the time he got to the edge, water was lapping at his friend's chest. "Get out of there! You'll get hypothermia! *Brian!*"

Rahul and John kneeled by the pool, their arms futilely straining to reach Brian. They shouted at him in a frenzy, ordering him to get out of the water. They couldn't tell how deep it was. They didn't know if Brian was a strong enough swimmer to tread water with the added weight of his backpack. No matter how loud and frantic they were, he ignored them and continued wading.

"Dammit, Brian, get back here!" John screamed. What he intended as a firm command ended up as a desperate plea.

The water was up to their friend's chin. Their shouting, demanding, and begging did nothing to help. Brian went under.

Rahul sprang into action and started taking off his gear to go into the lake.

"Hold on," John said, putting his hand on Rahul's arm.

"We can't just let him drown!"

"Look, he's not thrashing, he's not even surfacing, and that water's way too murky for you to see anything in there," John responded, trying to be the voice of reason. Even so, his voice quaked and cracked.

Before they could continue bickering, a figure bobbed up and broke the surface tension of the lake. The two men on land gasped when they saw the face. It was Michael. They couldn't see most of him, as his body was angled downward, but it was clear that he wasn't treading water to keep afloat. He was on his back, leaving only his face and chest visible. His features were bloated with water and patches of his skin were purple, while others were pale and marked with veins. His expression made it seem like he was in great pain, even in death. One of his usually smooth cheeks had been torn apart. They could see the slight wriggling movements of worms and other creatures on his muscular neck and shoulders.

Rahul muttered a profanity. He didn't think much about the fact that his legs wouldn't obey his command to step back.

With Michael's lifeless body swaying in the water, their hopes for Brian's survival dwindled. They knew well enough that it would be fatal to go into the pool without proper equipment. Though the situation was urgent, the sight of their friend's swollen corpse pulled them in and made them reluctant to leave. The surviving men tried to step back, but their feet felt heavy and stiff, almost like their bodies did not belong to them. The sensation was the least of their worries. They lingered by the edge of the water, waiting a moment for a miracle. Eventually it came: a tiny blessing in the form of voluntary movement.

Breaking out of his trance-like state, Rahul said, "We have to contact the rescue squad. At least they can get the body out."

"Alright," John said in a raspy voice, his throat hardly opening enough for the word to get out. "Let's go."

The men rushed out of the cave and out of the woods, not caring what they left behind. They could hardly get a firm grasp on their ropes, could only take a few steps without stumbling. They felt the prodding eyes of something on their backs.

When they were long gone, there was once again movement in the lake. This time, Brian's body rose and disturbed the stillness of the water. A permanently tormented grimace twisted his face as well. His and Michael's bodies drifted toward each other, their hands eventually making contact. Both corpses were at the same state of decay, though Michael had been dead for much longer. The bodies were to remain bloated until the sisters were done inflicting their punishment. The men were to pay for their intrusion on the sacred space. They would not walk with impunity after forcing their falsely entitled claim on the land. Worms and fish would feast on their pliable skin, which would build up again as soon as it was bitten off.

A wide mass emerged from the water and began to take shape. Slowly, three young women formed from the heap of clay. They cast their eyes down into the water.

"Their battle is lost," the lady on the left said.

"Mother would have been pleased," the middle woman added, looking down with unfocused eyes.

The sisters would finally reclaim the stillness that was rightfully theirs.

The woman on the right let a melancholy sigh slip out. It wafted upward and swirled around the stalactites before dissipating into nothingness, as if it had never been there at all.

– THE END –
ENJOYED THIS? CHECK OUT:
UNDER THE CHURCHYARD IN THE CHAMBER OF BONE
BY JR BILLINGSLEY

GREETINGS LITTLE GHOULINGS! DO YOU HAVE-OR HAVE YOU EVER HAD-AN IMAGINARY FRIEND? WELL, WHAT IF THAT FRIEND WASN'T SO IMAGINARY? WHAT IF THAT FRIEND WAS A MONSTER? AND WHAT IF YOU MADE THAT MONSTER DO TERRIBLE THINGS TO PEOPLE YOU DIDN'T LIKE? FROM THE SERIOUSLY DISTURBED MIND OF M. BRANDON ROBBINS, WRITER, GAMER, AND LIBRARIAN FROM GOLDSBORO, NC, COMES "A MONSTER DID IT," THE STORY OF A VERY DEMENTED LITTLE BOY WHO ISN'T AFRAID TO UNLEASH A LITTLE DEATH AND DISMEMBERMENT ON THE PEOPLE WHO GET ON HIS BAD SIDE.

A MONSTER DID IT

M. BRANDON ROBBINS

Toby had met the monster while walking through the woods one day during summer break, when the sun was especially bright (save for in the woods, where the trees offered bountiful shade) and the air was especially thick. He didn't have permission to go into the woods, but his mom was at work and he felt brave. When he first saw the monster, it was crouched at the base of a tree, coiled and ready to strike. Its skin was scaly and black and a matted mane surrounded its face. Venom, spit, and blood dripped from its fangs and its eyes shone a virulent shade of green.

Before the monster pounced, Toby did something unexpected. He reached forward, presenting half of a ham sandwich. "Are you hungry?" the boy asked.

The monster cocked its head to the side and stopped snarling. It took a step forward and snatched the sandwich out of Toby's hand. It gulped it down too fast to enjoy the salty, fatty taste of the ham and the creamy smoothness of the cheese, but the snack satiated its hunger and cost it little effort. The monster was pleased.

The monster came from a world where there were rules, rules like "Never tell a stranger your true name" and "Never accept gifts." It had accepted a gift. Now, it had to pay.

The monster bowed to Toby. It then looked up at the child. "I serve you," it growled.

"What?"

"I do as you say." The monster spoke as if doing so caused it pain.

"I can tell you what to do?"

"Yes. You feed. I serve."

Toby furrowed his brow in thought, then smiled with the deepest satisfaction. "Can you kill people?"

"Yes. You tell me name. I kill."

"How will I find you when I'm ready?"

"Summon."

"I can just call for you?"

"Yes."

"What's your name?"

"I no name. You summon."

"So just like, say, 'Hey come here' or 'You there' and you'll come?"

"Yes. Summon. I come."

Toby smiled once more. "Okay. I'll get you when I'm ready."

Toby walked back toward his house. The monster went back to the dark place, deep in the woods, covered with dirt and stone and dead limbs, where it slept.

☙❧

Toby sat in the highest chamber of the playhouse, far away from the rest of the children, reading a book. He liked it here. Most of his classmates didn't bother him when he sat up here and read. He knew the other kids thought he was weird, but he didn't care. If it meant they left him alone, then they could think whatever they wanted.

He heard stomping coming up the steps to the chamber he was in. Toby knew who it was without even looking up. Ryan was one of the few kids who would approach him when he was alone. In front of the teachers, Ryan was well-behaved and polite; but when the grown-ups weren't watching, Ryan was a bully. Toby was his favorite victim.

Ryan smacked the book out of Toby's hands. "What's up, freak?" He cuffed Toby's ear. It hurt very badly.

Toby covered his hurting ear and turned to the side, refusing to make eye contact with his antagonist.

"So did your mom go out on any dates this weekend? I bet she goes out with anybody that asks her. I bet she does it with them too. I heard your mom's done it with every guy in town!"

Toby rarely answered Ryan. Most of the time, he just let the bully have his say, suffered through a few slaps and punches, and then went back to whatever he was doing before Ryan had started in on him. But bravery seized him, and he spoke up. "Does that mean she's done it with your dad?"

Ryan gritted his teeth and balled his fists. Toby had his hands up to cover his head before the blows started raining down on him. He dropped to lay on his side and pulled his knees into his chest to deflect the kicks to his ribs. "Don't you talk about my dad like that!" Ryan yelled. Toby was sure a teacher would hear Ryan and come running to his rescue, but nobody came.

After nearly a full minute, Ryan stopped punching and kicking and stood over Toby, panting and with a vein popping out of his neck. "You don't ever talk about my dad! He would never get with a bitch like your mom."

Ryan ran off. Toby sat up and picked his book back up, but he didn't resume his reading. He waited for the teacher to call them in from recess, and then he waited patiently to go home at the end of the day. As he walked across the parking lot to his mom's car, Toby made eye contact with Ryan and smiled.

⊰⊱

Toby's mother, Angela, steered around a left turn. "So how was school today?" she asked.

Toby shrugged.

"You had your big spelling test today, didn't you?"

"Yes."

"How did it go?"

"I don't think I did too good."

"I'm sure you did just fine. You're pretty good at spelling."

Toby was quiet for a moment before speaking again. "Ryan hit me today."

Angela furrowed her brow. "Did you tell Ms. Hatch?"

"No. She wouldn't believe me. She never does."

"Honey, if you don't tell your teacher when something like this happens, how is she supposed to do anything about it?"

Toby rolled his eyes. He had explained this to his mom several times, and it frustrated him deeply that she never seemed to grasp it. "I told you: She wouldn't believe me. Ryan has bullied me before and he's never gotten in trouble. He always gets away with everything because he's a teacher's pet."

"I'll email Ms. Hatch tonight to ask to come in for another conference. I'll see if Ryan's parents can come to this one."

"It won't do any good, Mom. Ryan is just going to pretend like he never does anything wrong and then he's going to keep hitting me and picking on me. And it's not just that he hits me. He says bad things about you. He says that you do it with every guy in town."

Angela swallowed hard as her eyes narrowed. "And I'm sure he gets those ideas from some grown-ups he knows. That's why we need to talk to his parents."

Toby huffed. "You don't understand, Mom." He wished that his mother understood. His mom seemed to think that all he had to do was tell his teacher everything Ryan did and all would be well. Maybe if his mom knew it wasn't that simple, she could actually help.

Angela reached over and stroked Toby's hair. "I do understand. I was bullied when I was your age. I know how bad it hurts and how hopeless you feel. But one day Ryan is going to get caught, and he's going to get the punishment he deserves. Until that happens, we'll keep doing what we need to do and talk to your teacher, okay? I might even try to get in to talk to the principal."

Angela stopped the car in their driveway. She looked over at Toby and smiled. "How about something that makes this bad day a little better. You want to have spaghetti tonight for dinner?"

Toby nodded enthusiastically. Spaghetti was his favorite meal. "Can I spread the butter on the garlic bread again?"

"Sure thing. Just maybe don't put as much on it as you did last time. Mommy is trying to fit into her 'before Toby was born' clothes again."

ʘʘ

The spaghetti was good. Angela told Toby they were trying a new sauce tonight. Toby had enjoyed it quite a bit, though it was rare that he didn't enjoy spaghetti, no matter how it was cooked. He liked that it was squishy and made sucking sounds when you stirred it and he liked that the noodles looked kind of like worms. He loved spaghetti with meatballs, but his mom only made meatballs on special occasions because they were a lot of work.

She had made meatballs tonight. When Toby asked if it was a special occasion, his mom told him that she just wanted her boy to be happy.

As Angela washed up the dishes, Toby walked through the kitchen to the door that led outside. "I'm going outside to play," he announced.

"Stay out of the woods."

"Can I get close?"

"As long as I can see you."

Toby walked outside, crossed the backyard, and stood at the line of trees beyond. "Are you there?" he whispered.

The monster came creeping up from somewhere deep within the forest. Its tail whipped and snapped as its body twisted through the underbrush. It stopped just within the canopy of trees.

"I want you to kill Ryan." Toby said, barely above a whisper. "He's the kid at school who bullies me and says bad things about my mom."

The monster growled low and rumbling. Not unlike a dog, it barked the ugly, rough, and forceful bark of a hungry beast. It glided across the ground and lurked back into the deep woods.

❧

In his own backyard, Ryan was kicking his soccer ball into the net his dad had set up for him. Ryan set the ball a few feet away from the net and backed up ten steps. "Ryan Steeler going for the penalty kick," he whispered, his imagination placing him on the pitch of a major league soccer field. "If he makes this one, it will put his team in the lead!"

Ryan ran forward and kicked the ball with every bit of strength he could muster. It went flying over the top bar of the net and plopped into the woods beyond. He huffed and kicked some dirt up in frustration, then stomped toward where the ball had landed.

Ryan stepped forward; the fading sunlight was shut off by the trees overhead. Darkness enveloped him, but he wasn't afraid. He just had to get the ball and go right back to playing soccer again.

As Ryan stooped over to pick up his ball, the monster came out from behind a nearby tree. The boy never even saw him. There was the snap of jaws, a muffled scream, and a splash of blood. The monster dragged Ryan deep into the woods, back to his lair, where he would finish what he had started.

ᘓᘔ

Three days later, a volunteer aiding with the search for Ryan found his body in the deepest, darkest part of the woods. Ryan's parents couldn't positively identify him; it was only after DNA testing that the identity of the once-human form was confirmed as the lost little boy.

ᘓᘔ

At a school assembly where he spoke to the student body about Ryan's passing, the school therapist made it very clear that his door was open and if anybody wanted to talk, all they had to do was come to his office before or after school and set up an appointment. They didn't need to ask their parents to do it for them, though they could if they were comfortable doing so.

Angela had heard about the therapist's offer from another parent that she sometimes had coffee with. When she picked Toby up from school, she asked him why he had not said anything to her about talking to the therapist.

"I don't need to talk to anybody about Ryan dying," he said, as matter-of-factly as the most detached professional. "I'm glad he's dead."

Angela took a sharp intake of breath and dropped her jaw. "Toby, I know that Ryan was mean to you, but you shouldn't be glad that he's dead."

"Why not? He was mean to me. Now he's not here to be mean to me anymore. Why can't I be happy about that?"

"Because it's terrible when anybody dies. Think about this: maybe one day Ryan would have started being nice to you and apologized for all the bad things he said and did. You two could have ended up being good friends. But now that will never happen."

"So? It's not like I'm missing out on anything."

Angela shook her head. "You just shouldn't be glad that Ryan's dead, sweetheart. His friends and his parents—his entire family—are grieving."

"So they can grieve. I've got nothing to be sad about, and Ryan isn't here to bully me anymore. I still don't understand why I can't be happy about that."

Angela shook her head once more, this time in defeat. "You'll understand one day, honey. In the meantime, I think it's a good idea that you talk to Dr. Langham. Maybe he can help you understand why it's bad when somebody—anybody—dies. I'll call and make you an appointment tomorrow."

Toby turned to look out the window. He knew that if he spoke out loud what he was feeling at the moment, he would get in very big trouble. His mom might not even let him go outside, and he had to talk to the monster tonight.

⋘⋙

The monster came creeping out from the dark, its blood-encrusted claws cutting into the earth.

"Yes?" it said when it had reached Toby.

"My mom's going to make me talk to the therapist at school. I don't want to. I think he might figure out that I made you kill Ryan. Can you kill him?"

The monster nodded. "Name?"

"Dr. Langham. I don't know where he lives."

"I find."

The monster dashed away into the darkness, sniffing the air.

☙❧

Dr. Langham poured a measure of scotch into his tumbler, then carried his refreshment over to his favorite reading chair. He set the drink on the coffee table in front of the chair and turned to his bookshelf. He decided he would unwind by reading some Shakespeare tonight; there was something about the Bard that always relaxed him.

The doctor sat down in his chair and opened his book to a random sonnet. He began reading, reciting the poem out loud in its singsong cadence, enveloping himself in the rhythm and imagery of it. He finished the piece and took a deep sip of his whiskey before moving on to the next one.

He didn't hear the monster come up behind him, but he felt its cold breath on his neck.

As Dr. Langham turned to see what was blowing across his skin, the monster bit into his neck and pulled him down to the floor. It ripped at the doctor with its claws. A storm of blood sprayed against the wall and poured onto the floor. Bits of flesh and guts splattered onto the coffee table and the chair. Dr. Langham screamed and begged for help, but there was no one to hear him.

The monster didn't stop until long after Dr. Langham had stopped making noise and moving, and even then he severed one more artery and ripped out the doctor's liver just to be certain that the deed was done. Satisfied with his work, the monster crept back out through the window and scurried across the lawn, quick and unseen, back into the woods in the distance.

❧

Dr. Langham's housekeeper found him the next morning. It took some time for the news to reach the school. The principal decided to keep it quiet for now; if any of the students asked where Dr. Langham was, the teachers would just tell them that Dr. Langham was very sick and couldn't come to work today.

The death was the headline for the town newspaper that evening. With only one elementary school for the entire community, Dr. Langham was known to nearly everyone; he had been at the school for twenty years.

❧

Toby came downstairs for dinner as soon as his mom called. They were having spaghetti again tonight.

Angela let him eat some before speaking to him. "Toby, did you hear about Dr. Langham?"

Toby shook his head.

"Dr. Langham died."

Toby made no response.

"Toby, did you hear me? The therapist at your school is dead."

Toby shrugged. "Okay."

"Toby, I know that you didn't know Dr. Langham well, but aren't you just a little upset about this?"

Toby shook his head. "Nope."

Angela curled her hands into fists, simmering with frustration. "Toby, it really bothers me that you're not upset at people dying."

"If one of my friends died, or if you died, I'd be very sad. But I'm not sad when someone I don't like or don't know dies."

"Not even a little bit?"

"No."

"But you knew Dr. Langham."

"I kinda knew him. I never spent any time with him. Why should I be all sad that he's dead?"

"Well, I can tell you this much: You're not going outside to play alone anymore."

Toby slammed his fork down and furrowed his brow at his mother. "What do you mean I can't go outside alone anymore?"

"Honey, there are horrible things happening in this town. I don't want you to be all alone and defenseless. I should have cut off your outside playing after Ryan died, but now I'm certain I don't want you out there without me."

"How long is this going to last?"

"I don't know. Until I feel that you're safe again."

"But I am safe!"

"No, you're not. Nobody is. Not even me. But at least I'm a grown-up and I stand a better chance of defending myself."

"You don't understand, Mom. I know I'm safe!"

"How?" Angela snapped. "How do you know you're safe?"

Toby nearly told her the truth: That he had a pet monster who killed people for him, and it was that monster who had killed one of his classmates and his school therapist. But he didn't. If she believed him, he would never be able to go out and speak to the monster again. He sunk his head down and mumbled, "I just know I am."

"Well, I'm not convinced. You'll still have some time outside each day to play, but it will be with me watching over you. If things calm down around here and nobody else dies, maybe I can let you outside without me again. But right now, I just don't want you to be in any danger. Do you understand?"

Toby sighed. "Yes, ma'am."

"Okay. Now, finish your dinner and we'll go outside for a few minutes."

Toby finished his dinner. As promised, Angela went outside with him. He absent-mindedly swung on his swing set and jumped on his trampoline. In less than ten minutes, he was ready to go inside.

Angela messed with his hair as Toby walked into the house. "I know it's a bummer having your mom always breathing down your neck, but it's my job to protect you."

Before walking inside, Toby looked over his shoulder toward the woods. The monster wasn't there. Toby wondered if he would ever see it again.

CRENGD

The days went from being drenched in sunlight and warmth to being short and cool. The wind picked up and howled as it cut through the trees, now stripped of their green leaves and left with a blanket of dead foliage at their trunks. Scary movie marathons started coming on TV and the local library put up a display of thrillers, mysteries, and horror stories. Retail stores took down their displays of lawn furniture and pool toys. They replaced them with costumes both whimsical and frightening, plastic skeletons, foam tombstones, and all the other disposable decorations that people bought for Halloween.

With no further shocking and violent deaths in town, parents started feeling safe. Curfews were lifted. Children—including Toby—were allowed to play outside unsupervised again.

The monster stirred in the woods, quiet and slow, waiting and watching for its next summoning.

⊂⊃

Toby had a bag full of candy in hand when Angela picked him up from school on Halloween. The school had sponsored a carnival for the students. There were games, costumes, and candy of every type: soft, hard, chewy, chocolate, fruity, caramel, bubble gum, peppermints, and even full-sized candy bars. "Goodness!" Angela exclaimed as Toby climbed into his seat. "It looks like you've got quite the haul."

"The carnival was the best thing ever!" Toby shouted as he shut his door. "I wish we had one every Friday!"

"But then they wouldn't be so special." Angela pulled out of the driveway and started heading to their home. After a few quiet moments, Toby spoke up again.

"Mom, I know I've got a lot of candy, but we can still go trick-or-treating tonight, can't we?"

Angela sucked her teeth. "Honey, you're going trick-or-treating tonight. But you'll be going with Mrs. Yelverton's kids. You know our neighbors, Mr. and Mrs. Yelverton?"

"Are you not going?"

"I'm afraid not. You see, a very nice man from work asked me if I'd like to go to the movies tonight with him."

Toby screwed up his face in anger and frustration and more than a little hurt. "You don't want to go trick-or-treating with me?"

"Oh, honey, it's not that! It's just, this is my only chance to see this movie and spend time with this guy. If Mrs. Yelverton couldn't take you trick-or-treating, I would have turned him down and we'd go. But Mrs. Yelverton can take you, so you can still go and have a good time and get lots more candy. And I can go to the movies and spend time with my new friend. We both get what we want!"

He had heard his mom call a man a "new friend" before. It usually meant that they were going to go out lots of times and the new friend would eventually come over to meet Toby. He never liked any of his mom's new friends. He knew what the new friends were. They were people who wanted to replace his dad. Toby huffed and sank into his seat. "What's your new friend's name?"

"Roger. He's really very nice. I think you would like him. Maybe you two can meet soon."

Toby didn't answer. He sunk into his seat and pulled another piece of candy out of his bag. He unwrapped it and popped it into his mouth. He was going to offer his mom a piece, but he decided that she didn't deserve it.

When they pulled into the driveway, Toby asked, "Can I go play outside for a little while?"

Angela told him he could. Without another word, the boy walked through the house, shrugging off his backpack in the living room and leaving his bag of candy on the dining room table. He went to the backyard and strode purposefully to the woods.

"Are you there?"

⚬⚬⚬

Toby dressed up as the Grim Reaper while Mrs. Yelverton's sons dressed up as superheroes. Toby liked his costume the best because it was scary. He thought that the whole point of Halloween was to scare people.

When they got back to Mrs. Yelverton's house, everybody changed out of their costumes into their pajamas and gathered around the kitchen table to dive into the massive haul of candy. Toby had just ripped open a king-size pack of peanut butter cups—the most prized gift of the night—when there was a knock at the door.

Mr. Yelverton answered it, and a moment later he escorted Angela into the kitchen. In between smacking bites of the rich confection, Toby said, "You missed the best Halloween ever, Mom."

Angela laughed. "Well, maybe you'll share some of that candy with me."

Mrs. Yelverton took Toby's bag and started dumping his share of the candy into it. "How was your date?"

Angela beamed. "It was great. I had a wonderful time. We plan on getting together again this weekend."

Toby grimaced.

Angela extended her hand for Toby to take. Mrs. Yelverton handed him his bag. "Don't eat too much candy or stay up too late!"

Angela assured her neighbor that she'd get Toby to bed soon.

As soon as they walked outside, Angela saw Roger sprawled across her driveway beside his car. Coiled intestines spilled from a gaping wound in his stomach. A mass of flesh was missing from his neck; it lay nearby. His face was torn open and his jaw was unhinged. A lake of blood surrounded his mutilated body.

Angela screamed.

Toby looked to the woods on the other side of his house, he saw two green eyes shining in the darkness.

He smiled.

ೞ

Toby had been waiting inside his house for his mother to return. When she did, she sank onto the couch. Toby crawled up beside her and snuggled at her side. Angela put her arm around him. "I'm sorry about your new friend," Toby said, his voice thick with sweetness. "Do you know what attacked him?"

Angela shook her head again. "No. The police didn't find anything."

Confident that his mother couldn't see his face, Toby smirked. "Maybe a monster did it."

– THE END –
ENJOYED THIS? CHECK OUT:
MR. HAUNT
UPCOMING FROM
BY M. BRANDON ROBBINS *SLEY HOUSE!*

HUSBANDRY

GORDON B. WHITE

Danny is a lamb. When I pull the knife down along the inside of his bicep, a white cloud of wool springs out to meet me, the faint dampness it holds from beneath his skin already drying before my fire. Still, he screams like a boy being murdered.

"Mad woman," he squeals. "Witch!"

I cram a bulb of garlic into his mouth. It's not required of the process, but it is very effective at tamping down his piercing curses into muffled sobs.

His young wife, Carla, watches from as far across my one-room cottage as she can press herself while I slip the knife to Danny's elbow. My knees pin him to the floor and, although he thrashes mightily, he can't slow my excavation. The shared origin of all mammals means that most have similar boney bits and bobs, just not necessarily the same size or placement, and experience has taught me how rough I can get with the outer layer, so I work the blade deeper to free Danny's forelimb and hoof from the human-shaped arm he'd mistakenly thought was his. It's an unpleasant task, but one must simply dig in and do it.

"Do you see?" I ask Carla as I make new incisions across Danny's throat, down his naked sternum, across his soft belly.

She nods from the wall.

"It's not that he was lying to you." I lay the knife down, grip the new wound's lip with one hand and plant the other against the floor to pull back hard. With a wet tearing sound, Danny's garbled sobs turn into plaintive bleats. "He didn't know either."

Like shearing a sheep whose wool has been left to burl and knot, the first cuts are the hardest. Once you get a through-line, though, the outer layers practically peel away. Where Carla likely expected bones and organs, the stuff inside Danny which holds the lamb upright as if on two legs is akin to the pale insides of a pumpkin, albeit more cartilaginous. The chunks of honeycombed gristle wilt in the air, practically deflating now that the husk is breached, leaving just a few moist bones behind. I whistle a tune the forest taught me, push back in, and soon the skin and bloody extra ends are just a pile around the confused animal's cloven feet.

Before my fire the Danny-lamb stands, snow-white wool flecked with crimson buds of blood, but otherwise voluminous and dry. Black eyes gleam like hematite in shadow, and I feel connected on an almost mineral level as I slip the briar harness around his muzzle. The thorns are just long enough to reach through the fur as a gentle reminder, provided he doesn't pull.

I loop the strand of vines that holds the harness around the leg of my stool and sit, leaving enough slack for the lamb to remain standing in the split man-skin on the floor. Its dark eyes are irritated but not angry, like a child caught during Hide-and-Seek who must now wait quietly until the rest of the game is over. And him with no thumbs left to twiddle.

"I want you to know, I'm not judging you," I say to Carla as I wipe my hands on my apron. "But I do hope you'll tell me the truth."

She's released herself from the wall and already shaking her head in answer. She knows the indecent questions the Mad Woman asks, but she knew what I would do to Danny, too, and yet still she lured her husband here to my cottage. Suspicion and modesty are always strange bedfellows, though.

"Did you copulate?"

"No," she says.

I wipe the knife blade, long as my forearm, against my thigh to clean it and watch as Carla floats towards the creature that was inside her husband. "It's not the end if you did," I say, "but I do need you to be truthful: Did you consummate the marriage at all? Even with a covering?"

For the first time tonight, Carla laughs. She shakes her head again, but she is a cat shaking off rain rather than swallowing secrets. "He fucked my leg," she says.

I'm not easy to surprise, but even I blink.

"On purpose?"

She laughs again, a dam unstuck. "I mean, he meant to fuck me. Did he mean for it to be the crease of my thigh? I don't think so, although he was certainly vigorous about it."

Wherever these beasts are coming from, they're unprepared for even the most basic tasks, it seems. Back when this was wild country, when the town was but an outpost, such things were never heard of. What are the town fathers *doing* down there, I wonder?

"When was this?" I ask.

"Last night." She reaches out as if to pat the Danny-lamb, but her fingertips hover just above. "Our marriage was arranged, of course, but he wasn't in a hurry. Early doors, he wasn't very impressive—a bit dull, no help around the house—but I've heard enough whispers from other wives that I wasn't going to wait and see."

A lightness attends this information. I am no stranger to the more intimate shearing that might have been required had Danny—poor fool—made a lay of her, and I am glad not to be there. But that Carla was aware enough, had heard enough, to bring him to me early is a new development. It makes me wonder not only how far word has spread of these creatures, but how common have they become?

"Forgive me," I say, "and again this is intended as no reflection on you, but do you still have the bedsheet from his…error?"

CRRO

After I put the knife away and let Charry and Cinder—the sister cats—back inside, I send Carla home with Danny's old pink skin and extra bones. She's to take them to Annette, the tailor's widow, who will tan and stitch them into a Danny-bag which can hold everything Carla needs to set out from this dying town. The Danny-lamb I offer to her, too—sell him, eat him, train him—but she won't take the briar harness from my hands. Fair enough, I say, and when she's gone, I take him out back and across to the woods behind the pasture.

The next evening, Carla brings me the marital bed's sheet and points out the white on white stain where Danny made his mark. A sniff confirms, so into my iron pot it goes.

The wad of linen stews at a low simmer above the fire. In time, the concoction becomes cloudy white—not like milk, but more a suspension of salt in water. It becomes thicker as it cooks down, the cottage air taking on a damp and earthy musk.

When morning breaks, I pull the bed sheet out and wring it above the pot. Every drop counts. Afterwards, the remaining broth of secretions continues to bubble away, reducing as I take the sheet out to the burn pile near the pasture's edge. The chill mist still hangs low, yet to burn off in the early dawn, and it stiffens my joints as I tread over uneven ground and sharp bristles of sheep's grass.

As I toss the sheet—already rigid with frost—onto the pile of garbage, a dozen or more eyes watch me from the forest's edge. Dull lead and copper orbs with square pupils like keyholes that have nothing on the other side to see or be seen, their mechanical observation annoys me. Even shed of the pretense of being men, these lambs still mill around, desperate for direction and pleading for attention. Not a ram among them, it pains me to see.

"Shoo!" I wave my arms and stomp towards them. "Get!"

They disappear into the recessed branches as the rising sun sweeps the shadows back up under the canopy. The only traces left are their little two-toed hoof prints in the soil, the bearded crusts of frozen dew already melting back into the earth.

☙

Charry, the smaller and darker of the sister cats, is waiting outside the back door as I return. Someone's inside.

I ease the old door open. A man, enormous, is perched on the stool before the embers in my hearth. The iron pot with the boiled-off juices of Danny-lamb still hangs over the coals, a faint ghost of steam rising. The intruder is hunched over as if afraid of hitting the low ceiling despite being seated. Cupped in his massive hands is Cinder, the other sister cat, frozen solid as he pets her with a squeeze.

"Good mother," he says as he turns to me. "Forgive my intrusion, but I was passing by and stopped in to ask directions."

A plain but well-made black traveling coat falls like wings around his sides, a clean linen shirt beneath and sturdy trousers tucked into mud-caked boots. His ruddy skin has been tempered by sun and wind, but he seems as little bothered by the elements as would be a horse. The teeth he bares when he grins are big and orange. He squeezes Cinder while Charry rubs beside my ankle and I shoo her back. This stranger is no guest.

"Forgive me, sir," I say, entering and moving towards the small area where I prepare my food. A peeling knife should be at hand, or even my pestle, if things get desperate. "But I do not think I have had the pleasure to make your acquaintance?"

"No, good mother." He gives the sister cat a slow pulling stroke that wrings out a whimper. "You have not."

"Are you new to town?" I ask. "You had mentioned passing by?" Where is my peeling knife? The blade I opened Danny with would be good, of course, but it is with my other tools beneath the bed.

"Are you looking for something?" the man asks as he rises.

As if bit, I freeze. He's watching me. Waiting. I must not look towards where my tools should be hidden.

"Only a piece of bread or meat I might offer you, sir." I slowly smile broadly as if in apology. "I have so little to give, out here on my own, but all hospitality is yours."

The man tucks Cinder beneath his arm and grins. "I eat no meat, mother," he says, "save that I catch myself."

He shifts and, in one swing of his long legs, he could be on top of me, but instead he curls down over the iron pot. Although his dark hair brushed the rafters when he stood, bent over double he looks practically broken.

"Soup?" he asks.

"Ah," I say. "No soup."

Still bent, he twists and his arms coil more tightly around Cinder. Her sister yowls from the corner and then scampers under the bed. I watch her go and from the shape of the shadows see that my tools and their bag are still secure. Whatever the stranger is looking for, he didn't look there. Not yet.

"No soup?" he asks.

"No soup," I repeat. "That's lye. It's for soap."

He smiles wide, teeth glowing like goals. "So, soap. Not soup."

"Correct," I say.

"You are clever, good mother." He takes a whiff, then wrinkles his nose. With a swift movement he rights himself and plucks Cinder from beneath his arm to hold the limp, defeated cat out in front. Her tail tip dips just into the cooling brew.

But then he kneels to place Cinder to the floor. She's off even as her feet touch, under the bed with her sister cat. From the pool of darkness four green eyes stare at me in terror.

The man now spreads his jacket to reveal a flintlock pistol on his left hip—butt set forward for a duelist's draw. He turns to display a matching holster on the right, this one cradling the silver head of an ax.

"Clever good mother," he repeats. "Hazard a guess at my business here."

His hands are heavy and ribbed by scars. The wicked spark in his eyes says more than any weapon. With thick fingers he pulls a tiny gold medallion on a whisker-thin chain from beneath his shirt and presses it to his lips.

"A guess," he says.

I smile sweetly. "From the ax, good sir, a woodsman, I'd wager."

He stares for a hard moment but then guffaws.

"Yes, mother. Chop chop." He drapes his coat's wings once more over the gun and blade. "Lots of work to do here, with so many good men vanished and their wives run off. Hard to keep a town running, wouldn't you think?"

At these words, I start looking around again, moving as slowly as I can bear in the hopes that he'll mistake *searching* for *puttering*, although I am prepared to club him to death with my kettle, if I must.

There is a creaking and I turn, braced for him to be above me, but instead he has opened the front door. He dips beneath the threshold and smiles again with his orange teeth.

"Thank you, good mother, for a moment by your fire and a hearty laugh, but I must be off to the village now to meet the fathers." He rises and his head vanishes.

"Wait," I call to him. "Did you not say you needed directions?"

He leans back down to look in and smiles even more broadly, eyes burning in the sun.

"Did I? Well, no need, mother. I always find what I'm looking for." He taps his head twice and closes the door behind him.

౭౪౦

Carla comes by the next evening, as the sun is going down and the woods begin to hum and stir. The breeze that sneaks with her through the open door is brisk but doesn't yet whisper of snow. The girl sits by the fire and the empty iron pot takes in every word she says and seasons it with a little metallic echo.

"A hunter has come to town," she says. I offer bread and fresh butter, compounded with sage and thyme, as I take a seat beside her.

"Big fellow," I say. "Teeth like trowels."

Mouth full, Carla nods.

"He came by here," I say. Charry and Cinder watch from the corner, still uneasy. "Did he come to see you yet?"

Carla swallows. "Yes," she says. Her eyes widen as if she can't believe what she has said.

"To ask about Danny?" I continue.

She tries to cover her mouth, but from behind her hands she confirms. Then she asks, "Am I—what's happening?"

I pat her knee. "Hospitality, dear. One cannot lie to gracious hosts, that's a rule."

Rising, I take the iron poker from beside the hearth and prod the glowing wood. The layer of ash flakes away, revealing bones as bright as the sun. I let the poker's tip rest among the coals, slowly beginning to take their color.

"Has Annette finished the bag of Danny's bones and skin?"

"Aye," Carla says. She is watching the metal rod warm from cold iron into something more.

"But you haven't left yet." It isn't a question, so she doesn't answer. "Did you tell the man—the hunter—about the bag?"

"No, mother," she says.

"Did you tell him about Danny?"

"I did, but—"

"Stop." I phrased that poorly and would get a poor answer. "Did you tell him about what we did here?"

Carla's face is the same color as the cold ash.

"No, mother." Her voice cracks like a branch. "I lied and told him my husband had gone to market two towns over."

"Oh?"

"Aye," she says. "I told him this so that I might have enough time to pack the Danny-bag and flee."

I take the poker from the fire, its tip red as the devil's manhood. Carla winces.

"He'd know you for a liar if you ran," I tell her.

"Yes, mother, and likely hunt me, too." She stares at the floor and then, quite without the magic, she says, "I don't think there's a way out now, is there? No way to stay or to run."

I sigh and place the poker back in its stand, the tip already cooling and the fire's glow returning to one even shade.

"Two more questions, dear," I say. Charry has come out and brushes around my ankles like a warm shadow. "Did you mention me to this hunter?"

She shakes her head.

"Say it."

"No, mother," but there's a pregnant pause. "I didn't, but that's because he mentioned you first. I think he already thinks you're— well, what you are."

This is true. His intrusion two days before hinted as much, but I know his type. The kind to wait and pay out the line, to relish in the "sport" of what they do. Nothing new in the world of men or beasts, it seems.

I hold out a hand to Carla and draw her up from her seat. We walk over to the wall where my herbs and poultices are arranged. The jar of milky white suspension is covered by a homespun cloth but seems to glow like the moon through a gauze of clouds.

"Last question," I say to Carla. "What was it you came here tonight hoping to find?"

⁜

After the moon has risen, after the chores are done and the cats are fed and the rubbish taken to the burn pile, I stoke the fire again. I bring in the small copper tub, fill it with three trips from the pump, and wash with a cloth and the last nub of scented soap that reminds me of the purple flowers from the meadows of my childhood. I let it linger on my skin until it becomes too cool and starts to leave a film, then I rinse and dry off.

From beneath the bed, I take my leather bag and open its clasp of white bone. Reaching in deep—past my elbow, past my shoulder, past the ridge of cold air and into the depths—I pull out the yellow candle. The color of fresh butter, I place it in the window facing the pasture. Its wick takes a spark easily and offers a downy cast throughout my small home as I lay myself in bed and roll to face the wall.

Even though I don't mean to sleep, I do, and images of orange teeth and copper eyes with square pupils melt away against the wall as the creak of the back door opening returns me to the present.

The candle is out, house dark, and for a moment my breath catches as the heavy tread crosses the floor. But then the familiar weight bends the straw mattress as I am joined.

How I have missed his warmth. The presence of his body beside me. His hot breath on my shoulder. His beard, curly as wool and stiff as a bird's nest nuzzles against my skin.

"Husband," I say, reaching back, hand running down the fuzz of his chest and belly. "I have missed you."

He doesn't speak, but the touch of his lips on the nape of my neck makes me shiver.

Eyes closed, I roll to face him, pressing front to front. He smells of the pines and rich earth and rain on the mountain stone as I press my face against him. His is the smell of a place far from burn piles, lamb shit, and the fetid musk of unclean laundry. I want to bury myself in my husband, even if only until the sun interrupts us.

"Husband," I say again and push back, eyes still tightly shut. "I need to ask something from you." He doesn't speak but his great chest rises, his heart beating like a slow barrel drum. The tender movement of his inhalation and release answers me.

From beneath my pillow, I retrieve my knife. Even my closed eyes can't stem the tears.

⟨§⟩

In the morning, the hunter's lackeys come for me. Fortunately, I rise early and so the chores are done—the sister cats put out and the leather bag from beneath my bed buried out in the burn pile's ashes—before the village men kick in my door.

The hunter is not with them, but he has taught them his ways. The stammering of words they expect will bind me. A series of overly elaborate knots no more magical than a sheepshank. The only thing they do get right is to put a burlap sack over my head, but that works on everyone. I don't fight them, of course.

As the cart beneath us trembles east along the road toward town, it strikes me again how easily molded young men must be. It has taken no time for the hunter to whip this lot into his preferred shape, down to aping his dress and rubbing ochre on their teeth in imitation of his own orange grin. Do they all have lambs within them too, I wonder, or is it merely that all men are so easily nipped and barked into order?

⟨§⟩

They leave me sitting in the cart for the trial, drawn up in the town square next to a hastily built dais where the town fathers sit behind a long table. A similarly slipshod gallows pole leans beside them, exhausted at having to wait through their pomp to get on with its duty.

One by one, the fathers read the charges—the Prelate condemns me for a consorter with devils and perverter of order, the Mayor for a corrupter of youth, the Doctor for a nuisance to public health.

Their powdered wigs and gray beards shake with indignation that I have hidden in their midst for so long and that I would be festering still were it not for the brave hunter who sits at the far end of the stage. Heavy hands cupping crossed knees, he winks whenever he thinks he's caught my eye.

The assembled town is silent. In the crowd are so many faces of women and men alike who have come to my cottage for aid and yet now do nothing. I set that one's bones; I lifted a curse from the other. She can sleep now; he can speak. What was it I did that went too far? Shearing the lambs, of course. There is a tolerable amount of non-conformity the town fathers' rigged scales can hold before the illusion of balance tips and my finding out—cutting out—the lambs hidden in their dullard sons and husbands has done it. They cannot abide my rooting out the naïve little beasts, so easily swayed and fawning over fathers and hunters but more burdensome than children to the rest.

The fathers' parade of witnesses and lies holds no interest for me, so instead I pass the morning trying to pick out which of the town's men still hide pillowy, malleable creatures beneath their skin. A few are easier to spot than others: the mawkish adherence to the fathers' sartorial fashions, the dull and open-mouthed stares, the distant eyes of the women beside them. Some are harder to spot, and I find it intriguing to observe which faces are swayed and which are doubtful. A few, bless them in the slightest, even look upset at the charade before them. Of course, no one does anything to stop it.

By the time the sun is high, the energy of the "court" is flagging. As the final witness, they call Carla. Emerging from a scrum of hunter's men, she picks her way up the rickety steps, carrying a leather bag. My leather bag. The ashes from the burn pile still dull the gleam and scars of its skin. She does not look at me as she takes the witness chair.

She states her name. They ask if she witnessed me do magic and she says aye. The crowd murmurs and the fathers' gray hairs again tremble.

"And what is this you bring?" the Prelate asks.

Carla bows her head. "I believe it to be hers, your holiness."

"And how did you come by it?" the Mayor asks.

"It was buried in the ashes of the burn pile out by her pasture, near the edge of the forest, your honor."

The Mayor looks to the pack of hunter's men where they mill like curs by the steps. One of them speaks up: "It's true. We saw it. We escorted her there and had to chase off almost a dozen lambs circling the cinders, bleating at it."

The Prelate frowns, lips quivering. "And how did you know it was there, woman?"

How indeed? For the first time, Carla steals a glance at me, but quickly dips her head again.

"Where else to hide evidence of her crimes?" Carla replies.

The Doctor harrumphs. "Yes, yes, very logical." The other fathers grumble and nod.

The Prelate snaps his fingers, gold rings flashing in the noonday sun, and beckons to Carla to hand him the bag. She rises and places it before him, returning to the witness seat again when he waves her back. The Mayor takes the bag from the Prelate and runs his fingers over the leather, the clasps. He passes it to the Doctor, whose face curdles when he realizes this is not cow or deer leather, and that the bone clasp is of a very specific sort.

"Foul!" he shouts to no one and everyone. He wipes his fingers on his shirt but glares at them as if stained when he points at Carla.

"Evidence, did you say?"

She nods.

"Of what?" the Mayor asks.

She looks at me again and I can't help but laugh out loud. The fathers and the crowd, the hunter too, all turn to me.

"Of whatever you want," I say. "Of witchery or murder or marrying the Devil or anything else."

"That's enough," the Doctor says.

"Of being a woman," I yell. "A wicked, wicked woman, come to shear your lamb-sons who pretend to be men and to corrupt your daughters with freedom. An enemy to—"

"Enough!" the Mayor shouts.

"Baaaaah," I bleat back at him.

"Silence!" the Prelate roars.

"Baaah!"

The Prelate rises, face red as a cardinal beneath the gray cloud of his wig. He raises a hand to condemn me further but is interrupted when the hunter slaps his own thigh. As tall as the Prelate even while seated, the hunter strikes his leg again like a gavel and the crowd's attention turns again.

"Let her act out, if she must," he says. "Soon the verdict will come and with it an end to her hysteria. Do not let yourselves stoop to such indignity." He waves dismissively.

Still standing, the Prelate smooths his robes. "Very well," he agrees and takes my leather bag from in front of the Doctor. "Let us have the last bit of evidence introduced and be done."

The Doctor sputters to stop the Prelate but isn't quick enough. The Prelate opens the clasp and is reaching his hand inside. Now his forearm, now his elbow, bicep, shoulder—so much deeper than a bag that size could be and colder, too. His breath comes in little rasping clouds as he realizes something bad is happening.

With a piercing shriek, he yanks his hand out. Three fingers— thumb through middle—are missing. Blood fountains out from the wounds and my bag is trembling, its leather sides heaving in and out like the throat sac of some naked beast. Then the tip of my knife emerges, covered in the Prelate's blood. This is my cue to close my eyes.

From the screams and commotion in the crowd that accompany the strong punch of cedar and pine, I can see what is happening without looking. I can see my husband, terrible in his wrath, emerging from the bag as if born from a well of flesh. He is horrible and he is unwavering, and he loves me as fiercely as I love him.

The screams take on a different timbre as the heavy fall of my husband's leaps and crashes across the stage now land out among the crowd. Iron buries the moss of my husband's scent and I know the chaos that accompanies him like a daughter. The fathers are screaming and the hunter shouts at his men. The crowd is breaking like a flood out of the square, high keening wails that waver between the holy and the damned. Eyes closed, I slip the silly knots of rope from my wrists and blindly leap from the seat of the cart toward where I hope I remember the fathers' platform being.

I hit the boards, thankful not to have missed, and crawl. All around are howls of destruction; the clang of metal and slap of flesh; shouting and rending; the whimpers of the fathers and the bleats of their lambs. As I press forward my elbow bumps an ankle that pulls away with a shrill squeal. My fingers cross a bearded face, still warm but no longer attached to anything below the neck. Finally, I reach the table leg and work my way up, patting across the surface until I feel the stiff and waxy skin of the bag.

Beside me, I hear Carla whimpering beneath her breath, still in the witness seat. "Don't worry," I call. "Just keep your eyes shut."

"Aye," she whispers.

With the bag found, I push my arm inside—deeper, deeper, deeper—there! A dim light I can see behind my eyelids like the moon through a curtain. I grab hold of the jar with the concentrate boiled down from the Danny-lamb's fumbling and drippings and pull it out, the glass smooth and round in my palms.

Then there is a crack of thunder and a tremendous groan rattles the earth. I smell burnt gunpowder and I know what has happened and my heart explodes. I open my eyes.

All around are piles of skin and bits of bone like bloody laundry left wet upon the ground. Dozens of terrified lambs are running in circles, covered in the gore that makes mud of the square. My husband has been busy, cutting and tearing all these cowards free of their shells, but some of them remain only half done. One jogs by with the Doctor's scalp still on its wooly head like a cap. Another keeps tripping over the Prelate's arm and ringed fingers that still cover its forelimb like a rich woman's elbow-length glove. Women and men—not lambs, at least—peer from windows and around corners, witnesses now to the weak beasts hidden in the town fathers and so many, many men. So easily undone, all of them, by the slightest opposition.

But in the bright sunlight of the aftermath, I see that what I feared would happen has. The hunter stands around the empty rag-corpses of his footmen, but in his hand is the smoking pistol and at his feet is the great and shaggy form of my husband, face down in the muck. The cruel barbs of swords and daggers stud his naked back and thighs like steel quills, but the silver head of the hunter's ax crowns them all, beak buried in my husband's neck.

Panting, the hunter looks to me and he, too, is gravely injured. The orange teeth have been split by my husband's fists. The skin across his face is torn and from beneath it tufts of white and black badger bristle protrude. He wobbles in the middle, his bottom half seemingly under separate control from the top as he staggers towards the platform where I stand.

Carla is still seated beside me, trembling, eyes closed. I nudge her foot with mine. "Better go," I say, but like a sister cat, she's gone before I can finish shooing her away.

The broken hunter lurches towards me. The lambs have stopped running and gone still. One by one, they raise their pink noses to the sky and sniff. They fall in around the hunter now like drifts of snow and stare up at where I am holding the jar of cloudy white. Even on the platform, I am only just slightly above the hunter's head.

"Clever, clever," he rasps. Spittle flecks the fur along his jaw and inside the broken orange teeth I see smaller, sharper ones hidden like golden needles. "To bring the devil."

"No devil," I say. "My love."

"Love?" He laughs so hard he convulses, swaying back and forth, almost splitting in half at the waist. "How can you love that?"

What is the answer? I know many things, but not how to explain love to a hunter who does not believe it. Not how to put it in words for lambs who have been told love is the subservience of one spouse to another, and both of them servile still to the fathers.

"I can't teach you," I say.

And with that I hurl the jar and it smashes across the hunter's battered face, covering him in sparkling shards of glass and the viscous brew. He howls and grabs for me but, before his fingers touch, the lambs are on him in a swarm. Pawing with their split hooves, biting at his fingers and lapels, they clamor for the drippings. He swings his arms, scattering a few, but there are too many. One butts him in the knee and the top of the hunter falls over, his body splitting in half at the waist. His legs stumble but stay upright even as his torso claws through the red mud towards the platform steps, only to be buried under the lambs.

They make quick work of the hunter's upper body, stamping and chewing. They tear away his coat and shirt and flesh and I can see the black and white fur of whatever was hiding inside him, but then it too is ripped apart. The hunter's legs only get to run a few steps away from the herd before they're also tackled and devoured, a similar fur exposed beneath the buttocks before that second hidden creature is also devoured as it screams.

And then nothing is left. The lambs mill around, black and white faces covered in blood, tatters of cloth and skin in the corners of their mouths. One of them bleats plaintively and soon the rest follow. Asking for something I don't know how to give them.

Carefully, I descend the steps and, as the town watches, I cross the battlefield of the square to my husband's enormous body. Face down, his arm is outstretched, my knife still clasped in that hand that was only ever tender to me. I pry open his loose fingers and take the knife by its handle.

His body is too heavy for me to roll over, and so I am slipping there in the mud, one hand clutching the knife while my tears stream. But as I struggle, I become aware of someone beside me. Carla. And then Annette. And soon they are all coming from around corners and out of unbolted doors, helping me to roll over the enormous corpse of my wild husband. And with many hands and one great heave, he is over. Face to the sky, his wrathful visage is almost peaceful beneath the mask of mud.

"What will you do now?" Carla asks.

I straddle my husband once more and I raise the knife into the sun. Then I bring the blade down and begin to carve away the skin and extra bits. From within his body the shape of ram's horns begins to emerge; then, through a slit, the golden curls of wool; and I press harder—sure now that I can feel him breathing.

– THE END –
ENJOYED THIS? CHECK OUT:
PERSEPHONE'S ESCALATOR
BY JOE TAYLOR

BENVENUTO, BAMBINI! WHO ISN'T A FAN OF ITALIAN CUISINE? IN THIS TALE, ONE TRAVELER WHO FAILS TO APPRECIATE LOCAL CULTURE LEARNS THAT THE NONNAS ALWAYS TAKE THEIR RECIPES SERIOUSLY. MANGIA, MANGIA!

SALTIMBOCCA

DANIEL A. RABUZZI

"Invaders, intruders in the forest, help, help, come quick, quick, quick!"

Magpies are pirates and crows are loudmouths, but they're not liars, so when we heard them calling, my brother and I ran towards their racket. We burst into the clearing where the charcoal burner Massimo had his kiln. Massimo stood looking nonplussed, confronted as he was by a figure on a horse—which meant trouble because only a fool or a tyrant would ride a horse into a forest. The rider was an upstart sort of fellow, in city garb with a high collar and very fine boots—in other words, not one of us, not a *vicino*, a dweller in the forest, a member of the woody commons. He sat the horse like a clothespin clamped on a laundry line. A bedraggled man-at-arms stood beside the horse, both he and the animal looking as if they wished to be anywhere but here. The birds jeered at them.

"I don't understand a word he speaks," said Massimo, turning in relief to us. "Some sort of Latin, like a priest, and then it gets really strange."

The rider peered down his nose to inspect us. He wrinkled that nose, then pulled out a sheaf of papers from a satchel by the saddle. That could only spell more trouble—when they present documents and get all official, it means they aim to take something from us or deny us some freedom.

Darting a glance at the rider and seeing that he was being ignored, the attending man-at-arms rolled his eyes and made a furtive gesture with his free hand, the one we make when we've been cheated by a merchant or thwarted by a functionary.

"Per voluntatem dei et iussu ducis," said the rider, in the voice of a man used to being obeyed. "I am authorized to find and bring to justice the witch, known to be harbored within these woods, who lures innocent children with her house built out of gingerbread, therein trapping them for her cannibalistic pleasures."

That was a mouthful, to be sure! The foxes looking on from the hazel thicket, the squirrels in the beeches, the woodpeckers on the oaks…we all took a moment to understand what we thought we had heard. Even the crows and magpies fell silent. Massimo shook his head and looked at us with a resigned "See, what did I tell you?" look.

The rider spoke some sort of Italian but not a Tuscan tongue. We were used to the dialects spoken by the hunters and gleaners who came from the villages near Pieve Fosciana and Barga, by the swineherds whose rambunctious passels feasted on the mast from the oaks and the beech, and by the friars who held services at our chapel once every quarter. We could understand the lordly *padroni* and their retinues from Lucca and from Pistoia when they visited every third or fourth year to pay homage to the forest and maintain their ancient privileges over specific tracts of timber. All these people belonged to the forest, coursing within its green waters in regular, time-honored channels, offering due deference to the spirits of the wood. But this rider, with his bizarrely accented Italian and his ostentatiously embossed and printed papers, was the very definition of an interloper.

"Sir," I said, after conferring with my brother. "Welcome."

The rider interrupted, his sniff accentuated by his posture atop the horse.

"Welcome is not what I am after," he said. "I want the *strega*."

The man-at-arms looked down at the ground, his pike sagging. The charcoal burner shook his head. My brother and I stepped forward.

"Well, sir," I said. "Be welcome nonetheless. Clearly you are from…somewhere north, I would guess? Your words have a sound of Modena…maybe Reggio Emilia?"

"In a manner of speaking," he snorted. "I am an emissary from the Holy Roman Emperor himself, the most illustrious Charles VI, *Gott erhalte den Kaiser*. It appears to have escaped your attention that we Austrians have taken the Duchies of Modena and Parma. We are now bringing necessary light to your rusticated precincts, all the most modern ways of thinking, rooting out the old and backwards and all that is wicked."

My brother and I gaped at this. The birds erupted with an even more clamorous din. One of the magpies swooped low upon the man on the horse, who drew a very large pistol from the satchel and waved it about.

"Creatures!" he cried. "Bandits and devils!"

I vaguely recalled that there had been some big war out there, beyond our green veils, something involving a bloody dispute over who would be the king of Poland, great armies from faraway France and Spain fighting Austrians in Italy, none of it making any sense to us.

"Well," I said, looking to my brother for support. "In any event, this is Tuscany, not Modena. You've come over the top of the mountains, into the forest of Serchio."

"It matters not," said the Austrian, with another slurry of chancellery words and references to treaties and rights we had never heard of.

My brother looked at the man-at-arms.

"I think I know you," he said. "Aren't you one of the Agostianos from Sillico?"

"Nearly," said the pikeman, brightening, even as he threw a quick glance at the rider. "One of their cousins, through my mother. I'm a Barciani from Pastina."

"Oh yes," said my brother. "The bakers."

The man-at-arms broke into a big smile.

"Enough!" said the rider. "Don't talk to him. He's just a servant."

"But how do you come to be in *his* service?" said my brother, pointedly ignoring the Austrian.

"They came with their guns and papers, and used lots of words we didn't rightly comprehend but in the end it amounted to stealing the bakery from us," said the baker from Pastina, very quickly and with as much local dialect as possible, to minimize the likelihood of being understood by the man on the horse.

"*Schweigen*, silence, impudent wretch!" shouted the Austrian, waving his pistol for emphasis. "Per martial law and with all proper procedure, this man's bakery was requisitioned for the war effort. And we offered him personal service as due compensation. A privilege, really, for one so slovenly."

The baker looked desperate, and we nodded in sad understanding. So it always went with those who came on horseback into our community of roots and leaves.

"Enough," said the intruder. "Where is the witch's house? Do you know it? All rumor and legend have led me here. Don't lie to me—or your fate will not be one to your liking."

My brother and I recalled a time of woe, when the forest had taken us in and succored us. Like so many others, we had been orphaned by famine, pestilence, and the marauding of troops. Deep into the woods we fled, helped by the birds and the beasts, until at last we found a beloved *nonna* in her cottage between the beech trees. *Brutto ma buono* as we say, not pretty but good, that little house, as comforting and sweet as the uneven *pizzelle* and the lumpy *cantucci* baked there. It may have been ramshackle but it smelled like small heaven, with an intertwined aroma of anise, rosemary, crushed hazelnuts, olive oil brought up from the valley. It was wreathed with yellow broom, sage, dried wood-anemone. It was guarded by an elegance of wrens and a caution of crows, and a fox was its herald. A *nonna*, not a *strega*, lived there, providing us with a home, feeding us until we regained our flesh and our wits, and loving us so that our hearts hummed with the bees and sang with the thrushes.

We knew what we had to do. The charcoal burner and the baker looked at us expectantly. So did the horse. We felt the pressure of many eyes gazing at us from the rim of the clearing, and from the sky above. So, we did what we must: We convened the *magnifica comunità*, the congress of the forest. The Austrian continued to sit astride his horse, haughtily oblivious, while time became as glutinous as *zabaglione*, and the light slowed, with an undertone of *verde chiaro* suffusing the air for those who had the eyes to see such pale green. We asked the magpies to convey the call. We sent the squirrels across bole and bough. We roused the owls, badgers, and bats, and old *bruno*, the bear of the mountain. No one would convoke the assembly except for matters of mortal importance. No one present took their duties lightly, but in short order (if one can speak about discussions held beyond the clock's reach) all agreed to the judgment at hand. We would appeal to Silvana, the great dryad, the lustral and avenging

Titania. As custom dictated, the chief of the hares was our *scario* and *saltaro*, the messenger we sent to alert Her and to prepare the way.

"I ask this one last time," said the Austrian, ignorant of our debate and unaware as time and light returned to their ordinary workings. "Where may I find the witch?"

"We yield," I said, bowing my head to aid my pretense. "We will show you, if you promise not to harm us."

As we knew it would, our plea for mercy flattered him immensely.

"Of course," he said, flourishing his document in the one hand, and his pistol in the other. "We are nothing if not magnanimous."

"Her house lies only a league away, up that valley, where the chestnuts cluster," my brother said. "But the path is very narrow and winding, through holm oak, smilax, and hornbeam so dense that no horse could take you there. You will need to leave your horse here, with your servant, and proceed on foot."

The rider looked most displeased, but our further description of the difficult path finally persuaded him to dismount and hand the reins to the baker.

"You will be rewarded for this," he said, as if he were distributing precious gems. "His Imperial Majesty will know of this directly from me."

"Please give her our regards," said my brother. "Be sure to tell her that we, Ninnillo and Nennella, sent you."

"I will," said the Austrian, who scowled at the baker. "And you, knave...if you steal my horse, it will go very ill for you... understood?"

The baker mumbled his assent, but his eyes said something else. The horse whickered.

All the birds called out as the Austrian left the clearing along the route we had described. He thought they were saluting him.

"Well," said the baker, once his erstwhile master had vanished into the green. "What am I to do with this friendly horse?"

"His previous master will have no more need of him," I said. "Take him back to Pastina, treat him well. I think you will also find that your bakery awaits you."

"I'll put this here pike up in our loft," said the baker, smiling. "Just in case others like that one come over the mountain. Please stop in anytime—your bread I will always give to you for free."

He led the horse (who looked very pleased himself) in the opposite direction from the route the Austrian had taken. The charcoal burner whistled and got back to minding his kiln. The magpies and crows began their usual badinage. The forest breathed out.

Somewhere in the depths of the woodlands, the Austrian smelled the ginger and lemon-peel of *cavallucci* and the almond paste of *ricciarelli*. Bewildered, he entered a glade wherein stood a house whose walls were slabs of *panforte* and whose roof was made of *cantucci* and *bruttiboni* and many other kinds of *biscotti* besides. The windows reflected an orange-colored glaze. From inside, a sugary voice beckoned him to the supper table. He went in.

Three months later, to the day, just before dawn, we heard a knock on the door of our *nonna's* house. We knew not to open the door before sunrise. When the sun rose, we found on the doorstep an oak box, with delightful if slightly macabre carvings on it. We found inside a large pistol broken in two, and a sheaf of ripped documents, their edges scorched. At the bottom was a note written on a large beech leaf, in what might or might not have been blood (best not to look too closely).

"Thank you," the note said. "I appreciated the dinner guest you sent, who received his just desserts. Seasoned, sophisticated, oleaginous. In truth, he was *saltimbocca*."

WELL WELL WELL, AREN'T YOU JUST CHOWING DOWN ON THIS DREAD-DRENCHED, GHAST GALA OF A BOOK LIKE ITS GUTS WERE MADE OF PURE HONEY? YOUR PEEPERS MUST BE POPPING RIGHT OUT OF YOUR HEAD! STILL IN THERE? WE CAN HELP WITH THAT! COME ON, HAND 'EM OVER! NO? OH, YOU SWEET, SILLY, STUBBORN SOUL! YOU THINK YOU HAVE A CHOICE—HAHAHAH! UP NEXT WE HAVE A QUICK LITTLE STING THAT'LL LEAVE YOU . . . MESMER-EYES-ED.

CONSUMED ILLUSIONS

ALEXIS DUBON

There once was a beautiful princess. Her makers were certain they'd gotten her just right, they'd figured it all out—how to rule through charm. She was made of porcelain and gold, with sapphire eyes. Fed acrid meat with the promise that it would turn sugarsweet inside her. The more she consumed, the more her insides melted until they were jelly, where wasps fed at night and made her dream of venom.

The princess was kept in a castle made of spider silk, which glittered in the sun and held dewdrops like diamonds. Her makers crafted her with care, and were happy to allow her subjects to look upon her through those whisper-thin walls.

She was told she was modeled from angels and she believed it. While others walked on dirt and stone, she felt only clouds beneath her feet. She was imbued with nectarous poisons, which she believed to be potions, and told everyone her blood was sourced from star rivers. That she could cure any illness with a single drop. That celestial light ran through her veins. And they believed it too.

No one would have thought otherwise because at night, when she roamed the dark castle, she shined opalescent, haloed in glow.

No one knew this was only the wasps at work, beating their tiny wings inside her liquified belly, feasting on spoiled and sour victuals.

But lies, however enchanting, can only remain without cracks for so long. Her exquisite exterior was thin and delicate, difficult to maintain. Eventually, fractures crept through the ceramic; windows formed from shatter. Scuffs and warps exposed small gaps along golden trim. Whispers spread throughout the kingdom—the princess's beauty was nothing but varnish. She was ghastly underneath.

There were powerful people who served her makers, whose loyalty had been easily bought. They were given great riches, so long as the princess could keep their tongues on her nightstand. Pink and fleshy and studded with buds, they were much lovelier than the faces of those whose mouths they once filled. These she preserved in a bowl of rosewater and threw like bombs at anyone who dared call her a monster.

When they were no longer of use, the tongueless acolytes were fed to the princess one at a time—meat and bone and hair. She picked tendons from her teeth with sharp metal talons, her costume now entirely devoured by wasps, who had become so well-fed, they multiplied until her insides could no longer satisfy the swarm.

All who saw the ooze that leaked between the black wire of her skeleton were destroyed without question, and those who survived had been so privileged because they'd gouged out their own eyes. Some who saw, pretended not to and were spared, permitted to live without blood-pooled chasms in their faces. They swore the princess remained as beautiful as ever—immaculate, angelic, sublime—swore to exterminate what remained of the sighted who claimed otherwise. The most vocal of all in their devotion, the most eager to prove their piety, these loyalists slaughtered friend and family alike in the name of the princess's perfection.

She made a crown from all the eyeballs she collected during the massacre and declared herself Queen. Strung each orb one by one along a wire thread and coiled it around her skull. With so many eyes, she could see most anything, but she only directed her gaze at her mirror. She still saw that beautiful porcelain mask. Lustrous gold and sapphire, a luminously limned silhouette. Disguises which had long since been chewed up and regurgitated into nightmares by her winged bêtes, illusions she was certain were true. Even with a tower of eyes mounted on her head, the only ones that mattered were her own, and they saw beauty in that mirror.

She spoke only to her reflection and was pleased to find it always agreed with her. And though they loudly avowed their love and loyalty, her subjects could never comprehend the true fathoms of her perfection the way she did. After all, isn't that what made her their Queen? Superior to all in every way, there was no one who could delight her as much as her own reflection.

The Queen, paying no attention to anything other than the mirror, didn't realize she had eaten the last of her hired acolytes. She did not realize her makers had abandoned the kingdom in hopes of crafting a new princess in a new land, one who wouldn't rupture so easily. They had been tithed enough money in veneration of the porcelain princess's beauty, that maybe this one they could cast from pure gold. Fill her with honeybees instead of wasps. Feed her sweet things—fruit and caramel. These are valuable lessons they learned from the mistakes of the Queen's body.

Very few people remained to worship her. Some journeyed far away, to distant relatives who would greet them with open arms; some stood firm, killing each other because they did not believe their opponent was truly as devout as they insisted; some wandered sightlessly into the sea. She ate whoever was left after that.

And then she was alone. In her castle of shredded spider silk, its gauzy walls torn and splattered puce with carnage. Her brood of wasps fed on whatever they could scavenge, until they were forced to eat the withered, misshapen eyeballs that adorned the Queen's head. Once those were gone, there was nothing but each other to eat. And soon, there were no more beating wings and the kingdom was silent and still, inhabited only by the Queen and her beautiful nightmares.

> **– THE END –**
> ENJOYED THIS? CHECK OUT:
> *GODFESTATION*
> BY JENDIA GAMMON

IN THE SHADOW OF THE GHETTO

GREGG STEWART

U p until one minute ago, Vincenzo Sardella thought he was the cleverest son of a bitch in Little Italy. The heist he'd orchestrated tonight was set to be the stuff of legend. But hey, one minute you're an up-and-coming criminal mastermind, and the next, you've unleashed a demonic spirit upon an unsuspecting public. It happens.

How'd he get into this mess? Like most messes, it started with a pretty blonde from the ghetto. She was sixteen and pregnant with

Vinny's baby. Her father was a rabbi who walked the neighborhood carrying a shotgun. Don't ask. It just gets worse from here on out.

If I'm honest, Vinny's life was kind of a *spettacolo di merda* even before he fell for Sadie Goldheim.

Back in August of 1925, at the tender age of fifteen—and with no family, money, or prospects—Vinny left Naples on a slow boat to America. By the time he reached Ellis Island, over fifty passengers had died from dysentery. But Vinny tended to be lucky, right up until he wasn't. It didn't happen often, but when his luck ran dry, it turned to friggin' bone dust.

Eight days after settling at a flophouse on Mulberry Street with us other guineas, young Vincenzo met Sal Pimonte. Now, Sal was a good guy to know if you were Italian and new to the city, but not in Vinny's case.

Truth is this city hates us *Eye-talians*. No one will hire us. Vinny had been trying to drum up work since he arrived and was having no luck whatsoever. Remember that thing about him and luck?

Desperate and hungry, Vinny decides food is more important than the threat of a New York City jailhouse, so he steals a loaf of bread from the corner market—Sal's corner market.

Now, had Vinny just asked for the bread, Sal might have given it to him, but Vinny was the proud sort. Bad luck for him.

After Sal and his guys were done kicking Vincenzo's *dupa* up and down the alley and giving him a proper Lower East Side welcome, Sal informed the would-be thief that he'd be working off that loaf of bread until his new boss decided Vinny had paid his debt. Sal also told Vinny that if he didn't make good on his debt, one of his guys would gift the little *bastardo* with a pair of cement shoes and a nice, long bath in the East River—and that was a promise.

Vinny took the job on the spot, ecstatic to find work. Turns out he was good at it. He'd make deliveries, collect envelopes full of cash, and never act too curious about any of it. He'd even smack someone around if they tried to pull a fast one on Sal. All the while, Vinny would keep that trademark Casanova grin plastered on his face and that spring in his step. He took to his new vocation with such gusto that Signore Salvadore Pimonte—resident bigwig of the Italian Quarter—put Vinny on his payroll within the month.

This mutually beneficial arrangement went on for the next year and a half. Vinny even got me hired on as his extra muscle. It seemed like Vinny's luck was back, and like grabbing a tiger by the tail, he'd be damned if he was letting go of it this time.

Then he met Sadie. There was something about that girl—her sultry, heavy-lidded eyes, that wry smile, the way she walked down the street, the way she looked at him. Oh, she was trouble. We got one rule in Little Italy. Well, we got a lotta rules, but one of the big unspoken rules is this: Ya don't go messin' with the Jewish girls over on Eldridge Street. Ya stay outta the ghetto.

I was there the night Vinny met her. I tried to tell him. But he was feeling lucky. I was also there a few months later when Sadie dropped that baby bombshell on him. He didn't feel so lucky then.

He moped around for the next week, kept throwing down his chestnut brown fedora, kicking it down the sidewalk, and then picking it up again to dust it off.

Every day I asked him, "What are ya gonna do about this gal says she's havin' your baby?"

All he said was, "Lemme think on it, lemme think."

A few days later, we're heading down Delancey to deliver a couple cases of *vino rosso* to Bennie's when we see the wagons coming down the block. Rows and rows of 'em, all painted in crazy bright colors. At the end of the procession, there's this giant friggin' wheel on a flatbed.

"That one o' them Ferris wheels?" I asked. Vinny hates when I ask questions I already know the answer to, so I followed up with another real quick. "Hey, did you know the carnival was comin'?"

Vinny looked up and stopped cold. "Hey!" He called to a man clad in dungarees leading an ostrich on a leash. "Where ya settin' up?"

The man pointed to the empty lot down Eldridge Street.

"Next to the synagogue?" Vinny asked. The guy nodded, and that's when Vinny's eyes went wide with excitement. "That's it, Gio! The miracle I been prayin' for. I friggin' got it!"

"Got what?" I asked. "You gonna run away with the circus?"

"No," Vinny scoffed. "I been tryna think of a way into that synagogue for a week, and now we got ourselves the perfect distraction!"

"Get into the synagogue? You convertin'?"

"Nah, ya *stoonad*! We're gettin' Daddy Rabbi to pay for me and Sadie's big elopement."

"You're gonna marry her? Wait, you're *robbin'* the synagogue? But the carnival is right next door. All those people."

"Yeah, it's genius," Vinny said. "Don't ya see? No one's gonna be lookin' at the door on the other side of the building. Everyone'll be at the fairground!"

"You sure about this?"

Vinny leaned in with a conspiratorial whisper. "Sadie once let it slip that there's a ton o' cash just sittin' in there. So, why not go get it? Then she and I can head to Los Angeles and be together."

"Los Angeles? Why there?"

"C'mon, Gio! Grow a little imagination. I'm gonna be in the pictures!"

"Pshh! There ain't no Italians in the movies."

"Oh, ya never heard of Rudolph Valentino?"

"Yeah, but he's from Persia or Arabia or somethin'."

"His name's *Val-en-ti-no!* It don't get more Italian than that. *Mamma Maria,* God gave you all muscle and no brains, you know that?"

"A-right, a-right! So, what's the plan for gettin' in?"

"First, we gotta talk to Sal. We're gonna need some help to do this right."

⊂ℛℬ⊃

The meeting with our boss did not go the way Vincenzo had hoped.

"Ya wanna what?" Sal asked.

"You'll love it, it's a carnival," Vinny said. "They got clowns."

"I hate clowns."

"Oh. Well, they got one of them Ferris wheels, and we saw a real live ostrich! Didn't we, Gio?" Vinny's smile slipped as he saw Sal's sour expression. "And, uh, and a bearded lady. Ever seen that?"

"Yeah," Sal replied, folding his arms over his chest. "It's just a guy in lipstick and a dress."

"No it ain't! It's a bearded la—" Vinny paused. "*Mamma Maria!* Is it really just a guy in a dress? How did I never put that together?"

"You kids think you're so smart," Sal said as he lit a cigarillo. "Forget the carnival, Vincenzo. Forget this synagogue business. You don't steal from a holy place. Everybody knows that. It's bad luck—the worst kind. Giovanni, talk some sense into this boy."

I could only shrug. "He says it's a lot of money in there, Signore Pimonte." Vinny kicked my leg as I said it.

"Yeah? And who told ya that?" Sal asked, waving his cigarillo in Vinny's general direction.

"Just some girl."

"What girl?"

"Rabbi's daughter," Vinny replied, swallowing hard and giving me a look like he and I had some business to settle in the alley when this meeting was over.

"Oh yeah?" Sal said, nodding like he was interested now. "And she shared this with you? You're her priest or somethin'?"

"Nah, it's nothin', Signore Pimonte. She's just—" Vinny gave a dismissive wave. "Just a girl I talk to sometimes."

Sal took a long drag off his cigarillo and narrowed his eyes at us. "Ya ever hear of the Kabbalah?"

"The what?"

"Good," Sal said, exhaling a cloud of smoke. "Stay outta the ghetto, Vincenzo, and especially stay away from the Jews at the Eldridge synagogue. We don't mess with folks like that. You don't know like I know."

I gotta admit, that statement took us both aback. What did Sal mean? Sure, the Rabbi Goldheim carried a shotgun in broad daylight. From the little I knew, that was not typical Jewish behavior, but Sadie seemed like a decent sorta gal. And the neighborhood might be poor, but it was quiet and clean. The people kept to themselves. There wasn't no yelling in the streets or dishes thrown at the walls at two in the morning like we had over here on Mulberry Street. That struck me as kinda strange once I thought about it. What happens to a person when you don't blow off a little steam now and again?

"Maybe he's right, Vin," I said.

Vinny chewed at his lower lip, thinking. "Yeah, it's a stupid idea. Forget I said anything."

Sal gave Vinny a knowing appraisal. "Don't get any funny ideas. Nothing happens behind my back." Sal stepped in real close to Vinny and waggled a thick forefinger in his face. "You bring a war with the Jews upon us, and you'll be fitted for a new pair of cement shoes followed by a nice, long bath in the East River. Ya hear me? It's dark down there, kid, not even your shadow to keep you company."

"I hear you," Vinny said, his eyes turned to the floor.

Sal nodded. "Good boys. Now, I need ya both to head over to Chinatown. The Lady Li's got garlic coming in on her rooftop garden. It's the best, I tell ya."

Sal exhaled another smoke cloud, and his eyes went dreamy for a moment. "Bring me two boxes," he said, tossing an envelope of cash to Vinny. "Go now, before the friggin' Hungarians grab it all."

Vinny didn't say a word the whole way to Chinatown and back. An hour later, we'd delivered the garlic, and I followed him straight to the open lot on Eldridge Street to watch the carnival set up shop. The Ferris wheel looked enormous. I'd never seen anything like it.

"People go up in that?" I asked, feeling a cold tingle down in my fruits. Vinny nodded, eyes squinted, looking like he was cooking up some big plans.

I saw he was staring at the synagogue now. It was hard to miss with its bulbous spires and six-pointed stars reaching up to the heavens, and that huge, circular high window at its center, looking like a massive glass flower. The building cast a long shadow, and I realized we were standing in it.

"We're doin' this anyway, huh?" I asked.

I could tell Vinny's mind was working overtime, thinking about how he'd get it done under Sal's nose. "Yeah," he said, his voice low and flat. "We're doin' it anyway."

※

The next day, he'd spilled the whole plan to Sadie, which I thought was a terrible idea. Turns out she was as excited as all get out. Imagine that? If you ask me, I don't go in for a girl who would steal from her old man, but Vinny was in love, I guess. He also knew we'd need her help, so I had to admit, he was right to let her in on the scheme.

First, she gave us a rough description of the ornate wooden strongbox where her gun-toting father, Rabbi Goldheim, kept all the money. Next, on the first night of the carnival, she'd be our lookout, setting up across the street and ready to whistle if anyone was about to walk past us. The plan was simple, as it turns out. Most good plans are.

As we stood in the alley ready to break through the side door of the synagogue, we could hear the carnival on the other side of the building—music, chimes and bells, the mechanical hum of the Ferris wheel, and the squeals and laughter of children.

The smell of fresh pretzels filled my nostrils. "We gonna go to the carnival when we're done here?" I asked, my belly rumbling.

"Course we are. Anyone sees us here we'll lose them in the crowd. I told ya, Gio, it's perfect."

I hefted the crowbar from inside my jacket. A minute later, we were inside.

I'd never been in a synagogue before. It seemed about the same as any church, but there were differences. First off, did you know the women and the men enter through separate entrances and don't all sit in the same room? Yeah, that was news to me. We entered on the men's side, which meant that, other than breaking the law, we weren't also breaking any strict religious rules. I can't explain why, but this fact calmed my nerves.

Vinny made a straight line for the altar, or whatever they call it here. He went about rummaging through the place like the way the cops do when they're looking for contraband in the flophouse—tipping everything over, throwing crap around—as if you'd find anything that way. "Hey!" I said in a harsh whisper. "There ain't enough light in here to be tossing crap around. We're gonna trip and break our necks on somethin' on the way out."

Vinny stopped and stared. "That's actually good thinkin', Gio."

"I have my moments."

We went about moving a bit slower. Vinny figured the strongbox wouldn't be sitting in the open, so we started looking in drawers, under heavy books, and checking the back room.

After ten minutes, I heard an excited gasp.

"What?" I called, "Ya find it?"

Vinny was pulling a large wooden box from a closet. The thing was two-and-a-half feet long and one foot deep—way too big for a moneybox, if you asked me. Man, these people must be loaded.

I stepped closer and saw it had weird markings all over it. "What are these?"

"It's Hebrew."

"He-what?"

"It's how Jews talk."

"Oh. When your gal told us it had ornate carvings all over it, I thought it'd be flowers and vines or somethin'."

"Nah, this is it," Vinny whispered, his eyes glowing with excitement. "Think about how much money ya can fit in this thing. There's just a small lock. Here, gimme that crowbar."

I handed it to him and watched as he pried the lock with little effort.

Vinny paused. "Seems too easy for somethin' full o' dough," he said, growing wary. "Maybe it ain't the right box."

"Wanna keep lookin'?" I asked, feeling a growing uneasiness creeping up my spine and tingling at my temples.

"Nah," he replied, shaking off his concerns. "We already got the lock off. Might as well see what's inside."

I could tell he was feeling lucky, and I found myself caught up in the moment, thinking about the small fortune that must be inside this box.

With great care, Vinny lifted the lid. A puff of thick black smoke wafted up from within and settled tar-like along the back wall.

We looked down. The box was empty save for what seemed to be pale, whitish dust and a few tiny shards, like bone.

We gazed up at the wall and saw the smoke had formed into a shadow—horned, hunched, with a spiked tail and gangly arms that led to long daggers at its fingertips. It turned in profile as it opened its mouth, showing razor teeth.

I made the sign of the cross and then wondered if that would work in a synagogue.

The shadow's forked tongue licked the cool night air, and it let out a hideous cackle that dropped us to our knees, covering our ears from the pain.

On instinct, I scrambled behind one of the long rows of pews, crouching low and hoping the vile devil would simply get back inside the box we'd freed it from, but no such luck.

Vinny was screaming at it now, shaking the crowbar in one hand. Next to the shadow's hulking frame, he looked like a kid who'd had his lunch money stolen and was wailing for his teacher to come over and reprimand the big bully.

The shadow continued cackling as it stared down at Vinny from the wall.

"Vin!" I yelled, scuttling back to the side door like a frightened crab. "Run!"

He didn't need me to tell him twice.

As he raced for the doorway, the shadow slid along the wall at lightning speed, stretching its body and twisting to block our exit.

We barreled through the side door and into the alley like two maniacs fleeing the madhouse. Sadie's face went white as she saw us sprinting her way. Without thinking, Vinny grabbed her by the arm as we raced down Eldridge Street, heading toward the carnival.

Sadie was yelling something, but we weren't listening. I glanced over my shoulder and saw the shadow scurrying along the outer wall of the synagogue, looking small as a rat now, with its teeth gnashing and spiked tail flailing behind.

As we dashed into the fairgrounds, the shadow skittered along and leaped onto one of the tents, disappearing.

We paused to catch our breath, eyes darting, trying to spot the hellish thing.

"What have you done?" Sadie asked, her eyes like flames. "It took my father's great-grandfather almost a decade to hunt that thing down and trap it. We've gotta lure it away from here."

"What in Christ's name is it?" Vinny asked, chest heaving. "You said the loot was in an ornate box. That was the box!"

"Not *that* box!" Sadie scolded, growing angrier still. "Where did you even find that?"

"In the closet!" Vinny yelled. He was getting mad now.

Sadie crossed her arms, looking even angrier. "I told you it was under the bimah!"

"What the frick is a bimah!"

Sadie huffed and looked away. "I also said it had ornate carvings," she muttered. "Like flowers and vines."

"Ah, *Mamma Maria!*" Vinny yelled, throwing his arms in the air. He took off his fedora and threw it on the ground. "Damn it!"

I knew this was no time to say I told ya so, and so I kept my eyes on the tent, hoping to spot the vile shadow. Also, these two were going to have a long and happy marriage, I could tell. The best ones all started out this way. Didn't they?

"Well, how do we kill it?" Vinny asked, picking up and dusting off his hat.

"You can't kill it," Sadie said. "You have to trap it again."

"Fine. How do we do that?"

"You're not gonna like it."

"Christ, Sadie, tell us anyway!"

"It's going to start possessing people. We need to get it to go inside a baby. Then, we lock the baby in the box."

All the blood ran out of my head, and my eyesight blurred a moment. Carnival music rang in my ears, and the scent of pretzels made me want to puke. I looked away from the tent and saw Vinny's ghost-white face. He and I were thinking the same thing, I knew. The bone dust and tiny shards in the box—they had locked a possessed baby in there.

"How do we get it to go inside a baby?" Vinny asked with a voice that told me he didn't want to know the answer.

"We act like the infant matters to us. First, we protect it. Then, it goes for it."

"Maybe we oughta get the rabbi?" I cut in, "He may have a better—"

"No!" Sadie yelled. "This is the only way. If he finds out you've freed it, he'll kill you both first, before he goes to trap it again."

Vinny looked around at all the laughing children. He looked at Sadie's belly. "I…I can't."

"We have to," Sadie replied, her voice stern. "Otherwise, a whole lot of people are going to die."

"Die how?" Vinny muttered, looking back toward the tent.

"Once it possesses someone, we'll need to kill them to get it out. The faster we get it to choose a child, the less people it'll possess. Now one of you, go get the damned box!"

"I'll go," Vinny said.

"Wait," Sadie said, grabbing him by the arm. "I'll get it. You freed it, so I don't think it'll possess either of you. Me on the other hand, well, best if I steer clear."

From our initial encounter with the shadow, I wasn't sure if she was right about us being free from possession, but I held my tongue.

"Fine. You go get the box," Vinny said. "And we need to find…a baby."

Sadie gave him a somber nod before running back to the synagogue.

Vinny watched her go. By the look on his face, I could tell that he was considering jumping the next train to anyplace other than here.

"Hey," I said, giving him a nudge. "What's the plan?"

Vinny bit at the inside of his cheek and furrowed his brow. "We gotta find that thing. We need to get it away from here."

He spun on his heel and ran in the direction of the tents while I lumbered along behind. As I rounded the corner, I found him standing stock still, staring at an ostrich not ten strides away. Its handler lay bloody at Vinny's feet. All at once, I saw the evil glow in the bird's eyes, and I knew. "Christ, it's inside the ostrich."

Vinny nodded, lifting the crowbar from his jacket.

The bird charged.

The fight lasted all of three seconds, all orchestrated to the sounds of carnival music, which made the entire encounter something well beyond the weird and strange. I'd never seen a fight between a guy and an ostrich before, but let me tell you, if you're ever about to get into a skirmish with a bird that big, do yourself a favor and run.

First, the ostrich kicked out with its enormous foot, sending Vinny and the crowbar flying in separate directions. I thought he was dead right there, but as the bird leaped to peck out his throat, Vinny kicked it away. It did not go flying the way he did and was right back at him in the next moment. Still, it gave me enough time to snatch up the crowbar at my feet. With a lunge, I spun my arm like a windmill, bringing the crowbar down on its head. It collapsed in a heap on top of Vinny, leaving blood and bits of skull and brains splattered on his chest.

"Ew! Christ, Gio!"

"*Prego*," I replied, gripping the crowbar tighter as the ostrich's shadow morphed back into a devil and dashed along the line of tents, skipping like a flame as it went.

With a kick, I knocked the bird carcass off Vinny and pulled him to his feet. In a flash, we were pursuing the shadow again. We had to stop this demon. Killing an ostrich was one thing, but I knew the next victim would be human. I didn't want to have to kill someone. Not tonight or any night. As I ran, I looked from one smiling and laughing kid to another, feeling my heart sinking lower and lower at the thought of putting a baby inside that wooden box.

When we reached the Ferris wheel, things took an even worse turn. The machinist lay in a pool of blood with his throat ripped and torn open. The wheel was going around with no one to stop it. Children and adults screamed from their tiny gondolas as they spun wildly around.

Vinny slapped my shoulder, and I glanced over to see him pointing at the center of the wheel. I looked up to find a demure figure in a large hoop skirt scaling the rotating girders. Blood covered its face and dripped off its beard.

"Nooo," I whined. "Not the bearded lady!"

Vinny gave a grim nod. "We gotta go up there."

"Do we?" I asked.

"She's gonna go from car to car killing everyone. We need to stop her."

I shook my head. "Well, I'm not climbing this thing while it's moving." I shoved the crowbar into Vinny's hands and jumped over the machinist's body. Without stopping to consider my actions, I pushed and pulled at levers until the wheel jerked to a stop and hung suspended.

"*Buono!*" Vinny called. "You get these people off, one car at a time, while I scale it and take care of that thing."

I didn't like that idea, but I disliked the alternative even more. "Sure, you climb it!"

While Vinny scaled the Ferris wheel, heading for the possessed bearded lady, I ushered folks off and told them to steer clear until we had the situation under control.

News spread fast up and down the fairground. I heard the kids all yelling, "The bearded lady went crazy!" but I stayed focused, getting people to safety one car at a time while keeping an eye on Vinny, now halfway up the enormous wheel. "Please, God, don't let him fall."

I reached a point where the cars only contained blood-soaked bodies. The creature was picking people off with ease. I cursed and yelled up to Vinny. "Finish it!"

To my astonishment, I found him standing in one of the cars, already midway down, while the bearded lady balanced on one of the cross beams, ready to pounce on him.

With a swing of his crowbar, Vinny walloped the bearded lady on the side of the head, sending her careening to the ground with a sickening thud.

I watched with dread as the bearded lady's shadow shifted away from her limp body, slithering along the bottom edge of the arcade, now in the form of a shadowy serpent. I raced after it, though I had no idea how to stop it. With a jolt, my heart leaped into my throat as I saw the shadow make a side-winding dash across the fairground, heading straight for Sadie, who stood frozen, gripping the wooden box.

Before I could move to help her, Vinny raced past me, dropping the crowbar at my feet and yelling, "Tell Sal he has to make good on his promise!"

With a hop and a skid, Vinny reeled around to face the slithering shadow, placing himself between the demon and Sadie. I called out, but it was too late.

Vinny turned his body to force his shadow to cross the demon's shadow.

The shadows merged.

Vinny turned to face Sadie, and she let out an ear-splitting scream. Before I knew what I was doing, I charged forward, striking my best friend on the side of the head with the flat of the crowbar.

Sadie and I stared down at Vinny's body.

"Is he dead? Did I kill him?" I mumbled, feeling numb all over.

Sadie's choked voice sounded a hundred miles away. "If he were dead, the shadow would be on the move again."

I breathed a sigh of relief. "Maybe we can get this thing out of him?"

Sadie shook her head and then broke down crying. "I thought he'd be safe. Why would he do that?"

I looked around at the chaos and carnage. "Cops will be here any minute. We need to get him out of here."

"Where are you taking him?" Sadie asked through her tears.

"You're absolutely sure there's no way to get this thing out of him? Can we try an exorcism or something?"

She shook her head. "That might work on some, but not this one."

I let out a heavy sigh as I thought about his final words to me. "Hey, if he's someplace dark, I mean real dark, can the shadow still escape?"

"No," Sadie whispered. "In total darkness and without a shadow, it can't move. That's why we locked it in the box."

"Then we only got one solution," I said, and I hated everything about it.

I tucked the crowbar back inside my jacket and lifted Vinny's limp body over my shoulder. I kept thinking of Sal's words: It's dark down there, kid, not even your shadow to keep you company.

"Where are you going with him?" Sadie asked.

"First I'm takin' him for a new pair of shoes."

"And after that?"

I kept walking.

"After that, Gio?"

"After that he's gonna take a nice, long bath."

"Well, what about me and the baby?"

I whirled around. "He saved you and the baby. Don't you see that? He sacrificed himself for both of you! I think that's enough. You can figure it out from here."

Sadie shrank back from my outburst. I felt like an asshole, but I didn't care. My best friend would be dead soon, and I was the one who had to do it.

I thought long and hard about hopping a train to Los Angeles the whole walk back to Little Italy.

Later that night, Sal and I sat in a small rowboat on the East River, neither of us saying a word. It had to be three in the morning, but we sat staring down into murky water, listening to it lap against the boards.

"Well," Sal muttered at last. "There goes the cleverest son of a bitch in all o' Little Italy." He gave me a long look. "Never forget what I said, Giovanni."

I looked to the shoreline, past the park, up East Houston, until I glimpsed the shadowy arc of the Ferris wheel in the far distance. Next to it, a single spire from the Eldridge Street synagogue pointed skyward, looking like a menacing black-taloned finger held up in warning.

"I know," I murmured. "Stay outta the ghetto."

- THE END -
ENJOYED THIS? CHECK OUT:
BLACK ECHOES
BY J.B. McLAURIN

CONSTELLATIONS

MARY MAXWELL

I wished on a star last night. I haven't done that since I was a kid. I don't know what made me do it; I'm not superstitious. It was a regular weeknight, nothing special in the air. I had taken Jo to the dog park; we share a love of solitude in our middle age, so we go after dark when everyone else has cleared out and she can sprint to her heart's content without interruption. As I was kicking around the patchy lawn for a spare tennis ball, something made me look up. It was a clear night and I could see some stars sprinkled across the sky. Never as many as there used to be, back when I was a small-town kid who had never heard of light pollution.

In my memories of those days, filmy with nostalgia and the corrosion of time, the sky is splattered with them like a Jackson Pollock in black and white. My dad would spread out the tattered old quilt and lay with me shoulder-to-shoulder, pointing at this or that celestial body and whispering their names as if afraid that they might overhear. My favorites were the Big and Little Dippers—or as my dad called them, Mama Bear and Baby Bear. I remember the first time he pointed them out, right after we lost them. I was seven years old and fidgeting in a stiff black frock, my lacy collar wet with tears. His warm hand had wrapped around mine and aimed it up to the sky.

"See that?" he said, tracing a trapezoid in thin air with my finger, a heavenly game of connect-the-dots. "See how the tail points to the smaller one?"

"Uh-huh." My raw eyes had followed along as the constellations took shape.

"They're called Big Dipper and Little Dipper, but those are just nicknames. They're really called *Ursa Major* and *Ursa Minor*. Know what that means?" I shook my head "no."

"It's Mama Bear and Baby Bear, looking down on us. And whenever you miss them, you can just look up in the night sky and remember that they're always watching over you."

Since then I always look for the Dippers first. I can usually find them, even in my neighborhood where there are streetlights lining every block and 24-hour gas stations beaming their fluorescents through the night. If I look up to find a clear night sky, I'm going to start looking for constellations. So last night something came over me; I looked up and then I looked *for*.

Mama Bear and Baby Bear first, faint but always always there. Then Papa Bear, the title I had bestowed on Orion nearly a decade prior—the completion of my celestial family. I hadn't believed in that stuff for a long time by then, but it felt right that he should join my mom and sister. It made me feel less alone without him. So I stood in the summer air and looked for my Papa Bear—he's easy, you just have to find his belt first, "Tic-Tac-Toe, three in a row," then the rest of him fills in—with his legs set in a sturdy stance and bow aimed forever at nothing. I put up my finger to trace his shape and that's when it happened. As I watched, a falling star streaked through Orion's heart like an arrow of light. My skin prickled at the sight and I was seized by an impulse.

I closed my eyes, and made a wish. I sat with it in the stillness of the night, felt the ghost of a breeze whisper against my skin.

Then Jo shattered the calm with a fit of barking at the other end of the enclosure, shocking me out of it. The moment passed. I spied a half-bald tennis ball in the dirt, grabbed it, and whistled Jo away from the fence and whatever presence had caught her attention out there. We played fetch until my shoulder was sore and she had flopped on the ground at my feet, tongue lolling and sides heaving with effort. I loaded her up in the car and left.

We drove through the drinking district to get back home. A whole strip just shy of downtown with bars lining either side, a couple of restaurants sprinkled in; the obligatory Waffle House. I wasn't planning to stop for a drink, but as we got towards the end of the strip I noticed something different. *Must be a new bar*, I thought, trying to remember if I had seen any construction going on there lately. The building didn't look particularly new. The red brick front was dingy, and there was black scum lining the windowsills. The windows themselves were that sort of warped glass that makes it impossible to see inside.

Neon letters in the door burned a bright invitation—*Come on in!*—beneath a plain white sign that read *BILLY'S BAR* in block lettering. I had pulled into the parallel space by the door without making the conscious decision to do so. Jo, happy to be anywhere no matter where it was we stopped, hopped into the front seat and whined to be let out.

"Okay, little girl," I said. "Let's check it out." She stuck to my heels the whole way to the door and snuffled through the cage of my ankles as I poked my head in. The air was thick with the smell of malt and hops. The only person inside was a middle-aged bartender with his back to me.

"Excuse me, can I have my dog in here?" He turned to the sound of my voice and leaned against the bar with an easy smile.

"Of course," he said in a voice as dry as paper. "Come on in." I pushed through the door and Jo kept right along beside me, sniffing at chairs as we passed through. There were four or five wooden barrels bolted to the concrete floor to serve as rustic tables, each one flanked with mismatched barstools.

"She a golden retriever?" the bartender asked. His eyes were still creased into a smile, but something about their cold blue set me on edge. His thick hair was streaked through with silver, what some might call salt-and-pepper, and he had a wiry build. It took no effort for him to reach over the bar and let Jo sniff his slender, long-fingered hand.

"A mix," I said, swallowing my uneasiness. "Golden and who knows what else."

"What's her name?"

"Joanna. Jo for short, or JoJo Bean."

"Hi there, JoJo," he crooned, a crease in his paper-thin voice. "Thirsty?" I thought this last was directed at me, but he ducked into a cabinet and produced a stainless steel dog bowl. He filled it with water and came around the bar to set it down. Jo dove into the water like she was dying of thirst, letting him scratch behind her ears as she drank. Her ease with him settled my nerves a bit; Jo had always been a keen judge of character.

"And you? Thirsty?" The bartender's ice chip eyes were on me and I turned toward the taps to avoid his gaze.

"Yeah, I'll try the brown ale on draft."

"Coming right up." While he poured my beer I settled my tired bones into a barstool and took a closer look around. I was surprised to find paintings covering every wall: prints of classic scenes and modern art; sweeping landscapes and muted watercolors. Behind the bar, hanging over the taps in swirls of blue and gold, hung Van Gogh's *Starry Night*. A chill ran through me and I drowned it with a deep swallow of beer.

"I've never noticed this place before," I said, making conversation to fill the stuffy silence. "Did you just open up?" It felt strange to ask, when nothing about the place looked remotely new.

"Naw, we've been here forever. My pops was Billy, he used to own this place. We had to shut it down for a while, after he got too sick to run things. Then he left me everything when he—" His eyes flashed to mine and away again. "Well. It's mine now." His face had darkened and my stomach cringed with impotent regret.

"I'm sorry. I didn't mean to—"

"No, it's okay," he cut me off. "It was a long time coming."

"That doesn't make it any easier."

"No. It doesn't." The bartender busied himself wiping down shelves with his back to me while I took cover behind another swig of beer. The silence stretched thin between us. I wished I hadn't come in. More than anything I wished that I had never gotten on the topic of dead fathers. I didn't want to think about Dad. I had spent the better part of a decade trying to forget, to erase the last raw images of him which tainted my memories.

His face, yellowed skin pulled tight over porcelain cheekbones. The sunken flesh around his eyes bruised with permanent fatigue. His wispy white hair, once so thick and richly brown, clinging like cobwebs to my fingertips when I stroked his temples. I sat with him—long, horrid days—and listened to the rattle of every breath in his cancerous lungs until there was no more breath to pull. I remember so clearly the red and blue veins which stood out across his cheeks, a roadmap leading to the inevitable end which all roads must meet.

I took another gulp of beer and cast around for anything to distract myself. My eyes fell on a print across the room: a nightmare scene of human and humanoid creatures depicted in intricate *tableaux* of unspeakable anguish—probably a Bosch.

"You an art collector or something?" I asked the bartender, gesturing to the wall. He let out a short puff of air through his nose.

"They're not mine."

"Oh." My beer was down to the dregs now and I was starting to feel sick.

"You want another?" No. I didn't. I wanted to grab my dog, walk out the door, and never come back. But something made me stay. Maybe it was the guilt of reminding him of his dead father, or the pain of remembering mine. Whatever it was held me fast.

"Yeah. Not a beer though, something else." I could feel the suds of the beer foaming up the back of my throat, and anyway I suddenly found myself in the mood for something stronger.

"Give me a…" I blurted the first cocktail that came to mind. "A Cosmo."

"You got it." In short order he presented a martini glass filled to the brim with rosy liquor. When I looked up to thank him, his cold eyes held mine and I couldn't look away.

"So. You've lost someone too."

"Yeah…"

"That sucks. I'm sorry."

"Yeah. It's okay," I took a sip of my drink. "I mean, it's not *really* okay, is it? But it has to be okay. Everybody dies. Everybody loses someone. You can't just go around moping about it forever. You have to get over it." I was starting to feel the alcohol then, a faint buzzing in the edges of my brain. I was vaguely aware of Jo's warm head pillowed on my foot in an oblivious doze.

"And did you get over it?" He was leaning on the bar now, watching me intently.

"Yeah, of course I did. I had to. It was a long time ago. You have to move on." The cocktail was sweet, coating my mouth and spinning my words until they were as thick as meringue. "I have to live my life, I can't do that if I sit around all the time and wish it never happened." *Mama Bear and Baby Bear, looking down on you.*

"Why not?" His voice was so dry, like leaves rubbing together in the fall.

Tic-Tac-Toe, three in a row.

"Because—" It was becoming harder to focus. I could barely force out speech around my prickling tongue. "Because it isn't going to get you anywhere. You waste years on what could have been and then one day you're gonna wake up and realize you wished your life away."

"What if you didn't wish it away?" His voice rasped right in my ear though he was no closer to me than before. "What if you wished your life back?" The room was spinning. My eyes landed on *Starry Night* and it was melting, the colors running together and swirling into a new galaxy. My blurry vision fell to the near-empty martini glass, then the bartender's cold eyes.

"What did you give me?" The words pushed out clumsily between numb lips.

"What you asked for." Everything went black.

⋘⋙

The piercing light of dawn woke me. My limbs were stiff and my head must have weighed about a thousand pounds. I realized with a jolt that the light was coming from the wrong direction; this wasn't my room. I sat upright and a sharp pain ripped through my skull, temporarily blinding me. *The bartender,* I thought through the haze. *That fucker drugged me.* I should never have gone in that damned bar. I pressed two fingers to each temple until the throbbing receded, struggling to take stock of the room. Strange, it didn't look like the seedy apartment one would expect of a date rapist.

I was in a full sized bed with a floral quilt in pastel pink draped over me. There were delicate lace curtains over the east-facing window, and a whitewashed dresser beneath it with a matching vanity table across the room. Next to the window hung a cork board covered in photographs and shiny technicolor stickers. A few posters featuring some old pop singers adorned the walls. It looked like a little girl's room. I crept out of bed, shivering at the cool wooden floor beneath my feet.

"Jo?" I called in a whisper. "JoJo Bean?" I didn't care what happened to me, but if that man did anything to my dog…

"Jo!" I called a little louder, glancing at the door and straining my ears for any sign of life. I tiptoed to the window to get a peek at my surroundings. "What the—" I froze. This was not my city. There was a smooth green lawn dotted with wildflowers and enclosed by a delicate iron fence. Beyond the lawn was a copse of trees swaying gently in the morning breeze. A magnolia tree stood at the edge of the yard, dangling a rope swing from its thick lower branches. As I took in the scene the first word that came to mind was "idyllic."

"Where the—?" I turned away from the window and crept across the room. When I passed the vanity mirror, I had to do a double take. My blood froze in my veins and I swayed on the spot, barely catching myself on the foot of the bed. A girl was looking back at me, her rich brown hair pulled into a braid over her shoulder, her dark eyes wide with fright. It was me, but it wasn't *me*. I couldn't have been more than nineteen years old. But I didn't look like that at nineteen, *my* hair had been cropped short and bleached blonde; I didn't have so many freckles, and you wouldn't have caught me dead in the frilly nightgown that I realized I was wearing.

I stumbled to the vanity, kneeling on the stool to get a better look. Those were my eyes. I grimaced and saw the crooked front tooth that I had gotten fixed in my thirties. I prodded the cheeks, the eyebrows. The give of flesh beneath my fingers. It was real. I was thirty years younger than I had been when I passed out, in a strange place surrounded by strange things. And I didn't even have my dog.

I felt a pang in my heart for Jo, but I had to brush it aside. Had to figure this out. Maybe it was a dream? I was having some kind of crazy vivid dream caused by whatever that fucker had slipped into my drink. That made more sense. So I would just have to wake myself up, or at least ride it out until I *do* wake up. Settling into investigation mode, I scanned the room again, landed on the corkboard and staggered over to it.

The surface was covered in overlapping pictures with big-eyed Lisa Frank stickers filling the spaces in between. I saw him first and the breath left my body in a *whoosh*. Daddy. A shot of him with curly dark hair just greying at the temples, his blue eyes warm with delight. He was holding a brown-eyed baby in his arms. I've seen this picture. I have this picture. It was taken by my mother, and you could feel her love echoing in every inch of the frame. This was my first birthday. The image blurred and I scrubbed the tears from my eyes.

The other pictures were unfamiliar, though I recognized myself in them. Seven year old me, beaming over a pink bundle in my arms. Me again, older—maybe twelve—holding a little girl's hand and cheesing at the camera in our matching flower-print dresses. The little girl smiled shyly, her honey-blonde hair falling around her face in gentle waves, her blue eyes a carbon copy of Daddy's.

"Janet?" The name passed my lips in a whisper. Another one, all four of us: Daddy looking proud with his arm around my mother, the girls stood stiffly between them and trying to be serious. My family. The family that could have been but *wasn't*, it never was, because they were dead. They died together before Janet could draw her first breath. I stared at them, those unfamiliar phantoms who left us so long ago. Mama Bear and Baby Bear.

Overcome with a wave of dizziness, I backed away from the board before I knew what I was doing. My blood thrummed in my cheeks and lips, my fingertips grew cold and my feet felt like heavy blocks at the ends of my legs. I didn't know where to go, couldn't see around the panic bubbling up inside me. I tripped in my confusion, flung my arms out to catch myself and knocked a music box off the vanity with a clatter.

I crouched on the cold wooden floor, knees burning and throat burning, trying to bring myself back when I heard footsteps up the hall. They stopped at my door and my heart stuttered.

"Lisa?" came a small voice from the other side of the door. "You okay?" I couldn't answer. I was frozen in place with fear and wonderment and a sudden, wild hope. The knob turned and a girl of about twelve popped her honey-blonde head through the doorway.

"Hey, what happened?" Her blue eyes widened in alarm when she saw me on the floor. She burst into the room, her small hands pushing under my arms as though to heave me to my feet. I found my voice.

"Janet?" She met my eyes, so close now, and a wave of emotion washed through me.

"Yeah?" My sister said. This was my sister. Her nose looked like mine. She had our father's eyes. Her mouth quirked just so, just like

Mommy's had in pictures and the faint memories of her that I had carried with me all this time. Overcome with all that had happened, I flung my arms around her and burst into tears.

"Did you start your period or something?" She pulled back and gave me a look of such puzzlement that my tears dissolved into hysteric laughter. I let her help me to my feet as I tried to catch my breath. I knew logically that this couldn't be real. What was happening was impossible. Whether it was a hallucination or dream or—whatever—I had woken up in a manifestation of my deepest desires. So I decided I might as well make the most of it.

I found a sweater and jeans in the closet and changed out of my frilly nightgown, then followed Janet out into the hall. It was strange, this wasn't anything like the house I grew up in. Maybe in my mind I had created the ideal home—somewhere I *wish* I had grown up. The house we would have had if Mommy and Janet had survived. We passed framed family portraits in the hall: Janet and myself at different ages, Christmas and Easter, special occasions.

I froze in front of an unfamiliar picture. A graduation photo, me proudly displaying my diploma. That's odd. I never did the cap-and-gown thing when I graduated high school. Dad and I both decided it was a waste of money, we never really saw the point. *Dad.* I shook myself and tore away from the picture. From the top of the stairs, I could hear the murmur of their voices. The familiar timbre of Dad's groggy morning voice; an answering coo, a feminine tone that plucked at the core of my memory.

I found myself seized with apprehension. What would they be like? Would they be how I remembered? Would they notice something was wrong with me? My fingers gripped the bannister and the wild impulse to throw myself over—force myself awake from this bizarre dream—rushed through me.

"Lisa!" Janet popped up at the foot of the stairs in a huff. "What's taking so long? Everybody's waiting on you." The moment had passed. I took a shaky breath and tried to smile.

"Sorry, I'm coming. It's just…cramps." I clung to her period theory as an excuse for my odd behavior. She rolled her eyes at me.

"Well, hurry up!" And she was gone again. I floated behind her, clutching at the cuffs of my sweater and making an effort to swallow my fear. When I entered the dining room it felt like I had stepped into the pages of *Better Homes and Gardens*. The bay window faced a blooming rose garden, an oval wooden table draped in a sunny cloth tucked into its curve. The table was spread with platters of bacon, scrambled eggs, buttered toast, waffles, and a bowl of mixed fruit. There was a pitcher of orange juice on the table, and a glass of milk at each of the four place settings.

At the head of the table sat Daddy, his brow furrowed over the newspaper. Not as I had last seen him, hollowed out by the ravages of disease. This was Daddy as I remembered him when I was a little girl, back when we were still happy and he smiled all the time. Just the way he smiled now as he looked up to greet me.

"Morning, Daffodil. Sleep okay?" I swallowed the lump in my throat and nodded.

"Yes, Daddy." I sat next to Janet, who was already spooning eggs onto her plate.

"That you, Lisa?" came the bell of a voice from the kitchen. "Do you want some coffee, honey?" Warmth flooded my frozen fingers, and when I answered my voice was surprisingly strong.

"Yes, please! Thank you!" And before I knew it she was sweeping into the room, her chestnut hair pulled into a ponytail with wispy bangs brushing over her eyes. My mother. Not quite as I remembered her—she was younger in my mind and in all the pictures I'd ever seen of her. This Mom had streaks of grey in her hair, lines in the corners of her eyes and creases around her smile. This Mom had lived.

I broke my stare as she set a cup of coffee in front of me. It was milky brown, and when I took a sip the perfect hint of sweetness softened the bitter taste. This Mom had lived, and she knew how I took my coffee. My eyes welled with unbidden tears and Mom shifted from warmth to sharp concern.

"Hey, hey." She placed a gentle hand on my cheek which made me cry even harder. "What's wrong sweetie?"

"She has her period," said Janet.

"Okay now, not at the breakfast table." Daddy shifted in his chair.

"Oh honey," said Mom. "You need some aspirin?"

"No," I choked out, then took a steadying gulp of coffee. "No, thanks M-Mom. I'll feel better when I eat."

"Amen to that!" Janet led the charge in filling her plate with one of everything, and I slumped with relief to have the focus shifted away from me for the moment. Once we had all served ourselves everybody joined hands while Mommy said a prayer over the meal, and then we were permitted to dig in.

My head was whirling and I had to force down the first couple of bites, but once I realized how hungry I was it was easy to clean the whole plate. I even found myself going for seconds, and accidentally dropped a piece of bacon on the floor in my haste.

"Jo-Jo!" I called automatically, whistling for the little furry vacuum to zoom in and clean up my mess. Everybody at the table stopped and stared at me, and I felt my heart sink down into my stomach. *That's right. She's not here.*

"Lisa?" My mother was looking at me strangely. "What was that?" I cast around for a reasonable excuse and blurted the first thing that came to mind.

"I was just thinking, if we had a dog, then she could clean up for us when we drop food on the floor." I followed this with a shrill laugh. My mother's brows pulled together in a frown.

"You know we can't have a dog, your sister's allergic. Maybe just try *not* to drop food on the floor?"

"Jo-Jo's a stupid name for a dog anyway," Janet snickered.

"No it's not!" I said petulantly, heart freshly stinging with the loss of my pet.

"Now, girls," said Daddy, having finished his breakfast and burrowed back into the paper.

"Well it is," Janet said under her breath.

"Enough," Mom cut in, and that was the final word. After breakfast was finished, Janet disappeared upstairs and I helped Mom with the dishes. Gloom lingered over me. It was strange, I was happy to have my family and see what I had been missing out on all these years, but it felt wrong. I was like a puzzle piece that had fallen into the wrong box; a picture of the same subject, taken from a different angle. This was someone else's life.

"Don't be too hard on Janet. She just misses you." Mom spoke up out of the blue and startled me from my musings.

"What?"

"Ever since you started the semester all she could talk about is how she can't wait for you to visit. I know she's been picking fights, but I think she just doesn't know how to handle the distance." I turned to look at Mom, but she was gazing out of the window as she spoke. "She's never had to be without her big sister before. It's lonely."

"Yeah…" Lonely. I knew enough about that. "I'll talk to her."

CRSO

When I went looking for Janet, I couldn't find her anywhere in the house. I searched the unfamiliar layout, opening doors to closets and bathrooms, Mom's sewing room and Dad's office. I found what must be Janet's bedroom, the twin bed obscured by a mound of stuffed animals, but she wasn't there. I finally circled back to my own room in desperation, and spied through the window a tiny figure swaying back and forth on the rope swing.

I found my way outside, taking in the spring sun and the scent of the rose garden on the breeze. It was peaceful out here. I understood why Janet would come out here to think. I understood why our family moved here, and found myself wondering again where we really were. I wondered where *I* really was, the real me, while I was living in this fantasy. Maybe the Lisa of this world had been transported to *my* body, to my life.

Maybe she had grown sick of her younger sister and wished she had never been born, and the universe granted both our wishes by swapping each out for the other. But that's preposterous, of course.

"Janet?" She was sitting on the knot of the swing, straddling the rope and walking backwards in a spiral, winding it up for a good spin.

"What do you want?" Her voice was thick, and when I got a good look at her face it was blotchy and swollen.

"Just wanted to hang out with my baby sis," I said lightly.

"Yeah, right." She was struggling to twist the rope now, digging her heels into the ground against the resistance.

"You don't believe me?" She didn't look at me, just scrunched up her face and shook her head. "That's okay. You don't have to believe it for it to be true." Her blue eyes finally met mine, just for a second, then she lifted her feet and she was twirling around and around with her legs straight out. Her colors blurred until she looked like a top, and the thrill of it elicited a high-pitched *Wheeeeeeeee* from her diaphragm.

When she finally stopped and pried her hands from the rope, she was giggling just like a little girl. She turned her unfocused eyes toward me and as I reached out to catch her, a fierce well of affection sprang up in my heart. I pulled her against me and held her tight. My little sister whom I never got to know. Who never got to play on swings and giggle in the sun, who never got to pick fights or pig out at the breakfast table.

"Lisa? You okay?" Her voice was so small, muffled as it was against my breast; she must have felt my tears in her hair.

"Yeah, honey, I'm okay. Just missed you."

"I missed you too." Her arms tightened around me. "Do you have to go back to college?"

"Yeah. It's important." I, the real me, never went to college. I didn't need it, and I was okay without it. But I could feel it, this me here in the life that never was, *she* needed it. She had her own wants and dreams.

"You won't forget about me, will you?" Her voice was quivering now and I pulled away to look into her sweet face.

"Of course not, Jellybean. I could never forget you. I love you."

"I love you too." Janet gave me a watery smile and I squeezed her hand.

"Now it's my turn!" And with that, I dove for the swing and called on her to help spin me around. We goofed off together for the rest of the day, breaking only for a lunch filled with approving glances from Mom and Dad. After dinner that night, Daddy spread out a quilt on the lawn and we all sat together to look at the stars. Out here in the country, we could see thousands smattered across the sky. I tried to find my usual constellations.

"Where are the dippers, Daddy?" I asked, squinting at the countless points of light.

"The what?"

"You know, the dippers. Mama Bear and Baby Bear?" I turned towards him to find that he was looking at me strangely, the way he had when I'd called for Jo at the breakfast table.

"I'm afraid you've lost me, Daffodil."

"Never mind." Something cold crept up the back of my neck as I turned my eyes back to the sky. I guess he didn't need the bears in a life where we didn't lose Mama and Baby, but he'd still know about the Big and Little Dipper, right? I scanned the stars more closely now, looking for my old holdout. If all else failed, I could still find Orion by his belt. *Tic-Tac-Toe, three in a row.*

But no matter how hard I looked, he wasn't there. The more I searched the sky the more I had the feeling that the pattern of the stars didn't seem right. A puzzle piece in the wrong box. Cold sweat broke out over my body. This was all wrong. I wasn't supposed to be here. I didn't belong here. I willed myself to wake up, squeezed my eyes shut and pinched my arm until it bruised. When I opened them again I found Janet staring at me. Her blue eyes in the dark reminded me of another pair of blue eyes—ice blue and cold over a paper thin voice.

My gaze snapped to the sky again, and I saw what I somehow knew I would see: a falling star streaking across the sky like an arrow of light. I shut my eyes again, the streak of the star burning even against the darkness of my eyelids. I made a wish.

⚬⚬⚬

The next morning I fully expected to be back in bed, my *real* bed back home, with Jo snuggled up next to me. When I opened my eyes to find the light coming from the wrong direction through the window, my heart sank down into my stomach. I, the dream me of this world, would be going back to college today. I didn't know what else to do but go along with it, continue to ride it out until I found a way back home.

After a somber breakfast I packed my bags, loaded up the Honda which had apparently been my graduation present last spring, and turned to face my family. I wondered if I would ever see them again, hoped that I wouldn't and hoped that I would. Longing clawed at my throat as my father put his arms around me for the last time. Vibrant and strong as I remembered him, smelling of soap and coffee (no cigarettes—*this* Dad had quit before I was born and never picked the habit back up again; he never needed to).

Next my mother embraced me. Her tears wet my cheeks as mine wet hers, and I breathed deeply to catch the scent of her hair. I would try to remember it better, to hold this image of her in my mind and let it brighten the dim memories of my real past. I felt a twinge of regret that I hadn't gotten to know her better in this fantasy dream world of mine, but I hadn't gotten to know her in real life either so I guess it evens out.

She held my face in her hands and brushed her thumbs across my cheeks to catch the tears, just as she had when I was a little girl.

"We're so proud of you, sweetheart." Once she released me, my dad tucked her into his side, gripping her shoulder with suppressed emotion. I turned to Janet then and was nearly knocked off balance when she launched herself into my arms and buried her face in my shoulder.

"You better call me every week," came her muffled voice. I stroked her honey-blonde hair and held her tightly.

"Of course I will." And then I left, rolling down the gravel drive which led away from our little paradise, my family waving me off as they grew smaller and smaller in the rearview mirror. I had no idea where I was going, no plan for how to get back home except to keep driving. I drove all afternoon through unfamiliar country roads, past signs for country towns I'd never heard of.

Finally, while passing through a little speedtrap town shortly after the sun had set, I found what I didn't even realize I had been looking for the whole time. It was a standalone building of dingy red brick with a white sign. The block lettering read *BILLY'S BAR*. As I pulled into a spot out front, the neon sign in the door flickered on. *Come on in!*

He was behind the bar as I expected, his back to me. The same wiry build, the same salt-and-pepper hair. When he turned to greet me in his papery voice, they were the same ice chip eyes which met mine.

"Lisa." I found it didn't surprise me that he knew my name.

"Billy." I knew too, that his story the night we met—about his dead father leaving him the bar—had all been bullshit. It wasn't *his* father we talked about that night. I strode up to the bar and sat in the same stool that I had occupied the first time I came, just two days ago.

"Let me guess," he said, already pulling bottles from the shelf. "Cosmo?"

"You got it," I said coolly. I looked around while he mixed my cocktail, finding everything exactly as it had been—down to the Bosch on the opposite wall and *Starry Night* above the taps. My attention returned to Billy only when he set the rosy drink in front of me.

"I wished on a star last night," I told him.

"Yeah? And did it come true?"

"I don't know yet. I think so. It did the last time." *Two days ago*, I didn't say. I took a sip of the cocktail. "I don't think it was real though, any of it."

"I don't know about that," he said, leaning against the bar with a crooked smile that didn't reach his eyes. "It was real to somebody." I tried to work that out, make it fit in my head with the stars being wrong and the mismatched puzzle piece.

"Hey Billy, do you believe in parallel universes? Like everything that *could* be, *is* somewhere out there? Even…different versions of yourself?"

"What do you think?" His cold eyes pierced mine.

"I think I'm probably losing it. Imagining someone living the life I wished I had. I don't think I can believe it."

"That's okay. You don't have to believe it for it to be true." I had nothing to say to that, so I drank my cocktail. Billy wiped down the counter and waited until I had finished my drink before he finally broke the silence.

"So, was it what you had wished for then? The life you wished you had?" I shook my head, which had started to buzz around the edges.

"I think I *thought* so at first, but that wasn't really me. I like my life. I wouldn't trade it; the time I got to have, and the memories I made. They're so much more precious than any might-have-beens could be." He nodded, and for the first time I saw a hint of warmth behind his blue eyes.

"So, did you get over it?" The colors of the world around me were starting to blur, and I heard a high-pitched whine.

"Yeah. I think I'm over it." The bar pitched and swayed and was swallowed into nothingness.

೧೫

The whining was what roused me into consciousness. A keening sound, over and over in my ear. *Now what,* I thought groggily. *What else could the universe have in store for me?* Something warm and wet on my cheek jolted me right out of drowsiness.

"Jo-Jo Bean!" Her sweet yellow face filled my vision and then I was drowning in puppy kisses. I fended her off long enough to get my bearings; I was slumped sideways on a bench beneath the stars. The warm summer wind rustled the grass around me and I was hit with the realization that I was back in the dog park. Or, still in the dog park. I threw my arms around Jo and squeezed her until she squirmed and whined to get away, then pushed myself up off the bench. My limbs were stiff and there was a sharp pain in the left side of my neck, my penalty for falling asleep in such an awkward position.

I stretched, joints creaking in protest, then led Jo through the gate and back to the car. She hopped right in and sat in the passenger seat, turning her bright eyes to me with open adoration. I couldn't help but plant a kiss on her soft muzzle, enjoying her doggy scent.

"I love you, ya little peanut. Wouldn't trade you for the world." I stepped around to the driver's side, opened the door, and hesitated. I didn't know what had happened, whether it was really a dream or if something less substantial had taken place under the stars that night. I thought of Dad, and the image that came to mind was no longer the haunted husk, replaced now by the vibrant Dad whose eyes twinkled like they used to. My eyes were pulled up to scan the open sky, and there he was. *Tic-Tac-Toe, three in a row.* Right where he had always been.

"Good night, Papa Bear."

– THE END –
ENJOYED THIS? CHECK OUT:
GROUND CONTROL
BY KA HOUGH

NO ONE HAS EVER SAID RESTAURANT WORKERS HAVE AN EASY JOB, BUT POOR LINCOLN AND HIS COWORKERS ARE ABOUT TO EXPERIENCE A TRUE NIGHTMARE, FOR THEIR RESTAURANT IS HAUNTED, AND AFTER THE PATRONS LEAVE, THE GHOSTS COME OUT IN FULL FORCE FOR A 4-STAR MICHELIN HAUNTING. STAY TUNED, FRIENDS, FOR . . .

BRICK AND MORTAR

ADAM FALL

The mop water sloshed across the speckled linoleum floor in a gray slather of soap and piss—runoff from whatever trickled down the front of the toilet bowl, remnants of a lazy shake, a half-hearted dribble. Lincoln swept the handle deftly from side to side. His hands curled around the handle, holding it like an upside-down baseball bat. In lieu of pine tar: a pair of latex-free, too-tight gloves and a dream—maybe one that died a few dozen bathroom cleanings ago.

It was a Saturday night. The dinner shift had ended with a whimper after a flurry of calls for 'hands' and plenty of 'yes, Chef' being hollered over the roaring din of a filled dining room. *Foundations* was a new concept restaurant, or rather *was* a new concept six months ago, but how long do those trends really last in the industry anyways. Its open kitchen layout offered an intimate view of several dropouts, an alcoholic or two, and a head chef trying his best to keep his cool and the kitchen running smoothly. Things never went smoothly, like ever, nor did they go completely batshit off the rails. They remained in this perfect liminal space somewhere in between, treading water. Clientele was either old-money from the affluent neighborhoods to the West, or yuppy millennials that news station talking heads kept saying shouldn't be buying fucking avocado toast.

Located on the second floor, above a climbing gym of all things, the restaurant was situated in the heart of an historic neighborhood, one that you'd likely know about if you heard the name. Above, on the third floor, was the bar and lounge that supplied the drinks for those dining in the restaurant. No dumbwaiter ran between the second and third floors. Lincoln always joked and told tables who inquired at the sudden appearance of their beverages that *he* was, in fact, the 'dumb waiter.' Cue the laughter. Works every time. Easy five percent bump to the tip percentage.

Lincoln sopped up the amalgamation of fluids, wringing it out in the yellow bucket, soiled with the stains of previous use. He kicked the sloshing bucket as he went.

Backing into the door, he slid out into the hallway that connected the restrooms to the dining room. The only thing on his mind as he mopped was the extra dessert that Megan, the pastry chef, had secretly set aside for him and his girlfriend Kenzie, mostly for her—a woman who has not one sweet tooth, but a mouthful.

Behind him, a large window looked down to the climbing gym below. The wall rose higher, still, higher than the window and up another fifteen feet to the top of the wall. Handholds were firmly fastened into their respective routes, color coded and of varying degrees of difficulty. The only lights that illuminated the sprawling space at the base of the wall were the emergency lights, which cast the room in a dim and ominous half-light.

"You almost done in there?" Lincoln called, knocking on the door to the women's restroom.

"Just a minute!" Olivia responded, her voice reverberating off the white and black tile as she scraped soap scum off the bottom of the faucet.

THUNK

"What the fuck…"

One resounding noise echoed behind Lincoln. The window shook from impact.

Olivia tumbled out of the bathroom in a tizzy, checking to make sure Lincoln hadn't slipped in the mop water…again.

"You okay out here?"

"I…uh. I think so."

"What the hell was that?" she said, in a voice that expected to see him on his ass with the mop flailing in the air.

Lincoln turned, motioning toward the space behind him—to the mostly dark and desolate workout area below. "There was…I don't know…"

"Listen, if you tripped and busted your ass, just tell me! I won't tell the rest of those fools that you did it again." Olivia laughed nervously, referring to the heavy cream incident from several months before.

Lincoln shook his head.

"No. This was…different."

What little light there was behind the window caught the faintest glimpse of something on the glass, on the wrong side of it: behind the window, nearly a hundred feet from the padded mats that lined the floor at the base of the wall.

"Do you…do you see that, Liv?"

"See wh—" She stopped mid sentence, mid-fucking-word and just stared. "Oh. Oh shit."

There, on the window, was the most distinguished handprint either of them had ever seen. Five fingers spread in an open palm, each finger long and spindly, longer than it probably should have been. And below, two stories from the floor, nothing but empty air and darkness.

"Liv. That wasn't there before. Right? That wasn't *fucking* there. I walked past here five times tonight. That wasn't there. Nope."

Olivia slipped across the still-damp floor, over to the window. She took the long black sleeve of her cardigan and rubbed at it like her life depended on it. The thread threatened to come undone with each frenzied ruffle of fabric.

Nothing.

"It must just be stuck on, something sticky. You know how kids' hands can get." Her voice shook, betraying the faux confidence she tried to project, needed to project.

"Kids? Liv, are you kidding? Look at that…thing. What kind of kid has that kind of spread?"

The impact was an initial jump scare, but the impossibility of what they witnessed was reason enough for pause. Where the handprint had been placed, forced into existence, was a good twenty feet from the climbing wall. Not that being closer to the wall would have made things any better, the fact remained that Rock Hard Climbing was empty. At least if there had been folks climbing—near the window or somewhere down below looking up, mapping out their path to the top—at least then there would have been witnesses. Witnesses or an easier explanation, *any* explanation, no matter how roundabout of a mental journey it would have taken to get there.

Lincoln backed away from the window, pulling the mop bucket with him, not caring as water lapped at the edges, threatening to spill out onto the nearly dry dining room floor.

"Come on, Liv. Let's get the fuck out of here. I think we're done. We can tell Alice and Mandy about *this*," he gestured wildly at the scene behind him, "hand in our tips, and say we'll come in early tomorrow to finish cleaning. You know, when the sun is out."

"Yeah. You're probably right," Olivia said, never taking her eyes off the distinct greasy outline of what she hoped was an adult hand. "Let's dump this shit in the back and go upstairs."

Shaken, the two servers shuffled their mops and buckets through the dimly lit dining room, past the banquet table, down the main path between the 30s and 40s, and into the back hallway. They turned the corner into the dish pit, emptied the gray water quickly down the stained and crusted-over mop station drain. Olivia rinsed each bucket out, then passed them to Lincoln to flip upside down to dry against the wall.

"You think they'll be mad we're dipping out early?" Olivia asked.

"Mad? No, I don't think so. I think they'll probably be annoyed, par for the course on that one, though." Lincoln let out a laugh, trying to force a change in the energy of the moment. "You know we aren't the first people to see something…strange."

"Oh, I'm well aware of Mandy and Jacob in the basement. What was that? A couple months ago?"

"Yeah, Mandy was telling me they went down there to pound one out before dinner shift."

"Gross."

"Right? But Jacob had her bent over one of the half shelves with the condiments on it when they said one of those dangly light bulbs started swinging and flickering. They thought maybe someone had come in and was messing with them. You know, it isn't like they're shy about what they do down there."

Lincoln and Olivia turned left and rounded the corner of the 'L' shaped hallway, the door to the brightly illuminated stairwell in sight—not quite fifty feet away.

The door was one of those hulking industrial doors, which makes sense for a building that old. It used to be a power plant for the neighboring old city hospital. The hospital saw plenty of 19th century medical horrors; most locals thought it was cursed, or haunted, maybe both. Probably both. Destroyed by a fire after only ten years of operation, taken out by a violent tornado forty years after that, only to be reopened in 1907. By then, the hospital already had a sordid history to contend with. It didn't help that it predominantly housed the city's mentally ill, the cast offs, those with troubled minds.

Atop Foundations' third-floor lounge were two towering smoke-stacks. Reddish brown bricks met neatly, growing more scorched with soot and the ashy remnants of smoke long since dispelled. They had withstood the fire, the tornado, and stood silent guard over the neighborhood below. An iconic piece of the city skyline, a stark reminder of not only the Industrial Revolution and a once coal-powered world, but a reminder of the less savory things a power plant next to a hospital entailed in those times.

"Did they ever say if they figured out what it was?" Her voice took on less of the qualities of a scared chihuahua, the light of the stairwell having restored a modicum of Olivia's confidence.

"Jacob played himself up when he told us. He said he rushed over to the light, but all he saw was a shadow off the wall, saw it move from there toward the spot where old city hospital tunnels are boarded up."

"Does it ever freak you out that we basically work in a giant crematorium that they turned into a fancy schmancy restaurant?"

"You know, it didn't freak me out until about two minutes ago, but now that you mention it? Yeah, pretty fucking weird."

Echoes of their footsteps clunked and thudded up and down the thickly insulated concrete and brick chamber. Yellow and black pipes ran in every which angle through the stairwell: water, sewage, and who knows what else. The stairs had clearly been redone to be up to code, but there was still an air of something older, that no matter how many new coats of paint or new sections of concrete one poured, the building would still be stuck somewhere else in time.

"At least we've been here for six months and this is the first time we've seen some weird shit."

"If this kind of thing happens every six months, then I'm not sure I'll be around for the next one." Lincoln said, putting the full weight of his right shoulder into the door at the top of the stairwell.

The raucous and jubilant voices of intoxicated guests ambushed their senses as they exited the stairwell into the back hallway of the lounge. Music lay buried somewhere underneath the lively chatter, clinking of glassware, and occasional outbursts of excitement. Foundations' lounge, normally a chill, serene spot to take a third or fourth date—offering enough quiet for conversation and enough privacy for undressing each other with your eyes—was unusually busy for a cool spring evening. Both doors to the rooftop patio were propped open, letting out some of the noise and welcoming in a chill.

Olivia scampered past Lincoln and around the corner to where the office was hidden, nestled past an industrial ice maker and, surprise, more exposed brick.

"Geez, Liv. Ah, and Lincoln, too. Already done cleaning?" Alice teetered in the office chair, clearly having had a glass or three of wine. Leaning against the window overlooking the parking lot, Mandy stood, swirling a glass of pinot noir.

"About that," Olivia started. "We were about to finish up when some serious spooky shit went down."

"Huh-p?" Alice hiccuped, followed by a short giggling fit.

"Come on, Lincoln, tell her what you saw."

Lincoln shuffled awkwardly into the office from the relative safety of the ice machine alcove.

"Yeah, what's up? You see a shadow person like Mandy and Jacob?" Alice asked, rolling her chair to the side and nudging Mandy hard in the thigh. "I swear to Christ, if you're spinning some story to get out of finishing your side work, then you're back to being on mostly lunch shifts."

"No, we definitely saw something…" Lincoln trailed off.

"OooooOOOOoooooOOOO! What did you seeeeeee?" The sarcasm was palpable.

"There was a handprint. On the glass."

"Oh no! Not a handprint! Whatever are we going to do?" Alice teetered precariously in the chair as she exaggerated throwing her arms up.

"Oh. My. God. Shut *up*, Alice. I saw it, too. It was on the window to Rock Hard. Like, on the other side. Way high up. And it wasn't *just* a handprint, there was a huge *thunk* on the glass behind Lincoln. Like, this shit was fresh."

At the mention of the climbing gym Alice rocked back in her chair, back straightening to a tight ninety degrees. Her dilated pupils grew even larger as she took a deep breath. "Well, fuck me then." She said, firm and coated in worry. "I believe you. Yes, I believe you. I really do." She took another moment to sober up. "I wasn't ready to believe Mandy when she told me, well, you know…but after I saw what I did last week, I sure as hell believe her now. So, that means I have to believe this, too"

Olivia and Lincoln turned to each other, shared a look.

"What did you see?"

Alice grasped her wine glass tightly and gulped down the rest of her sauvignon blanc. She took one more deep breath.

"Last week, I was up here during the day on Monday doing payroll. I think it was around 2? But I was here, sitting right here, and everything was normal. I had just finished an afternoon iced coffee and was feeling jittery. Normally around that time I go down to the kitchen to sneak a taste of one of the pastries that Megan leaves behind on Saturday night. I went down the back stairwell.

"While I was down there snacking, I figured I'd post the paper schedule above the server station and make sure everything was stocked. The paper towels were low, so I went down the back hallway to the dry storage, grabbed some and walked back. I promise no one was there in the building with me—well, maybe at the climbing gym, but everyone is off on Monday except me.

"As I was unwrapping the c-folds and dropping them into the dispenser…I heard something scrape against the concrete floor of the lounge. And, like, I had just been up there, there wasn't anyone there. I'm as positive now as I was then, which makes it so much worse. It was the screeching rumble like when you're out to eat and someone moves a chair in just the wrong way and everyone jumps. The worst sound. But it was that—that noise, sustained and grating. What I'm saying is, it went on too long. Then it just stopped.

"I shrugged it off at first. Old buildings make weird noises, right? Like, that's what's supposed to happen, what's always happened. Then it was quiet. I actually heard one of the people downstairs yell 'take' to their climbing partner. I closed the paper towel dispenser and went back to my snack and then it happened again. Only this time, it was louder. Well, not just louder, it was deeper? No, it was like a chorus of voices screaming. Yeah, that's it! What I was hearing wasn't just one chair, but a couple, or more.

"Then came the voices, like there was a full house of guests on a weekend. Like the bartenders were working double-time to make enough drinks. And you know what? In that moment I imagined the bar in the Overlook Hotel. It went on long enough that it felt laughable. You know in a movie where they linger on a death too long and the blood spurting out starts to feel silly? I think I laughed. All I could think of was Mandy and Jacob fucking away in the basement with some spooky pervert watching them, listening to their sweaty bodies slap, again and again.

"The walk back down the hallway was quick. The stairs, though, I took those a lot slower. Closer I got to the top, the more I wanted to turn around, take them all the way to the first floor, go out the emergency exit, and never come back. I opened the door at the top and thought 'I'll just go straight to the office and lock myself in,' but the curiosity, morbid as it may be, pulled at me. 'Go and look, Alice. Go on. You have to see.' As I exited the hallway past the office, past the bathrooms, I took it all in. Each chair around the bar was pulled out. They weren't pulled straight out, either—it looked like they'd danced. Does that make sense? They'd twirled and moved in circles around each other and were just scattered around the room. In front of each spot at the bar were different pieces of empty glassware: a wine glass here, a highball there, a smattering of rocks glasses. I walked through the mess, pushing chairs out of the way, dumbfounded. I went straight to the elevator, unlocked it, took it right down to the first floor—and I fucking walked home."

No one spoke. The air in the room hung heavy with Alice's story, like a fog had rolled into the office. The ice machine might as well have been a dry ice machine. Lincoln and Olivia stood silently in the doorway.

"You know what the worst part was?" Alice said, fighting back tears. "I wasn't the first person in the next day. I was expecting someone to text me and be like, 'what the fuck, Alice?' But no one said shit. I came in later and the bar looked spotless. The chairs were more perfectly aligned than they'd ever been. No one said a goddamn thing. So, neither did I."

Olivia muttered under her breath, "Holy shit…"

Lincoln stood stock still, thrumming with unease.

"So, yes. I fucking believe you. Get out of here. Go home and forget it ever happened, tell yourself it wasn't real. Then, come back tomorrow, or on your next shift and pretend it never happened. Trust me. It's easier that way."

The two servers exchanged another wary glance and nodded to each other.

"Uhh…thanks, Alice. We'll do that." Lincoln said as they turned and left.

Olivia and Lincoln wove through clusters of intoxicated patrons: several women out for their weekly girls' night; a couple walking back and forth between the bar and the patio, taking turns hitting a vape pen; a gay couple laughing and having a seemingly delightful dinner date across from each other in two of the overly large wing-backed chairs near the window, beside the elevator.

There, with their backs to the cacophony of a Saturday night in the midwest, they waited for the elevator to arrive, to deliver them safely to the ground floor and into the night.

"With how the night is going, we'll probably get stuck on the way down."

"Don't."

"What? It's definitely on brand."

"Please, knock on some fucking wood or something." Lincoln just wanted to be home.

ding

The elevator arrived, empty.

"Hey, at least the light isn't flickering." Olivia punched Lincoln in the arm.

"Just get in," he rumbled, through gritted teeth.

The door closed and began to move with a lurch. They passed the second floor quickly, no chance of stopping. After hours the closing manager would make their way to the lobby, near the host stand, and insert their key into the slot next to the 'call' button and turn. While he would never tell anyone, Foundations' maître d', Brandon, loved to pretend he was stopping a nuclear launch when he inserted that key.

The elevator doors slid open on the first floor without incident and Lincoln and Olivia spilled out into the hallway. The lights were those fancy hipster Edison bulbs. Their dim glow cast long shadows: a wilting palm becoming a clawed hand, a cactus looming in the corner near the window. Rock Hard Climbing closed at ten on weekends, their receptionist long gone, the gym locked up tight.

Lincoln put his whole body into the front door and cast himself into the night air, into freedom. He took a step out but backed up and kicked a foot out to hold the door for Olivia.

"Where are you parked?" She asked, sheepishly.

"Second row over, you?"

"Fourth row," she paused, taking a beat. "Do you, uh, mind walking me?"

Lincoln sighed unintentionally, the exhaustion and fear escaping him in thin wisps of fog.

"It's okay…I can—"

"No, it's fine," he cut her off. "I mean, I want to. I'm sorry, this whole thing has just been, well, it's been a-fucking-lot."

Their eyes met and they shared a moment of relief and understanding, erupting in laughter, then tears. Olivia stood up straight, wiping the wetness from the corners of her eyes with her sleeve. "Man, never a dull moment in the service industry, is there?"

"Really made that ten dollar tip on a four hundred dollar check on an eight top worth it."

"Wait, really?"

"Yeah. Brandon even came over and tried to work things over a bit before they signed. Honestly, I think that just made it worse."

"Fuck, dude. And I thought I had it bad tonight, having only two tops and a little bitch section for being a closer." Olivia shook her head, "I wish they would have called someone off tonight."

"Me too. Not that I would have been lucky enough for it to have been me."

"What? And miss making those tens of dollars?"

"Stop. The night was bad enough before the…" Lincoln trailed off.

"Linc?" She never used the shortened version of his name anymore, not since they broke up the year before. "What do you think it was?"

Silence enveloped them, lingered in the space between them as they stood beside Olivia's Subaru. Lincoln fidgeted with his rolled up apron in his left hand, passed it to his right, then back again.

"It was nothing. Right?"

"Linc, don't do that."

"That's what Alice *told* us." His voice was full of frustration.

"But you saw it. We saw it. We *both* saw it." Olivia reached forward to Lincoln's arm, pulling back at the last second. A memory of something familiar.

"It doesn't matter. Tomorrow it'll just be a distant memory, like a bad dream. We'll be spinning wild tales about it in a few weeks during dinner prep. Kristen will probably scream. Dylan won't believe us. Hell, most of them won't believe us, but hey, it'll be a good story, right? Cause that's all it'll be, Liv. A story."

Lincoln grasped for the driver door and propped it open.

"Drive safe." He said, leaving it linger in the air, almost like a question.

Wordlessly, Olivia clambered into the seat. They shared one more look. She nodded, opened her door, and ducked inside without looking back.

Lincoln stood in place, watching, until she pulled out onto Carrol, heading south towards the on-ramp to the highway. He let out another sigh, this one for himself — conscious, insistent — and made his way to his Chevy Malibu.

The car started on the first try, which isn't a given, especially on cooler nights. Lincoln tossed his apron across to the passenger seat, his wine key, pens, and booklet tumbled out onto the upholstery, pens jumping like lemurs into the darkness of the floorboards. Seatbelt fastened, foot on the break, he checked his phone before putting the car in reverse.

Hey baby! Text when you pull in so I can unlock the door for you. Can't wait to try that chocolate turtle pastry thing that Megan sent home with you!!! Ahhhhh!!! ily

"Goddamn it."

Lincoln slammed his phone down into his lap. He beat his open palms against the worn tan covering of the steering wheel.

⊂ℛℬ⊃

The evening seemed colder than minutes ago as Lincoln emerged. He slammed the door. The Malibu rocked on its suspension, the clap of metal echoing off the surrounding brick edifice of the apartment building nearby. No, not an apartment building, Lincoln thought, a mental hospital wearing the face of luxury housing.

Lincoln tapped out a quick reply saying he's running a bit late, but that the dessert is in tow. Hit send. Sealed his fate.

The elevator took too long. He took the stairs.

Lincoln entered the lounge, taking in much the same scene as before, plus or minus a few guests. He pushed back through the fray, past the bar, the couches and cafe tables, making his way towards the back stairwell. He made it by the ice machine alcove and office without Alice noticing, where she sat slouched over the desk, wine glass empty, again.

Alice hadn't come back down to turn off the lights in dry storage or the back hallway. Thankfully their story had scared her enough to leave them on overnight, even though she'd claim tomorrow it was the wine.

No emergency lights lit the dining room. Each table sat quiet, each chair statuesque. The vinyl on the booths, normally a bright red, looked more like a deep crimson in the little bit of light the windows let in from the streetlights. The kitchen was equally dark, aside from the digital displays on various appliances. A large digital clock sitting on the pass showed the time was nearly midnight. The lounge would be winding down soon, hard to tell from the footsteps and voices he heard above.

Lincoln trudged through the dish pit. His non-slip shoes doing the Lord's work on the freshly mopped tile. It should be illegal to market these damn things as non-slip, he thought.

clink clink clank clink clink clank clink

To the left, where the dish pit opened up to the prep area, Lincoln thought he could hear the sounds of dishes being handled somewhere on the line. No, he *knew* he heard it. Over at Jacob's station, in the corner. He was in charge of the grill, straight across the pass from Chef.

Lincoln wasn't sure if the hair on his arms was standing up before he opened the door to the walk-in or not, but it was now. He shivered with each noise coming from the kitchen. It sounded muffled, like he was hearing it through the intercom at a fast food drive-in. Point being, it sounded like it was coming from somewhere *else*, an impossible place, anyplace but the kitchen of a closed restaurant.

Lincoln slid his phone out of his pocket and thumbed on the flashlight. The interior of the walk-in was all tubs and buckets and sheet pans of prepped ingredients or partially finished dishes. So much of working the line in a place like Foundations is prep. The further along a dish can be at the time of ordering, the shorter the ticket time—something that Chef prided himself on.

On the right side, atop a shelving unit filled with containers of homemade icings and sweet creams, was a small square clamshell to-go box. The top of the box had "Kenzie <3" written on it in black sharpie, the kind with the extra thick tip that you have to write at an angle with to come out legible.

Swiping the box from its perch, Lincoln backed out of the walk-in letting the door close with a quiet suctioning *kerphlp* as it sealed tightly to keep the temperature regulated.

Grab the dessert. Haul ass back up to the lounge. Get the hell out of here. A three step process on repeat in his head.

To-go container in hand, Lincoln exited the walk-in.

From the darkness of the unlit kitchen, a swell of voices rose from the line. No decipherable words could be understood, but the unmistakable cadence of speech was apparent. The words weren't so much in unison as they were babbling over each other, layered and growing in volume, like a group of fractured voices singing in rounds, only each voice sang a different song.

"Hello?" Lincoln called out to the pass.

Despite the overheads being off, there was enough light coming through the windows from the street to confirm that he was alone. No other living thing occupied the second floor, yet the voices persisted.

"We're closed! Go back up to the lounge or go home!" He yelled. Maybe Brandon had forgotten to lock the front stairwell, he thought.

All at once, the voices disappeared.

Lincoln slipped once more on the remnants of a puddle near the drain in the dish pit, and made his way back around the corner, down the hallway towards the dim overhead lighting, to dry storage, to the stairwell.

At the end of the first hallway, as Lincoln rounded another corner, he heard footsteps in pursuit.

What followed behind him weren't the footfalls of a single person, that much he knew. The familiar pitter patter of two feet rising and falling in an alternating pattern, while alarming, would have been more welcome than the quick succession of thuds that echoed down the hall. Each footfall was too close together, too many, too frequent.

clip thunk clip thunk clip thunk

No, what followed surely had more than two legs; how many, Lincoln couldn't be sure. He only knew that whatever it was, however many legs it *did* have, was moving fast. He couldn't stop repeating that line from Dracula in his head. Regardless, he wasn't sticking around to find out how fast the dead traveled.

Each of his footfalls smacking against the laminate was met with the clatter of several more yards behind. While it was the same hallway he and Olivia had walked down together not fifteen minutes earlier, it felt infinitely longer alone, even running.

Lincoln hit the door to the stairwell full force, exploding into the bright LEDs and sunny yellow paint of the stairway. He'd hoped the lights would scare whatever pursued off, or at least would make him feel better, more brave. Instead, the door remained propped open after he passed through, like someone had stuck their foot in the bottom corner to keep it from closing. Through the crack Lincoln heard a scratching and scuttling noise. Whatever had followed him struggled to find purchase and force the door open.

Crkkcrrkkscrkscrk

Talons. Claws. Nails. A horrid combination. Some invisible appendage pried the door back open and tumbled out onto the landing.

Lincoln kept running, not daring to look back.

Behind him, at the foot of the stairs, the heavy door clapped shut, giving way to a new sound. The sound began throaty, transitioning to a lower register growl, then deeper, past anything Lincoln had ever heard.

Grrrrrr GRWARRRRR GRAWGRUGUGUG

Leaping two, then three steps at a time, hands white knuckling the compostable clamshell in his grip, he climbed.

He bounded past the first landing, arm swinging to grab for the railing, pulling himself up, higher, faster. Each time he pulled against the handrail more desperately.

Behind, the footsteps stopped on the landing halfway up the stairs.

GRAWRRRRRRRUGUGUG

The thing's growling grew frantic, more frenzied.

Lincoln burst through the door at the top of the stairway, half expecting it would be locked or stuck with his luck. The noise from the lounge quickly overtook the roars fading away behind in the stairwell as the door closed.

Alice poked her head out into the back hallway.

"What the…Lincoln? What the hell are you doing back up here?" She teetered, again, forward into the hall, her heels working miracles to keep her upright.

Lincoln didn't say anything. He kept walking.

"Hey! Lincoln, are you good?" Alice called after him, but he was already gone.

Back through the crowd, thinner now, he dodged the same couple as before and danced through a group saying their midwestern goodbyes—they'd be there for another hour.

The elevator arrived as Alice stumbled through the lounge.

"Lincoln, wait!"

He stopped and turned to Alice, his face unable to mask the terror frozen on his brow, his eyes glazed over in a glossy sheen like the surface of a puddle in the sun.

"What…what happened?"

Without skipping a beat he responded in an unwavering drone, "Nothing. Nothing happened. And if it did, I'm not sure you'd believe me anyways."

Back outside, Lincoln stood in the gravel of the parking lot and let the cold air deep into his lungs. In. Out. In again. He pulled the door to the Malibu open with what little strength he had left, the adrenaline overflowing from him and seeping out into the night, leaving him fatigued in a way he'd never felt before. With his right hand he ever so gently placed the clamshell box on the passenger seat and stared at it. He laughed a little bit, mostly to keep from bursting into tears—adrenaline trying desperately to find another way to escape. The box looked insignificant, small. He reached over one last time and adjusted where it sat. He even considered buckling it in.

Before he pulled out of the lot, he typed out a quick text.

Omw.

Also.

Can you help me be on the lookout for a new fucking job?

—Everything okay babes?

I'll fill you in when I get home

—Oh

I got your dessert btw

—Awwww thank u! I'm not hungry tho

- THE END -
ENJOYED THIS? CHECK OUT:
BAD FORM
BY JOE TAYLOR

YOU THINK YOU'VE HEARD THIS STORY, BUT WE PROMISE YOU HAVEN'T. THE BRITISH ISLES HAVE A HISTORY OF SUCH MYTHS. FALSE, FAIRY-LIKE MOTHERS WITH BLACKENED EYES. SURE, THEY SEEM SO LOVING, SO READY TO BE THE PARENT YOU THINK YOU NEED. BUT THEIR DARK EYES AND SCARECROW FACES ARE HIDING A HORRIBLE TRUTH. EVERYONE YOU'VE LOVED, YOUR HOME, IS LONG GONE. YES, SHE'LL LOVE YOU, BUT YOU HAVE TO LOVE HER ALSO. DON'T WORRY, DEAR FRIENDS, IF THIS ARRANGEMENT SEEMS SUSPECT. AFTER ALL, ISN'T THE PRICE OF UNCONDITIONAL LOVE WORTH A LITTLE "GIVE AND TAKE"?

GIVE AND TAKE

SJ TOWNEND

A twist of a road, gravel, turned earth, wheat as high as his waist. The boy ran. He had never run so fast in his life. He would not return to his father's new house, not if he could help it.

Each time he craned his neck, his father's duplex apartment grew smaller in his wake. Doll's house, matchbox, lost. Heads of wheat drank up all that had been behind him as he ran deeper into the field.

His father was not a barbarous man, though. At bedtime, he'd comfort the boy and would reminisce about his son's mother in grief, but the boy's father had become forceful, callous even, since his wife had passed. He'd insist the boy should remain in his own bed in the flat they'd had to move into after selling up the family home.

Far smaller, with just one hopper window, dangling cables, and a bricked-off lintel door in the middle of a blank unfinished partition wall where the boy felt bookcases or paintings should be, the boy hated his new room. The unplumbed radiator would be sorted eventually, his father would promise, the boy shivering under his quilt—perhaps next month, they'd shop for curtains, for carpet together.

Alone in his junior bed, he'd cry himself to sleep. And then, the scratching would wake him. Without doubt, the scratching and thumping, like the flailing of soft meat on wood, would emanate from the thinnest wall.

"Next door is empty, unoccupied as of yet," his father would say while trying to soothe the boy. And the boy had tried to believe his father, had tried his hardest to sleep once his father had kissed him goodnight, but each night, he'd wake feverish from nightmares, horrid dreamscapes, to the sound of muffled thuds and scrapes.

The boy could not take another night in the unfinished building, a once-ample farmhouse house later cleaved into two located in the middle of some place in the countryside he'd yet to master the name of. And so, while his father had been washing dishes, and the sun, as if turning its back on an otherwise uneventful day, had begun its descent towards the horizon, he had run away.

Each inhalation hit his lungs hard. Ears of wheat brushed against his pumping arms. He didn't know where he was going. Just forwards, anywhere, away from his new bed, his new room.

An eerily dusk-lit scarecrow afloat on its post a few hundred yards in front of the boy informed him he must've been approaching the centre of the field, half way to the other side at least. He ran towards the scarecrow. The scarecrow became a person.

The boy stopped. Panting, and with his hands on his thighs, he looked up at the being which stepped down from its stump. He felt a little afraid, but held his spot; he'd seen far worse in dreams. At least it was not his father, standing in front of him in the field, forcing him to return home. It was an old woman with a face he could not find the thoughts to describe. There was something amiss with her, a peculiarity the boy could not fathom.

She moved closer, through the wheat. Her obscure features softened and reassembled, until, like mist clearing, the woman bore the face of his mother. The boy wheezed and choked as he inhaled with too much celerity, and the scent not of tilled earth or wheat but of bitter herbs stuffed his throat.

"Mother?"

"If that is who you long for, then I will give that gift to you," the woman replied. The boy tried to gather himself in raw handfuls—he knew it couldn't be her, he'd thrown dirt on her coffin at his father's command as she'd been lowered into earth on the other side of the country—but instead, his pneuma pooled like sand. "Mother?" he asked again. Tears rolled down his cheeks. The woman inched closer, crouched, and took the boy in her arms.

"Yes, my child." The heat of his mother's breath tickled the boy's cheeks, the lips of his mother kissed his tears away. "Would you like to hear a story?" The boy's tongue fell limp. He could not speak, his ability stolen by shock. Instead, he nodded. The woman smiled.

"Once there was a woman named Rebekah who gave birth to twins, one boy, one girl. The birth was swamped with problems, with pain, but Rebekah endured it, she had to, and was glad when, after careful examination by the midwife, both babes were returned to her bosom. Swaddled in rags and placed in her arms, her son, his cheeks as flush as blood, was bonny but screamed loudly. *'Tis normal, tis healthy,'* the midwife reassured her. The other baby, the girl, lay quiet, as if asleep, her skin as grey as the sheet in which she was wrapped. *'Your daughter has no heart,'* the midwife told Rebekah, *'but your son, the one who screams so loudly, has been blessed with two.'*"

The boy stiffened. The woman with the face of his mother cupped his chin in her hand and drew his face closer to hers. She pressed her ear against his chest. "A strong beat. Are you afraid, boy? Do you want me to stop?" The boy could not answer straight away. He inhaled sharply, balled his fists into tight knots, and thought of his father, the new bedroom, the noises which came at night.

He did not want this woman with the face of his mother to take him back there, did not want her to think he was scared, so he shook his head. "No. Please, go on."

"If you're sure." The woman continued speaking with the voice of the boy's mother. "'*She will not survive, without a heart,*' the midwife said to Rebekah and snatched up the babes from Rebekah's weak arms, '*but we can perform a procedure.*'"

"A procedure?" The boy asked. He'd heard this word before. A procedure had failed to save his mother. "An operation?"

"A procedure," the woman said. "'*Your son can be a donor. Let us share out the hearts.*'" The woman, with a firm grip, kept her arm around the boy, but looked away from him, as if addressing the heads of wheat, the breeze, and continued her tale. "'*But the procedure carries great risk,*' the midwife said. '*If successful, both your babies will be saved. But if not, you'll lose them both.*' Rebekah did not know what to do. She'd laboured for hours and lost a lot of blood, and did not want to lose either of her newborns, but she could not choose one love over the other. Aware she could not ask her own babies for opinion or consent, she agreed to the procedure. The midwife took the babies away."

The woman stopped talking, removed her arm from the boy, and turned her back on him, the air between them pregnant with silence. She stepped away, weaving through the wheat.

"The babies— Please tell me what happened to the babies," the boy cried. He chased after the woman with the face and voice of his mother, her familiar soft black hair ribboning behind her.

"If you want to know the rest of the story, best come with me."

The boy followed as she led him out of the field, as wheat became earth became gravel.

"Home," the woman said finally, and there in front of the boy, the field behind them, stood the stone cottage with shutters as blue as a summer's sky in which he'd grown up in with his mother and father, the house in which he'd moved out of a few months ago. The shutters had always reminded him of eyelids, ready to blink, and the cottage's windows, pupils, always watching over him, making him feel safe whenever he returned home.

The boy was confused. He recalled so clearly his father, a mess, posting keys through the letter box, escorting the boy into the car, bidding their old house farewell with tears in his eyes, before driving for many hours across the country to start their life anew. But there it was, just the other side of the field from where he was sure his father would be now, in the new home, darting in and out of each room, opening doors and shouting for his son.

A pang of guilt, of fear. He missed his father. But the woman, this uncanny echo of his mother, simply smiled and took the boy by the hand and led him along the path to the front door.

"Come inside, Kissyfer," she said. The boy's anxieties dissipated. Only his mother had ever called him that. His father only ever called him Chris. And so he followed his mother into the house, as young boys tend to do.

Inside, with a large oak drop bar, the woman bolted the front door closed and set about lighting candles. The boy quivered. As the first golden sphere lit up a patch of the cottage's interior, he realised inside was not familiar at all.

"Sit." The woman directed but there were no chairs. To his left, a rudimentary kitchen stood, with shelves packed with empty glass bottles and jars. In the centre of the room was a fireplace, and to the right of the hearth he saw a collection of hessian sacks and a single door. "On the floor, by the fire. And once I have lit the fire, I'll continue my story."

"Please, I want to go home," the boy said, his words reedy, his legs loose. The woman knelt by the hearth striking steel char cloth against flint. She ignored the boy and tended to the fire until flames burst warm and bright. The boy eked towards the front door and tried to lift the wooden bar to no avail. "I want to go home," he said again. "My father will be worried."

The woman sighed. She turned, looked up at the boy, her face no longer the face of his mother's but instead, that of a straw-stuffed hessian bag with two tortoiseshell buttons for eyes.

"I can help you with your nightmares. I know your father isn't handling that well. He has never had a bad dream before, how would he understand?" How the being spoke, the boy did not know, for it had no mouth. But the boy did have a mouth, he checked, made sure, felt it with his fingertips which felt like ice on his lips. He tried to scream but could not, no matter how hard he tried. Or perhaps, he did scream, but no sound came out.

"You can't scream, can you?" it said. "Just like in your dreams. Keep trying, one might come. Although there really is no need. Please, boy. Sit here with me on the floor. Allow me at least to finish my story." The being's button-eyes glinted on catching the light of the fire, and sparkled like the rows of empty glass bottles which, in the kitchen to the left of the fire, lined shelf upon shelf upon shelf.

The boy knew he had no choice. The door bar was as thick as his waist, heavier probably than him, so he sat cross-legged, keeping distance between himself and his captor.

"I'll make some tea, to help loosen your tongue, and then I'll finish my story." The being rose and moved to the kitchen area. The boy shivered despite the heat kicking out from the fire.

Drawers opened and closed, spoons twirled and tapped, and the being returned to the fireside with a mug of something which smelt bitter. "Drink" it said. The boy refused, shook his head. "It'll help with your nightmares, Kissyfer." Its face flickered back into that of his mothers: kind green eyes, shoulder-length black curls. How he missed his mother. He pinched himself on the hip, certain he was trapped within a dream, but he did not awaken and his hip skin smarted. "My darling Kissyfer, how I've missed you," his mother said. The boy pegged his nose with his fingers, lifted the mug to his lips, allowed himself to be lost in the fantasy of sharing space with his mother for just a moment more, and drank.

"The babies were taken away for their procedure. It was successful." The boy blinked hard, once, twice, remembering where the story had been left. How suddenly the story had come to an end.

"I am glad," he said, finding gravitas in the flesh within his mouth, in his words once more. "I'm glad the story ended well." On placing his empty mug on the floor, the being's mask faded once more

"Oh, better than well." The being lifted an arm and brushed its birch twig finger against the boy's cheek, then reached for his chest. He recoiled. From its head of cloth, the boy's mother's lips formed words. "You see, the son had given his sister the greatest gift he could, the gift of life, and in return, she had given him the greatest gift she could: a companion from the same womb, a sibling."

"Who are you?" the boy asked.

"Never mind that. Would you like another story? Perhaps the Widow of Zarephath? Rumplestiltskin? Some Faust? Another tale of give and take, tit for tat?"

"No." He shook his head firmly then rubbed his wet eyes. "I just want to go home."

"But what about those nightmares? Let me help you with those. I'll give you something you want, the face, the voice of your mother, perhaps, in exchange for your dreams?" And as it spoke, his mother's whole face reappeared. His mother's body nictated into existence. The woman embraced the boy and held his head to her breasts. The softness there, the softness of his mother, her silk blouse against his cheek. An aroma not of bitter herbs but of baked goods. The boy sobbed and wrapped his arms around his mother's waist.

"I'd like that," he said, yawning. "I think." She scooped the boy up, carried him through the small door to the right of the fire into the second room, and placed him there, on a bed.

Crouching by the boy's side, his mother stroked him until he dozed. "Sleep well," she whispered, then left the room, closing the door behind her, bolting it firmly from the outside.

ଦ୨ଐ

When the boy opened his eyes, he felt remarkably refreshed, no rattling or scratching had awoken him from his slumber. No nightmares. No dreams at all. But when he fumbled in the darkness for his bedroom light switch, he could not find it on the wall. And the wall did not feel like the unfinished wall, in his new room, where he lived with his father. He scrabbled around, searching blindly with his palms and fingertips for the switch he was sure was at the end of his bed, but found nothing. He felt around the perimeter of the room. No curtains. No chest of drawers. No window. None of his toys. In the dark, he looped the room's perimeter and found nothing except smooth walls and the roughness of the frame of a wooden door, a strange door with what felt like a small rectangular hatch in its centre. Patchy memories flooded back to him: racing through wheat, pungent tea, a story by the fire. He tried to scream but couldn't.

Running his fingers across and back along the hatch which was no bigger than a letterbox, eventually he managed to pop it open. He peered through it and saw the duplicate of his mother, boiling water, making tea, in not his mother's kitchen.

Upon the stacked shelves behind her stood myriad glass bottles, all of them empty bar one which was full of crimson smoke. "Help," he tried to shout through the opening, but only a quiet sound came out.

Carrying tea, the woman came over, unlocked the door and entered the room in which the boy had slept. "Drink," she said. The boy refused.

"Who are you? Let me go," he said, making loose swings at the woman. She placed the mug on the floor and restrained him gently.

"Dear boy, I wear *her* face for you. For you! In exchange, you'll sleep here and I'll extract your bad dreams. Look, to the shelf above the stove. Those red swirls of your rich imagination. See the full bottle, child? Now tell me you slept well, like a log. I know you did."

The boy's rage and fear diminished. He could not deny this. Perhaps this woman *was* trying to help?

"I need you to do a little more though, this time," she said, "for I've given you so much already." And with his mother's mouth, she kissed him on his crown. "You must write your dreams down for me, child. Scribe them out until you grow tired." She presented him with a pencil.

"My nightmares?" He shuddered, recollecting more clouded memories of a different room in a different house to the one he was in, another house with a person in it who'd cared for him. That person had been dissimilar to this woman—who he thought might be someone's mother, his mother?—but he could recall no more than that. Yet he remembered the content of his horrendous nightmares as clear as day.

"But what shall I write them on? You haven't given me any paper and it's pitch black in here when the door is closed."

"Simply prop open the hatch, sweet child, like this." She showed him how. "Use the walls as canvas." The boy breathed hard. "Such blank walls. They could do with some sort of decoration."

"If you're sure," the boy replied.

"Yes my Kissyfer, my darling, scribe your nightmares on the walls."

She sang to him sweetly—songs of twin toddlers playing in fields, chasing each other, tumbling through wheat, and listening to each other's heartbeats—while caressing the boy's scalp. He smiled softly. "Now drink, child." She passed him the tea and with his mother by his side, he drank. "Don't forget to write before you rest." She left. With heavy eyelids, he began to write.

C&SO

When he woke well rested from another dreamless slumber, all he could hear was his own breath, his heart beating beneath his ribs. He was glad to know it still there though, his heart. Glad it was where it should be. He fumbled in the dark, found the hatch, popped it open, and looked through it: his mother in the kitchen making tea. Two bottles full of red smoke stood side-by-side on the shelf.

He called out softly, his throat still weak in some strange way. She came to him accordingly and sang and stroked his neck. "More tea. Drink, boy." He did. His mother loved him so much, would only ever want to help. "Trust is an exchange, she whispered. "Trust me with your nightmares, and I'll love you like a mother."

This continued, the tea, the resting in her arms, the scribing of his midnight fears on the walls, the slipping into deep dream-free sleep. Each time he woke, he'd watch his mother pottering, through the flap. Smoke-filled bottles grew in number on her shelves, and his walls filled up with words.

Time passed. One morning or perhaps evening, the boy woke and rubbed his face, feeling the soft downy hair on his chin. He grabbled to prop up the hinged hatch door which had fallen closed while he'd slept. Light flooded in. His walls were almost full, and in the kitchen, so were all the bottles. He rapped on the door, spoke deeply, softly, as that was all his throat would allow, and called for his mother, called for more tea, for he had learnt it was better to be asleep, in a place of nothingness, than to be awake, even with his mother at his side, singing and stroking. Her face had become less soft with time, more like dry grass, rasping fibres, and her voice, less soothing.

His mother drifted towards his room. He felt some small twinge in his heart as she grew larger, closer – perhaps she'd continue with her story, about the adolescent twins who were arguing over something that one of them had borrowed and the other had wanted back while he drank. But this time, she did not open the door, did not have tea in her spindly hand.

She knelt and pressed her face up against the hatch hole from the other side of the door. "No more tea." Her voice was thick like turned earth, coarse like gravel, its pitch twisted like a country road, and her tortoiseshell eyes stayed pressed up against the hole, blocking most of the kitchen light. His mother said nothing more. The boy pleaded for more tea. He wanted to sleep. He begged her to come in and hold him and finish her story, even though the tale had become quite unnerving. What were the twins arguing over? But his mother said nothing. Her button-eyes threaded onto hessian sack, as dead as pinned butterflies, remained pressed there, filling up the only outlet of his room.

He placed his hands on the wood of the door, felt the shape of the hatch around where her eyes were, ran his fingertips over the rims of the buttons, and called out for his mother, tried to wake her up. She remained silent and stock-still. Fear and anger rose within him. Wide awake, he could never sleep without her, without the tea. He pushed on his mother's eyes. Hard. The hessian sack dropped to the floor and a wedge of light shone in. His mother was not in her kitchen. And all the glass bottles were gone.

Feeling quite untethered, the boy groped and scratched around the edges of his dimly lit room, searching for something with which to ground himself. He followed the walls around with his hands, reading over and over again his scribed words in his head: *I wake in a dark room. I cannot escape. I cannot scream.*

He scratched at the walls like a rat in a cage. His fingertips blistered and bled. He made his way around the room to no avail, finding nothing, and returned to the wooden door. His legs were heavy, his arms ached, but he could not sleep without his mother. He banged on the door, shook it as hard as he could. He brought his eye down to peer through the hatch. Through the hatch now, a different view, a room which felt familiar, like something from a dream: a small room, home to a too-tight bed which fitted the adult lying in it like a coffin. Could it be, his mother, sleeping? He shook the door and tried again to scream but alas, still no shriek came out. The hatch swung down, swung like a loose tooth, then snapped closed, and would not open again. Blackness. He hammered and shook and scratched at the woodwork. He hit and thumped the sealed-tight flap.

CRSO

He'd searched the countryside high and low, as had the police, because his little boy, his Christopher, had been missing for several days. "Try and rest," the officer had said on escorting him back to the duplex apartment. The man staggered into his son's bedroom and lay down on the small cot-bed, clutching his son's favored teddy bear to his chest. The man's eyelids five whiskies heavy, closed. He drifted off, but woke in the middle of the night from a terrible nightmare to the sound of scratching and thudding, meat on wood, coming from the bricked-up door.

— THE END —
ENJOYED THIS? CHECK OUT:
YOUR FINAL SUNSET
BY SJ TOWNEND

WE ROMANTICIZE SPACE TRAVEL, DON'T WE? BUT WHAT WE FAIL TO GRASP IS THAT SPACE IS COLD AND EMPTY AND ENDLESS. AMY KNOWS JUST HOW EMPTY SPACE IS, AND SHE IS MORE THAN READY TO GET HOME. BUT AS THE SPACECRAFT DRAWS CLOSER TO THEIR DESTINATION, AMY LEARNS THAT MAYBE NOT EVERYONE IS GOING TO MAKE IT HOME. WE BRING YOU NOW THE SCIENCE-FICTION THRILLER . . .

NEPHTHYS

JON LASSER

Amy shifted uncomfortably as she knelt on the corrugated titanium deckplate. Her bones resonated with the thrum of accelerating engines, silent trumpets of the dead. As if in response to their endless call, her back spasmed. A nerve pinched, a flash of electric pain flooded her body.

Low-G was supposed to be good for back pain. Maybe earthbound forty-five-year-olds had it worse. The pain would pass. She stretched out on her belly across the cargo bay floor. If only she could stay here forever! Somewhere above, Captain Senamun lay in wait, a lioness ready to pounce. The Corporation wanted Amy gone, and the captain was their agent.

They'd announced years ago, in a mealy-mouthed press release barely covered by the business journals, that the second age of crewed vessels was ending. They'd begun to convert their ships, thousands of seven-hundred-fifty-meter-long cargo vessels with crews of one or two, to fully-automated craft as quickly as crews retired. Amy imagined the process as a sort of friction, human capital evaporating in the heat of loss.

Even with a decade's warning, Amy wasn't ready to go. Here in the asteroid belt, where so many worshipped the sun, she stared into the black beyond. Outer space, seen with the naked eye, seemed blacker than black. Blacker than it appeared on any screen. They wanted to take it from her in the name of efficiency, of padded profit margins, of illusory safety.

She inched closer to the aperture tucked into the interior hull. Her heart beat faster as she stared into space. As black as it could get, but for the streaks and spots where cosmic rays stimulated the rods and cones of her eye as though from visible light. In this, physics betrayed her, allied itself with the Corporation.

Regulations forbade all windows, even peepholes. The high-energy particles that passed through this gap in her ship's shielding and inscribed themselves upon her eyes raised every risk of spaceflight: computer failure, cancer, structural fatigue. She'd done it anyway, back when the Nephthys was her own, in spirit if not in paperwork. She hadn't meant it as even the tiniest rebellion; she simply needed to stare through her tiny glass window into the eternal and empty heart of the universe. Nephthys: Goddess of death, goddess of service, of lamentation, of nighttime, and rivers.

ରୟଧ

Amy sat as the pain ebbed. The knurled plating bit at her knees. Soft footsteps tapped back and forth on the main deck above the cargo hold. The Captain was up there, perhaps searching for her, but Amy knew the ship like nobody else ever would, all of its secrets. Not just the peephole. The holographic guards, spears in hand, so often static as though carved in stone, which she'd programmed to guard the empty rooms. Nooks the security cameras couldn't reach. The small gold-leaf box with her son's ashes, welded in place between the hulls, so that he'd never be alone. Nephthys, goddess of death.

"Patel, what's your location?" The intercom crackled softly, perhaps tormented by the same cosmic rays that gave Amy her unwanted visions of light.

"Captain. I'm on the cargo deck. I'll be up in a moment."

She stood, still wobbly under the slight but still-increasing gravity, then launched herself at the porthole to the main deck.

Captain Senamun leapt backwards, her long red hair floating around her broad face, as Amy shot past her.

Amy grabbed the handrail and lowered herself gently to the deck. The captain picked herself up, scowled at Amy, and smoothed her uniform.

"Patel, I've been looking for you. What in Aten's name were you doing down there?"

"Sorry, sir." Six months earlier, Amy hadn't answered to anyone. She still served as engineer, sanitation worker, chief cook, and bottle washer, but the Corporation had assigned Veronica Senamun to captain the Nephthys. Nephthys, goddess of service.

The Captain stared at the floor and wouldn't meet her eyes. Was she ashamed of her role in this debacle? She didn't seem the type.

Amy coughed. "Did you need something, Captain?"

"Just wondering where you were." Senamun shook her head.

Looking for fault, no doubt. Reasons to terminate her employment, after which they'd convert the ship. It wasn't a problem for the Captain. They'd give her a bonus and assign her to the next freighter on their list. How many were left, after Nephthys? Not many.

"I'll be in my room if you need anything." She loped down the short corridor. "Thank you, Captain."

❧

Amy picked up her chair and sat it in the center of the room. She ran her fingers along its rough seams where the black and white aerogel met, and it crumbled a little beneath her nail.

She turned up the room's noise cancellation. The low hum she hadn't even noticed vanished completely. The audio blipped briefly as a video clip played.

The sound cut in a tenth of a second before the video. Amy knew it by heart, the last dying echoes of the cough of a dying man. Her husband, Stephen, in a loose turquoise one-piece. His brother, Chris, in a white shirt, maroon frills spilling messily from its collar, holding Stephen's hand. An office flooded with natural light. Water flowing in some fountain, splashing in full gravity, eerily silenced via software. In the background, a white-coated man sat stone-faced behind a desk, palms up as though to say there was nothing else he could do.

She had never needed to listen to his words to know the cancer was back. She'd seen it the first time she'd watched, in the way his hands trembled as he failed to lift them to his face. "Six months, maybe," he choked. Chris dabbed the corners of her husband's eyes with a handkerchief and looked at the screen as though to rebuke Amy for her absence, an absence that stretched nearly a year after the video arrived.

She stopped playback. Nephthys, goddess of lamentation.

Stephen hadn't wanted her to go to space. Her last time on Earth, he'd refused to let the matter drop.

"You could have died," he said. By which he meant that through some moral alchemy his cancer—by then in remission—was her fault, that she'd abandoned him and made him sick.

She never told him that she had died. She recalled staring across the deck at her shattered body. She'd watched as blood hemorrhaged in red waves, surface tension wrapping those red ribbons around her flesh. She never told Stephen of the pain that forced her back into that dead flesh against her will, even as she reached for the black beyond.

What had happened to her? Why hadn't she been allowed to die? Amy suspected she would never know, that the universe was stranger than she could imagine. Maybe his cancer balanced some sort of cosmic ledger.

Amy stripped, wrapped herself in the leopard-print netting tacked to her wall, and turned off the lights. Nephthys, goddess of nighttime.

⧬

Amy slept in silent darkness and woke refreshed. She unclipped herself and fell to the deck floor. More gravity than before, enough for a shower. She grabbed a canister and sprayed herself down, donned a fresh jumpsuit, and drifted to the main deck.

"Good morning, Patel." Captain Senamun smiled. "How does it feel to be heading home?" Nothing but business, no matter how she pretended. Not naming whatever causes she would list on Amy's termination paperwork. Not asking how Amy would cope with her first visit to Stephen's family. Just asking how the journey felt. Nephthys, goddess of rivers.

"Morning, Captain." The designation of hour a mere formality, offered by any recently-awakened officer.

The Engines burned so hot the air felt like a greenhouse, and the hull vibrated with a note Amy knew like her mother's caress. She closed her eyes and tasted ozone.

The klaxon squawked three times, the lights blinked red. Captain Senamun cursed loudly, but Amy ignored her. It had to be the cooling system. When traveling in vacuum, whatever parts were responsible for shedding heat were always the most difficult, most expensive, most fragile.

"I'll have a look, Captain." Proactive response to a crisis was the mark of a good officer. She wouldn't give Senamun any cause to file papers.

The captain nodded, her face composed and neutral.

Amy crawled into the duct with her repair satchel. There, ahead, the heat exchange coil spouted steam like a teakettle, hissing in the dim red dark.

She donned her gloves and took the brazing torch from the bag. She dug out a patch and the flux, which she sprayed on the coil and the patch. No time to clean it properly now; they'd need to replace the whole coil back on Earth in any case.

She clamped the patch in place, and was preparing the alloy when the coil exploded. Nephthys, goddess of death.

∞

She crouched outside her body, her feet seemingly firm upon the deckplate, as though her spirit couldn't escape the maintenance duct. It didn't look that terrible, her body. With the acceleration, the blood flowed normally from the hundred thousand shrapnel wounds. Her skin, charred and roasted, sluiced off under the powder and rain of the fire extinguisher.

She'd be with Stephen soon. Why had terrible things happened whenever she left his side? It was her fault. Always her fault.

Her spirit-body doubled over in pain. The flesh seemed recovered already: unbloodied, pink and raw with only minor burns. Her tormenter pushed her back inside.

She knelt, choking and coughing. Being alive didn't hurt half so much as being saved.

Amy crawled back to the intercom and pushed the button.

"Amy? What was that?" Captain Senamun sounded worried. She'd never called Amy by her first name before. "Are you all right?"

"I'm all right." She wasn't. "The coil gave out. Must've rotted from the inside when we weren't looking. You'll need to shunt—"

"Affirmative, it's already done. Though it looks like our long-range antenna array is offline, too. Can you put on a suit and take a look? We need comms."

"Roger."

⊃∘⊂

Amy hadn't ever liked wearing her exo-suit and working outside the ship. Too much opportunity for fatal errors. But now, sharing the ship with Captain Senamun, the suit offered her a little quiet, a little isolation. And with the Captain monitoring her, so long as she didn't get loose from her tether, chances of a fatal accident were far lower. One positive of two-crew ships.

She donned the suit, wriggling her fingers into its tight rubberized gloves. She tugged the heavy zippers closed, pressurized the suit. It inflated slightly. She pressed the button again and listened for the telltale hiss of leaks. Silence.

She squeezed into the small maintenance airlock and depressurized. The ship groaned and shuddered; even the negligible amount of air vented into space moved the ship. Outside, still connected to the ship, she felt the tug of gravity astern. She twisted reflexively as her perspective shifted, and now she felt herself cling to the windows of a two hundred story skyscraper with no Earth beneath it.

Amy's pulse pounded frantically in the tips of her fingers.

The radio crackled. "Everything all right, Patel?" Captain Senamun must have been monitoring her life signs. Nosy.

"Yes sir. I'm re-orienting and will proceed to the antenna array momentarily."

Amy turned off her radio and twisted her body to face the blackness of space. She smiled. This was home. In a hundred years, a thousand years, humans would adapt to space. Biological, mechanical, Amy couldn't predict, but it was too beautiful to believe it wouldn't happen. The darkness called.

Stars erupted in her vision; another burst of cosmic rays. Would they kill her one day, or would the God, Goddess, or space alien—whoever it was who dragged her back into her flesh at that moment of death—wrest her body from its home?

Poor Stephen, earthbound now forever. They'd saved his ashes, Chris reported in a terse text message. Left to themselves, they would scatter his ashes into the acid sea. She would bring him to space, where he could rest with their son, if only she could stay aboard Nephthys for another tour.

The long-range antenna array hung at an awkward angle, like a bent umbrella. It broke off in her hands. She disconnected the cable, and held the antenna in one hand while reaching for the small welding torch with her other.

She'd hardly pressed the ignition button when its gas canister burped flame. The burp blossomed into a starburst that remained even after she let go of the trigger. It whited out her sight even with the visor's auto-adjustment. The torch lacked oxygen enough for a significant explosion, but it had enough to burn her. She let go and shoved it away with both hands. Its now-tiny flame fell slowly down the side of the tower, the antenna following behind.

Nothing to be done for it now. Now that they were on-course, Management could track them on radar. Short-range radio would suffice for docking and last-minute course correction.

Amy turned and looked at the starry darkness.

೧೫

Captain Senamun ran her fingers through her long red hair and scowled. "You'd better pray nothing else goes wrong, Patel. We're on-course now, but we don't have any spare fuel for course—"

"I'm sorry, Captain."

The captain reared back like an angry bear. "Your apologies won't fill our oxygen tanks, Patel." Amy expected more: that they were going to die, that it was all her fault, but the Captain fell silent. The message had come across: Everybody was dying. Everybody but her.

Even so, they were headed home.

೧೫

Amy sat in her crumbling chair and punched up another message from her archive.

"I'm sorry," Chris whispered between sobs, "I think he just gave up. He asked about you, at the end."

Amy closed her eyes and sobbed with Chris, who had held Stephen's hand when she should have, who had been there for his brother the way that she should have been there for her husband.

It was her fault, that hundreds of hours of travel remained between this flying sarcophagus and Stephen's more modest coffin.

The Captain didn't say a word as Amy went below to the cargo deck. (Did she know about the peephole?) The only thing worse than

Stephen dying was knowing she would go on. Giving up wasn't enough to set her free.

Amy stared through the glass as the deep black of space. Cosmic rays painted her retinas with visions of dancing light. She was like those visions, an accident dancing through the cosmos.

સ્ૐૐ

Amy didn't know how long she stared into the darkness, minutes or hours, before Captain Senamun's voice crackled over the intercom. "Come up already, Patel." She sighed heavily, as though more resigned than angry.

"Aye aye."

Amy pulled herself up the ladder to the main deck. The Captain stood there with her bean-bag rifle. She pointed it at Amy.

"You weren't supposed to live," the Captain said. Her lungs wheezed with each ragged breath. Amy couldn't disagree. "I'm sorry—"

Amy peered into her eyes, distant and unfocused. Was this under orders? Even the Corporation wouldn't dare, would they?

"Veronica," she said, "I—"

Captain Senamun shook Amy off and smashed the rifle butt into her chest. Amy wheezed for breath and the captain's eyes turned hard.

"Walk." She gestured a'fore.

"Captain—" Amy said. Perhaps she could talk her down from whatever she intended.

"Stuff it, Patel." She shoved Amy up to the maintenance airlock.

The Captain intended to space her, didn't she? It wasn't right. She'd done nothing wrong, nothing but the window and that hardly counted. The welding tank, the antenna, the heat exchange coil—they weren't her fault, only terrible coincidences. Weren't they?

What if Captain Senamun did eject her into space? Would the decompression kill her? The lack of oxygen? Or would she float half-dead in space one hundred thousand years? Or one hundred thousand times that number? She swooned, dizzy with endless time.

Amy knelt on the deck. Her stomach convulsed, pumping rice and beans and bile and chocolate all over her uniform, and the stench brought with it a second round of convulsions.

"Blast it, Patel!" Captain Senamun smashed the rifle butt into her chest again, but Amy turned sideways, and the blow glanced off. She tugged the rifle away from the Captain in a sort of arcing motion, slow and deliberate in the reduced gravity. The rifle came loose from Senamun's hands, and she landed in the airlock.

With the Captain distracted, Amy pressed a button. Two guards materialized. Still as statues, they pointed their speartips at Veronica's torso.

"Please, Amy," the Captain begged. She'd never seen the guards, didn't know they were only holograms. They looked real enough, and she must have been too upset to question them. "I was only doing my job. Please don't do this."

Amy shook her head and poked Veronica with the business end of the rifle. "Stay there." She tried to sound tougher than she felt. "Or my guards will kill you."

Veronica paled. "You don't need to do this. I'm so sorry."

Amy latched the airlock and jammed the rifle in, so the Captain couldn't unlock it from her side.

"My wife, my son—" Veronica dropped to her knees, and Amy wasn't sure if the Captain intended to beg or vomit. She held the open airlock button with her left hand and the decompression override with her right, and the airlock opened into space before she could find out.

Without a tether, Veronica disappeared into the darkness.

Down wasn't down anymore, but off by a few degrees. Amy couldn't feel the ship spin, but the decompression override had ejected a tiny bit of atmosphere into space, efficient as any thruster.

Captain again, Amy connected to the computer and punched up the ship's log. Captain Senamun dead in airlock accident. Off-course due to atmospheric venting during incident. No steering thruster fuel remains for course correction. Could she vent some more air? Perhaps, but she hadn't a sense of how to time it. Maybe she could come close, but it seemed as though it would only make things worse. How long could she continue without air? It was best to wait, to save what remained.

⋙⋘

Amy stood and stretched. Water dripped somewhere. Under normal circumstances, the water loss would be fatal if not corrected, but she couldn't rouse herself to make repairs. On its new course, Nephthys would meet Earth in something just more than seven million hours. Eight hundred Earth years. Not never, but not in a lifetime. (Or was it, for her?) Until then, her ship would stay its course.

She sat in her chair, sprawled on her floor, replayed her messages a dozen times, a hundred times. She couldn't take her eyes off the doctor's upturned palms. There had been so much to do. She'd never sent Stephen a goodbye.

She recorded one, and another, and another. None of them say she left, and he died to punish her. None of them say that all of this is his fault. That Captain Senamun was right.

Time passed. Hours, hundreds of hours? Amy lost track. She missed Captain Senamun. Veronica. Amy punched buttons and browsed through the video archives.

Why had the Captain not disabled the cameras? Amy watched Veronica attack the heat exchange coil with a hammer. She watched her melt the long-range antenna pole with the brazing torch. She bent over the welding tanks and sabotaged them in some way the camera could not capture.

It took hundreds of hours, but Amy found the messages. Management had tired of waiting. The investors continued to pressure the Corporation to automate all of their ships. Where their contracts had promised permanent employment in the absence of performance problems, other methods must be identified. Their words were vague, professional, but Amy had seen the video.

She found Captain Senamun's reply in the affirmative.

∞

Nobody could stop Amy from weeping for Stephen, for Veronica. Nobody would stop her from staring out her peephole at the darkness beyond.

There wasn't anything out in the darkness except death for her friends, and for her enemies. There was nothing out in the darkness but life for her, a fate worse than death. The flying sarcophagus fell slowly toward the sun. Nephthys, goddess of rivers.

All rivers found the sea. Nothing ever ended. Something would happen next. Amy would be there to see it happen.

– *THE END* –
ENJOYED THIS? CHECK OUT:
A MIND FULL OF SCORPIONS
BY JR BILLINGSLEY

FROM THE DUSTY BACKROADS OF THE AMERICAN SOUTH, DAVID
CHANDLER OFFERS A TALE ABOUT TWO BROTHERS LIVING ON THE EDGE
OF AN OLD, DARK WOODS. THERE ARE STRANGE THINGS HAUNTING THE
TREES, AND WHEN THE ELDER BROTHER BECOMES A BIT TOO OBSESSED
WITH HIS NEW HUNTING HOBBY, THE YOUNGER BEARS WITNESS TO HIS
BROTHER'S . . . WELL, "CHANGES" MIGHT BE THE BEST WORD FOR IT. YOU
CAN BEAR WITNESS TO THE HORROR WITH HIM, THOUGH KEEP AN EAR
INCLINED TO YOUR DOOR AND BE PREPARED TO RUN OR COWER IF YOU
HEAR THE . . .

SCRATCHES

DAVID CHANDLER

I never really saw Jeremy as a hunter. No one did. Granted, everyone in Kilgore County went hunting, likely for a lack of other things to do, but in our family, deer season wasn't the pillar it tended to be for others in North Mississippi. I'm pretty sure even Dad, who would bring home at least one deer every year, would do so more out of habit or a sense of obligation than love of the hunt. He took us with him on occasion to the woods behind our house, showed us how to track and shoot like all our fathers did. I enjoyed the sport well enough for my part, but I never got the taste for it. While my cousins and classmates looked forward to deer season every fall, excited and hungry to take to the woods and bring home a well-earned kill, I mostly went hunting for lack of other options, and for the most part, Jeremy seemed to feel a similar sort of ambivalence about our community's favorite pastime.

I think his interest in hunting began the night our cousin Libby shared pictures of her first deer at the basketball game. Jeremy and Libby had always been close, her being just a few months older than he. They grew up as best friends; she was as much his sister as his cousin. She'd brought Polaroids of the young buck she killed to the game, and when she wasn't watching her boyfriend Trevor play, she was passing them around. Jeremy was one of the first people she showed them to. He smiled, said he was happy for her and meant it. But my brother's eyes had sadness in them, like he'd lost a race he didn't know he was running. He slipped his hands in his hoodie pockets and hunched a little—an attempt to make himself smaller so no one would register he was disappointed in himself. I don't think Mom and Dad noticed that his interest in hunting piqued soon after; I'm not sure they noticed much about their eldest son.

❧

Like most homesteads on the edge of Kilgore County, ours was unremarkable. The few hundred acres of land we owned was mostly pasture, but a good quarter of it was forested. My parents settled there when they were young, building a small farmhouse down a long gravel road, just off the county highway. Beside the house, the steel barn we used as a garage housed Dad's farm equipment. A fence with a cattle trap under the gate separated our yard from acres of pasture, and further still, a line of pines stood at the pasture's edge. When the sun set low, they'd cast their shadows across the pasture, blanketing the field and all that crawled there in a heavy gloom.

Beyond the pines, the woods grew older; the tall evergreens gave way to primeval oaks and hemlocks. Forced to weave its way through their branches, sunlight clung to Spanish moss and overgrowth that filtered the woods in a dusky haze, even at midday. It was easy to get lost among the disorienting shadows, but a few landmarks—the remnants of an old barbed wire fence that ran east to west, a toppled chimney that pointed due north—provided a means of orientation. Mostly, we navigated the woods by feel, following paths that mostly felt familiar rather than cutting a clear trail in and a clear one out. The woods had a way of overgrowing marks of our intrusion faster than we could blaze them. At the age of nine, I was too young to explore the woods alone, according to my parents. By the time they deemed me old enough, we had long since moved away; no one we know goes into those woods anymore.

Jeremy, however, spent time there almost every day that winter. He kept his hunting gear by the back door so he could throw on his overalls and orange vest as soon as he got home from school and take to the woods.

On the weekends, I went with him. We'd take the four-wheeler to the treeline and walk to wherever Jeremy wanted to hunt. We rarely saw anything, though, never anything Jeremy wanted to shoot. Even though we only spoke on the way out and the way back home, I felt lucky that my big brother let me tag along.

One Saturday evening, as we left the woods with nothing to show for our time, I asked him why he wanted so badly to shoot a deer. "I told y'all," he responded flatly. "I want to spend more time in the woods."

"But why?" I insisted, hearing the whine in my own voice and immediately hating myself for it. My throat tightened. Jeremy slowed and looked down at me, stone-faced and calm.

"Because I haven't brought home a deer yet. I want to know what it's like. It's not much more than that." He spoke resolutely, his words carefully chosen. I wasn't spoiling for a fight, but I was angry. Behind those words was an implication that I wouldn't understand, that he needed to cross some kind of threshold that I wasn't quite ready to navigate with him. Kids my age and younger had bagged deer every season. I got the sense that whatever Jeremy saw in his current fixation had little to do with bringing home a deer at all.

CR&ED

It was late in the season and late in the day when the kitchen phone rang; it was Jeremy, telling us he killed a buck big enough to mount. Mom and I both thought he was exaggerating until Dad took the phone from him and told us to meet at Jack's store. They'd drug it out of the woods and hauled it there because he didn't want to risk damaging the hide with a field dressing. I was delighted, not just for Jeremy but for myself. Instead of going to the woods every afternoon, Jeremy would be home.

When we got to Jack's, we saw Dad's truck. Its tailgate was down, and a thin rivulet of blood had pooled between the ridges that ran down the length of the bed. Mom parked, and we walked toward the skinning rack next to the store where they had already hoisted the deer. Jeremy was crouched down smiling, his face smeared with the blood of his first kill.

"What do you think?" Jeremy asked me. When I saw it up close, I understood more clearly the pride that must come with a successful hunt. The deer weighed about 180 pounds with a beautifully balanced rack of antlers. Each beam that protruded from the skull carried three perfectly-sculpted points, and the ends curled into elegant forks. It was larger and prettier than any of the deer I'd seen Dad clean at the farm, and I told everyone so. They all laughed, but it was hard for any of us to deny it was a stunning animal.

"Another year or two and he would've been a monster," Jack observed. Dad agreed. Instinctively, I started to come to Jeremy's defense, annoyed at their eagerness to disparage my brother's kill so casually. But if Jeremy took offense, he never showed it.

"So, tell me all about the hunt," mom insisted.

"Yeah, hey Jack, you're gonna want to hear this," Dad said. Jack joined us as Jeremy started to tell us a story we all knew we'd never stop hearing. It only exists in fragments now: my father and brother hunting from the ground, the buck bounding into sigh, a last-minute shot in the fading light. I can't recall the details, but I remember Dad's smile as Jeremy told it, never dropping the slightest hint as to any exaggerations made or details embellished. We all congratulated him again when he finished, and Dad started talking to Jack about the cost and storage for the deer's head.

Jack said, "I'll cape it for you, but you'll have to take the head home tonight and store it 'til the taxidermist can take it. Javier's about the only guy that does it around here, but he's damn good at it. Pretty backed up this late in the season, though. Last time I checked with him, he was about a month out."

Dad continued to press him for storage tips while Jack put his knife to work. I'd seen Dad dress several deer at the farm, but Jack's work was different. His host of tools made short work of it. Jeremy and I never had the stomach for the skinning process, but we watched in admiration when Jack began the process of removing the head. I'd never seen bloodied hands move with such dexterous precision—the delicate slicing at the shoulder, the gentle tug of skin pulled over the head to protect the rack and skull. It was thrilling to witness. After Jack finished, he hauled the carcass into the meat cooler to join the queue for processing. He wrapped the head and antlers in plastic and put it in the bed of Dad's truck.

When we got to the house, I watched Jeremy and Dad make room in the deep freeze in the barn to store the head until the taxidermist could take it. Jeremy lingered over the freezer, staring down at the head—an indiscernible shape of brown and red hazily filtered through layers of visqueen and encroaching frost. A smile of satisfaction rested on his face before he closed the lid and walked back to the house.

Inside, Jeremy called everyone he could think of from the kitchen phone to tell them his story. I stayed with him for a while, but I left to play video games in the living room when he called Libby. Their conversations tended to go on and involve the details of high school life that made me feel small. I made my way to the living room and noticed that Mom and Dad had already retired for the night; their low, muffled voices mixed with the noise of their TV. I'd just slipped a cartridge into the Super Nintendo when Jeremy's heavy footfalls thudded out of the kitchen and down the hall toward the stairs.

"I thought you were talking to Libby," I called to him, surprised that their conversation had ended so quickly.

He responded flatly without breaking his stride, "She and Trevor were watching a movie," and he plodded up the stairs.

Hopeful, I called after him, "Want to play a game?" But he didn't bother to glance in my direction; I told myself he didn't hear me. Disappointed, I played alone for a while then went upstairs. Jeremy had already turned in, his bedroom door pulled shut.

That night, after everyone went to sleep, I ran through the woods behind our house. I didn't know how I got there, no memory of leaving my bedroom and crossing the pasture, but I was compelled to move forward, faster than I'd ever run. Brush, bushes, saplings snapped under my feet. The woods grew denser, and as my momentum started to outpace the two legs that carried me, I leaned forward and caught myself with limbs that no longer fit the body I knew. Each propulsive stride stretched tendons and tore muscle beneath my burning skin. Nothing could compel me to stop, not even as flesh burned, ripping and sloughing off my body like discarded cloth. I opened my mouth to scream, and as my jaw hinged wider than it should have, a pained wail clawed its way out of my throat.

I awoke, startled and sweating, unsure if I'd screamed in my bed loud enough to wake the house. Shaking, I looked out my bedroom window, and through a sleep-addled fog, I thought I saw someone in the shadow of our barn—a figure opening its door and disappearing into the dark. I shook my head and convinced myself I'd imagined it. The world remained quiet and undisturbed—the barn, the yard, the pasture, and the immense sentinel pines that guarded whatever secret my dreaming mind pursued.

❦

Sometimes, it takes a while before a family can admit something is wrong. It's not that we're particularly imperceptive; it's just that it's easier not to notice when something is amiss. Once you name a problem, you have to confront it, and my family fears confrontation more than the inevitable disaster we'll allow to happen. So, when Jeremy spent his afternoons in the woods after the season ended, when his temper flared up unexpectedly, when he kept stealing glances toward the barn, we never spoke about it—not to him or to each other.

He'd follow the same routine almost every day: come home, drop his backpack by the door, throw on a coat, head to the barn for a while and then take off into the woods. He'd come back before dinner smelling like dirt and sweat, his clothes soiled like he'd been rolling on the ground. He told us that a short hike through the trees "cleared his head," but he would return looking haggard and tired, the furthest thing from clear-headed as far as I could tell.

Mom and Dad remained unconcerned. They ignored his wild eyes and terse speech. They weren't even bothered that every time Jeremy came back from the woods, he'd, again, disappear into the barn before coming inside.

That was the habit that bothered me the most. I asked him once what he did in the barn, and his response was a dismissive, "Just checking on things." Before I could ask what that meant, he was halfway up the stairs. I was left to wonder on my own. What was there to check? Was he just staring at the head in the freezer, lingering over that skull and antlers swaddled in frozen flesh?

Mom and Dad's indifference to it all filled me with dread. After a week or so, I confided in my mother about my loneliness. "I don't see Jeremy as much," I told her. "He's always in the woods. He doesn't talk to me anymore." I didn't even get to his strange fixation with the barn before mom delivered her prepared answer.

"Caleb, your brother's just growing up and finding new interests. He might not want to play right now, but that doesn't mean he doesn't love you. Things change; it's hard, but it's normal," she explained. I wanted to believe her, but I was nine. Whatever context I needed to understand why, on the cusp of his fifteenth year, my brother had begun to terrify me was years away, too remote for a lesson about patience to land. Her calm acceptance of it all just made me feel more alone.

⊂⊃⊂⊃

It had been about two weeks since he killed the deer when a cold late-January rain kept Jeremy from walking in the woods. He spent that afternoon pacing around downstairs, rustling about in his room, and staring outside the window toward the woods, toward the barn. He'd occasionally scratch at himself like a caged animal until the back of his arms and neck grew raw.

It didn't help that Dad was also in a bad mood. He'd been in the barn and had begun to notice a smell like some animal, a racoon or possum or the like, had found a way in and tucked into some corner to die. He hadn't been able to find it. He spent most of that afternoon in the barn working, and when he stomped into the house, angry at the inconveniences of living at the edge of the wild, we gave him his space. By the time we sat down to dinner, neither his nor Jeremy's mood had improved. Dad couldn't help but call attention to tension at the table.

"What's the problem?" Dad asked Jeremy, his question sounding more accusatory than concerned.

"Nothing," was the only response he received from Jeremy, suppressing a scowl. Dad grunted back at him. Dissatisfied with the conversation's dead end, he began a new one.

"Jeremy, you've been in the barn a lot. You noticed a smell in there? Or heard something moving around?"

"No." Jeremy stared at his plate.

"No, sir," Dad corrected him. "There's something dead in there, I can smell it."

"That's not table talk, honey," Mom interjected.

"Katherine, this is the only time I ever get a chance to talk to him," Dad countered. Jeremy stared down at his plate and picked up his fork. "Jeremy, you've been in there every day. You're telling me you never noticed the smell?"

"I said no," Jeremy responded, his head downcast at his plate. He was gripping his fork so hard his knuckles had started to whiten.

"No, *sir*. What's gotten into you?" Dad's irritation grew. He wasn't spoiling for a fight, but he was never one to suffer disrespect.

"God, I said it was nothing." Jeremy's tone and intensity matched our father's but he would not look up. Instead, he rested his head on his hand while he picked around his chicken and green beans.

"Elbows, hon," Mom said, automatically, as she'd done countless times correcting our manners. Jeremy groaned and muttered something mean and unintelligible. Dad picked it up, though. And he did not like what he heard.

"Excuse me? You want to speak up and address your mother?" Dad's face was stone, impassive and cold. Jeremy looked up, locked his jaw, and stared at Dad as he slid his elbow off the table.

"Moved. Happy?" he spat in my father's direction.

"Not until you apologize to your mother," Dad answered. The arms of his chair winced as his grip on them tightened.

"I didn't say anything!" Jeremy raised his voice.

"We all heard you, Jeremy," Dad rumbled, his voice growing heavier with each syllable. "You owe your mother an apology."

Mom turned to Dad. "It's ok, he didn't mean it," she said and smiled in a silent plea for Jeremy not to escalate. He did not return her kindness.

"I didn't fucking do anything!" Jeremy bellowed, flinging the plate and its contents against the wall and shattering the veneer of domestic manners along with it. A hurricane took its place—my father yelling, my brother screaming in response, my mother's vain attempts to pacify everyone. A shattered glass. A spat of curses. Crying.

I ran upstairs and shut myself in my room, muffling the chorus of shouting voices below. I heard Jeremy thunder up the stairs and slamming the door to his room. I heard my father calling loudly after him until the calmer voice of my mother talked him down. Then, a knock. Mom had come to check on me.

"Hey," she said apologetically. Her eyes were red and puffy, and her voice wavered. "You gonna be ok? It's quiet now if you want to eat. I'll sit with you." She held me as I cried, and when the crying stopped, we talked about what happened at the table, what to do when our anger gets the best of us, how to come back to each other in the end. My mother tried, with sadness and kindness, to reassure me that some things must run their course. I wonder, now, if her words were for herself rather than for me.

⚬⚬⚬

I don't suppose it mattered who needed the comfort more because the next day, my parents got a call from the school to come pick Jeremy up; he'd been arrested for damn near killing Trevor Harris.

It all occurred at the high school, so I wasn't there to see it, but over the course of the day and the fallout that followed, I pieced the story together. That afternoon between classes, Trevor was in the hall talking to his teammates, Corey and Shelby, when he brought up Libby. I don't know what he said exactly, and his friends insisted on the innocence of his words. But the way they talk about how Jeremy charged at him without warning, without stopping to see if he misheard makes me think it was anything but clean.

Regardless of what was said, no one expected Jeremy to dash across the hall and headbutt Trevor hard enough to shatter the bridge of his nose, stunning him and sending them both crashing to the ground. Jeremy moved so quickly that no one noticed the side of Trevor's head collide with the corner of a locker as he crumpled to the floor. All they saw was Jeremy beating him into the floor.

Panicked shouting in the hallways alerted the teachers, and someone called for the police. Coach Palmer bolted out of his classroom to help Corey and Shelby restrain Jeremy, who was hell-bent on continuing his assault. They eventually succeeded in pushing him out of the hallway into a nearby room where he bellowed obscenities about what he'd do to Trevor for "talking about his cousin that way." Teachers corralled students away from the scene, most too distracted to see blood that started to pool on the floor by the lockers.

I was told it was a student who first looked down at the floor and screamed. Trevor's swollen face had started to purple, and a long gash sliced his mouth into a wide macabre half-smile, rows of red-stained teeth peeking through a gap where his cheek had been.

The sheriff, police, and paramedics came almost as quickly as they were called. School let out not long after. The teachers and students were unable to stomach the disquiet suffocating the remaining hours of the school day.

In the principal's office, Dad spoke with the sheriff while I stood next to mom as she stared past them, her arm wrapped around my shoulder tight as a steel vise. The county jail next to the sheriff's office happened to be full, so they released Jeremy to us until Trevor's parents decided to press charges. Dad told the sheriff he understood, thanked him, and agreed to keep an eye on Jeremy. Mom said nothing.

ⳍⳍ

That night, I found myself wishing for an argument like the night before, anything to break through the apprehension that filled each room. We all kept stealing glances outside the window, looking for flashing lights. We listened for the crunch of gravel under a police car's tires. With each ring, the kitchen phone threatened to bring ill news about Trevor and the inevitable consequences of Jeremy's violence. We ate without nourishment, and we retired to our rooms quietly and early to do our best to sleep.

Sleep came, eventually, and I again dreamt of hurtling through the woods. I ran past the pines, past the oaks, past where the trees became gnarled and alien. I crashed through the forest, my body changing into something stronger with every bounding stride—first on two legs, then on four…

A rustle outside woke me. I looked out my window to see my brother, wearing only the gym shorts he slept in, walking toward the barn. I stepped into my slippers, threw on a sweatshirt, and cautiously, quietly made my way out of the house to follow him into the cold night.

The barn door was ajar, and I stepped inside. Shards of moonlight slipped through windows and occasional holes in the roof, settling on Jeremy, who stood near the bush hog hitched to the tractor. His back was slick with sweat, and in his hands he held the deer's head, still wrapped in plastic, but more loosely now than it had been when he stored it. The stench of decay rose wafted as he removed the plastic and let it slink to the floor. The head now exposed, he unfurled the cape with surprising ease, like it had never even been frozen at all. In the pale light, I could discern the antlers, the eyeless face that had started to rot, the tattered, distended hide of the neck that dangled from the base of the skull. I almost gasped seeing the trophy he had sought with such fervor now as just dead flesh, the putrid remnants of an annihilated thing.

Jeremy reached into the neck as if operating a puppet and, after several seconds working his fingers under sinew and fur, he pulled the skull out from the cape. He set it, black and slick with the ichor of decomposition, on the wheel of the tractor and worked both his hands under the skin, stretching it as if it were dough. Slowly, he pulled the hide, mottled and stinking over his head until the cape draped down to his shoulders and the antlers rested on top of his skull. The empty face of the deer dangled like a deflated balloon. The ill-fitting face looked absurd pulled sloppily over a human head, but as he knelt down into the dark, the cold intention of his movements stripped the macabre ceremony of its comedy. He started to cough, disgusted, I assumed, by the stench of the mask he wore. He never removed it, even as he moved deeper into the darker recesses of the barn with each gargled rasp.

Unable to see clearly, I crept toward the sounds that escaped the shadow: grunting, scraping, a tortured moan. I stepped closer, and my shuffling feet collided with some odd piece of junk we'd squirreled away with other forgotten things, sending it clattering across the floor.

Jeremy jerked the rotten mask from his head and shot up as his back straightened, and, finally, through a sliver of moonlight, I could see my brother's face. He was covered in a mucous film, greasy and black, and he stared in the direction of the noise, furious at this disturbance. A viscous column of drool slid down from his chin and disappeared into the shadows. His eyes, wide and alert, reflected a knife-gray glint.

I fought the urge to run. I knew that, if I started, I would never stop. I would run out of the barn, down the driveway, and into the next county; I'd run until my lungs burst and my legs were worn into the dirt of whatever Mississippi back road took me away from the gargoyle image of my brother hungry and cloaked in shadow. Instead, I looked down, turning my own eyes to the safety of the dark where moonlight could not illuminate whatever transgression I brought into this space. I did not chance a look to the door until he donned the head again and resumed crawling in the dark.

I crept out of the barn toward the house as silently as I could, terrified he would hear the thump of my heart, somehow smell the blood screaming through my veins. I shakily climbed the stairs to my bedroom. I locked the door behind me before settling on my bed, too tense to lay down. I tried to remain as still and quiet as possible, afraid that a single noise would further disturb the uneasy peace of a silent house.

Alone, I tried to process what I'd seen. Even then, I think, I knew that our family was about to break, that Jeremy was going somewhere I couldn't follow. The horror of him hunched over, his inhuman breathing, his face nuzzling the frost-burned hide into the cold concrete slab—it all played on a loop in my head. I was trapped. If I woke my parents, if I led them to the barn to see their son, the fragile calm that settled over our home would never return. I decided to give Mom and Dad their sleep; better to wait until morning, to face our demons in the sun.

But sunrise was hours away, and I heard movement downstairs.

Then up the stairs.

Then in the hall.

The footfalls landed softly and unevenly, as if whatever made them was stumbling on unsure legs. The floorboards in the hall creaked in quiet protest as each step got closer until I watched the gap under my door darken.

The scratching began—long, slow scraping down the length of my bedroom door. It started so softly that I mistook it for the roar of blood in my ears, but as the intensity grew, the sound of hard bone scraping across the wood became unmistakable. I remained frozen, certain that whatever was on the other side would find its way inside.

With growing eagerness, it heaved its bulk against the door with a thud, shaking me from my stupor. Instinctively, I met it at the door, countering its weight with mine. It escalated to frantic butting and stabbing through the wood to reach me. When it tried the doorknob, rattling it in its assembly, I swallowed the scream that rose in my throat. I gripped the knob and muttered desperately, *Please go away. God, please go away. Leave me alone.*

As if it heard me, a new, gentler sound of scraping began, beginning somewhere directly above me and sliding delicately downward. I swallowed dryly as it reached the top of my head and delicately traced the outline of my skull like it knew the contours of my forehead, my nose, the shape of my jaw. When it stopped at my ear, I pressed into the door and heard the creature shift. A deep, low growl rumbled through from outside. A chill ran through my veins, and I shut my eyes. When I opened them, the shadow under my door had disappeared. I heard something shuffle down the stairs and out the kitchen door.

I stumbled shakily toward the window and peered outside. My brother, naked and skulking his way toward the pasture, kept his back to the house. His body shone bone-white under the moon, and atop it was the antlered head of the deer. Under the moon, it looked fuller, healthier than it had in the barn. From the distance of my window, I couldn't discern the outline of his face beneath the fur, nor could I see the seam where the fur of the neck gave way to his shoulders. It fit him well enough to stay put as he jerked and twitched, occasionally falling to the ground and struggling back to his feet. Eventually, he stopped fighting to stay upright and crawled his way toward the pasture, toward the woods.

When he reached the fence, Jeremy stopped crawling and began to heave like I'd heard him in the barn. Coughing and retching, he threw his head back, and I could see his breath in a smoky wisp that curled out of the deer's mouth, no longer deflated but full and moving, its tongue wagging in pain. He arched his back and his skin split as dark wounds erupted along his body. Again he raised his head, the deer's head, to scream, and the groan that escaped it sounded inhuman, guttural and deep, and I shut my eyes and covered my ears, begged it to stop.

When silence crept back over the yard, I mustered the courage to peer outside again. Jeremy was gone. In the distance, something bounded across the pasture. I watched it until it was swallowed by the shadows of the pines.

ೞ

That was the last I or anyone else saw of him. Of course, I ran downstairs and through my parents' door screaming about what I'd seen. Dad leapt out of bed, checked Jeremy's room, and ran outside, shouting his son's name into the night. I listened to him take off across the pasture on the four-wheeler as mom called the sheriff's office and alerted our neighbors.

The whole community showed up to our house before the sun rose. We didn't have much time before the official manhunt went out to all of Kilgore County, before the police could come and make a mess of things. Dad and Jack led search parties that combed every patch of woods behind our house and the neighboring fields. A chorus of trucks and ATVs rose from every pasture within a six mile radius, but no one found him. The trees kept their secrets, as they so often did.

Soon, the gossip started. The running theory was that Jeremy knew Trevor's parents would have him arrested and convicted, so he bolted into the woods to be torn apart by wild dogs or whatever else crawled there; others thought he'd gotten hold of some hillbilly pills when he beat the hell out of Trevor, and he took off in a drug-addled mad dash toward his next fix. A worrying number of people thought the three of us were hiding him somewhere until we could smuggle him out of town. Without a body, each story was as plausible as the other; everyone in the county had their own version of events, each one of them true.

We never heard from Trevor's parents. Without Jeremy, they had no one to charge. Maybe they had their hands full re-teaching their son how to speak through his new injury and how to walk without aid. Or, perhaps, they felt too close to our grief, too familiar with family tragedy to add to our own. As for Libby, the whole ordeal left her heartbroken. Losing a boyfriend and a cousin in the span of a day took a toll on her. She still smiled, acted the part of herself, but her eyes held such grief. She graduated a few years later and went to college out of state. She rarely comes home.

Of course, Mom and Dad refused to acknowledge what I'd seen. It was a nightmare, they said—that I was too rattled from the day's trauma to separate reality from a dream. I seethed as Dad helped me paint over the scratches in my bedroom door, ignoring my explanation for how they got there by insisting that the old coat was just peeling. When I asked about the missing head, Dad told me he threw it out when he realized it was the source for the odor in the barn. Their grief wouldn't let them believe otherwise, I suppose. Eventually, I stopped trying to convince them. I didn't even bother bringing up the dreams that came to me each night–always hurtling in agony and exhilaration through the woods.

Mom and Dad didn't keep the farm but for a year after Jeremy disappeared. Dad said it was because he couldn't make enough money, but we all knew otherwise. With the farm behind us, our lives settled into normalcy. Mom and Dad found work; I finished high school and took a job with a trucking company. We were more or less like everyone else in Kilgore County. There was little to no mention of Jeremy among friends or family for fear of dredging up old ghosts. He became another phantom our town didn't acknowledge, his memory suffocated under a blanket of polite indifference.

The last time I drove out to our farmhouse, it seemed unchanged; whoever owns it keeps it as we did. It looks almost idyllic from the highway–tucked away down a gravel driveway, a weather-beaten barn beside it, a pasture dotted with grazing cattle.

And further still, boundless acres of pine keep watch over the field and farmhouse. When the sun sets behind them in the winter months, their shadows reach across the pasture toward the house, toward the road, extending an invitation for all who walk or crawl to spend some time in the woods.

– THE END –
ENJOYED THIS? CHECK OUT:
RISTENOFF
BY JR BILLINGSLEY

MAAMI

ABDULBASIT A. OLÚWANÍSHỌLÁ

after the earth sought for my mother as a fertilizer
                to supply her deficient nutrients—
her sister, my aunt, turned to rainbow &
                draws her lines over my nights.

i asked her: is this how miracles happen elsewhere?
                i doubt it is; there's a boy in our community—
he flies around with dirt, plastered on him like fate.
           people say, ọmọ tí kò ní ìyá ni ìyà njẹ.

she replied: this is not a miracle. do not make yourself
                a gardener of gloom. you're a card of crayons—
color the sky serenely. make your hand a firecracker.
                      i'm just an epiphany.

people say: it is God who frees a tailless cow
             from flies. & for a bald person, He gives beards—
i could not help but translate it to myself;
        a tailless cow mooing in the flock of my aunt's children.

if i tell you she flies trees to pluck mangoes
                  for me, just as for her kids—
you'd picture her as a lorikeet but believe me,
        she's just a hen with a duck's heart & an ostrich's legs.

fire outlives death by turning into ashes
           animals do theirs by turning into humus—
my mom did hers through the hands of her sister
        & i'm just a delicacy cooked by her dark pot.

- THE END -
ENJOYED THIS? CHECK OUT:
MELPOMENE'S GARDEN
BY CURTIS HARRELL

TELLING THE BEES OF THE BLOOD AND THE LAVENDER

AVRA MARGARITI

i.

When Father left for what we assumed would be the final time, Mother kept a seat for him at the head of the table, saved him the good silver while the rest of us picked wooden splinters from bleeding lips. She poured cream into his bowl while children mouths filled with watery, sour milk.

Mother hid the last of her fading bruises under dress sleeves as she heated the iron in the fireplace, burning herself in her haste to press Father's leftover shirts free of wrinkles. In her denial of his absence, she lied to the neighbors, her children, herself. She didn't tell the bees about his departure and soon their honey turned the ochreous yellow of figments, pus, and sickness.

Moribund bees relinquished their stingers in the viscous paste Mother insisted on calling honey. Mercifully, it merely filled Father's bowl, the stingers palpitating, disembodied, as if looking to prick the beekeepers who dared lie to their magical charges.

ii.

Mother and Father—who, like a disease, had by then inevitably returned, gambling debts and yet another teething baby in tow—thought girls should not don an apiarist's clothes. Girls should only be perforated by embroidery needles, penetrated by bridegrooms on wedding nights.

I had tried a different name before and it rang true and sonorous, but that was the year I knew for certain I was not the girl they saw in me.

The year, too, that the neighbors' daughter gave me a kiss upon the lips and a fistful of lavender seeds. My clever girl knew not to cut my bees' source of precious pollen, but to let my flowers grow into a feral jungle and only gift me with more means to my wilderness ends.

I told my hives about her, with the soil of my garden still staining my lavender hands, my lips tingling as if stung—I had never known such aching sweetness as when my girl's mouth first found mine over our parents' fences.

My fuzzy creatures buzzed with interest, plump, striped bodies bumping gently against my gloveless hands, caressing my maskless face. I knew the bees were proud of me. Her royal-jelly Highness the Queen even congratulated me herself.

Like house spirits, a family's bees care to know about the matters of their keepers: When someone dies, the bees are put into mourning, swathes of night-sky linen covering the hives, allowing them to grieve in peace. When someone abandons the household, the bees must be informed.

And when a family member is gripped by the vice of doubt (am I really what I see in the mirror?) or young love (please, give me more seeds, clever girl, more kisses for your beekeeper who hand-feeds you morsels of hexagon honeycomb), the bees ought to know as well.

I never made the same mistake as my mother, who lacked the good sense of superstition. Me, I've never kept a secret from my hives.

At least Mother and Father have stopped griping about my spending so much time in the fields. The neighbors agree no one has produced such sweet honey in all their years combined.

iii.

Father catches me in his stolen shirt and breeches pooled around my body, draped over the neighbors' girl as we come together in the lavender field born of her seeds.

What happens next is a vertigo of shouts, a flurry of beseeching words cut off by gunshots, a buzzing cloud risen over the fields my clever girl and I have baptized in our love.

Please, I tell my bees. *Please.*

And they, wrathful and magnificent, eclipse the sun in their yellow horde.

iv.

Mother drizzles honey over Father's empty place at the table. She's forgotten his porcelain bowl again, the sticky substance adrip over swirling woodgrain. My little siblings swipe their fingers through, bring to their mouths the sweetness. Ever since Father's latest departure, the neighbors say, our honey production has reached its most majestic height yet.

Mother claims she knows not what they mean, her husband is just around the corner buying her flour to bake more honey pies. Such is the surplus of bee-spit, floral paste.

I lick the residual sweetness from my thumb and head for my maze of hives, leaving Mother behind to rave about husbands and honey. I am in my shirt and breeches, yet the bees have never stung me for lacking protective gear.

The lavender field where my clever girl and I will meet tonight grows redolently wild; the grave-sized patch of bushes replanted, settling tall and purple—bonemeal nourishment; bee-boxes not covered in mourning black but left to thrive golden.

Thank you, I tell them, and they buzz gently as I feed them secrets. The Queen henceforth calls me the man of my household.

On days of advanced lucidity, Mother averts her gaze from the lavenders feeding on dead father flesh. She calls my soul honeycombed with sin.

The bees whisper to me a secret of their own. At their instruction, I slather honey over my old gunshot wound, aching with the imminence of rain. Like they did that fateful day in the field, their sweetness soothes the pain.

Their humming lullaby absolves me of all guilt.

– THE END –
ENJOYED THIS? CHECK OUT:
GIRLS GIRLS GORE   UPCOMING FROM
BY JAY TOWNSEND   SLEY HOUSE!

THE DEBTOR'S SANDWICH

ERIC RAGLIN

Compared to what they served at Langley High, the pizza at South Crest was practically gourmet. Waiting in the lunch line, Amir drooled at the sight and smell, so much more appetizing than the greasy cardboard he'd endured at his old school.

He often missed his Langley friends, but his mom assured him the trade-off was worth it, especially given South Crest's college prep courses, more experienced teachers, and abundance of extracurriculars. "You'll thank me when you get a better job than mine," she said whenever he complained about feeling like the odd kid out in class—noticeably brown and poor in a sea of pale faces and designer shoes.

He'd found only one new friend here—a boy one grade above him named Finley he'd met at basketball tryouts. After they both made varsity, they started sitting together at lunch, connecting through conversations about Call of Duty and their favorite NBA teams.

Today, the boys stood beside each other in the lunch line, grabbing sides of crispy sweet potato fries and cinnamon applesauce. Amir knew he didn't have the money to pay for it—he'd been in the red for a while now—but he hoped the lunch lady would let it slide with just the slightest stink eye.

"You don't know Coach 'cause you weren't here last year," Finley said, snagging a second slice of pizza, "but he's, like, the *cool* kind of asshole, you know?"

"Yeah, I get what you mean," Amir said. After yet another morning with only a spoonful of peanut butter for breakfast, his stomach grumbled. "Fuck, I'm hungry."

A lunch lady glared at him, and Amir mouthed an apology.

Finley snatched a chocolate milk and continued on: "He'll probably keep giving you a hard time because you played for Langley, but it's just part of the initiation process. You know, like, getting you in shape and—"

"Man, I'm *already* in shape," Amir said, smiling. "We beat you guys last year, remember?"

"'We?' See, this is what I'm talking about!" Finley jabbed Amir in the ribs. "You're not with them anymore; you're one of us, bro. South Crest is best."

One of us. Amir had been waiting for someone at this new school to tell him that. Hearing it from Finley made his face flush, but Amir pretended to stay cool.

Soon, the boys reached the end of the lunch line. Finley scanned his student ID to pay, then hustled off to claim a table. Amir held his own ID under the scanner, and the machine let out a dissonant beep.

"You're too far in the negative, hon," the lunch lady behind the counter said, eyeing the line that stretched far behind Amir. "Do you have a check to deposit? Cash?"

Amir stopped himself from cursing, knowing it would only piss her off more. He fumbled through his pockets for money he knew wasn't there. It would be a while before his mom's next paycheck, and even then, he doubted she'd have much to spare. Maybe enough to cover a handful of lunches. To make matters worse, South Crest had slashed their reduced-cost lunch program for poor kids. Maybe because the leadership assumed—mostly correctly—that none of their students needed it.

"Sorry," Amir said. "Can I bring some tomor—?"

The lunch lady snagged his tray before he could finish his sentence. Handing it to another worker, she grumbled, "Get me a debtor's sandwich."

A few seconds later, the worker returned with a sandwich alone on a tray: dry white bread and yellow filling that jiggled almost like a grotesque Jell-O. Egg salad, maybe. It looked more like a Langley meal than a South Crest one. The lunch lady behind the counter shoved the tray into Amir's hands.

"You'll be eating these every day until you pay off your debts," she said, her tone flat and compassionless.

"No more pizza?" Amir asked, but the woman shooed him off and called to the next person in line.

One sandwich wouldn't be enough to fill him up, but he'd have to make do. Hopefully Coach would take pity on him with a protein bar at practice today. Amir doubted it though.

Walking toward Finley's table, Amir felt his gut twist. He didn't want his friend to ask questions. Something told him Finley had never eaten—what had the lunch lady called it?—a debtor's sandwich. That sort of meal was reserved for kids who had hand-me-down clothes and phones with cracked screens, six generations out of date. Oh well. Maybe Amir could turn the sandwich into a joke. Or even something badass. *If she thinks I'm gonna pay for the shitty food they serve here, she can get fucked.*

As Amir neared the table, Finley waved to him, but someone tapped Amir's shoulder before he could close the distance.

"Mr. Davani, correct?"

Amir was tall enough to play good defense for the basketball team, but this man was a good six inches taller. He sported a goatee and a shaved head. A walkie-talkie hung from his belt loop. Amir recognized him—one of several administrators who supervised the cafeteria—but he didn't know his name.

"I'm Mr. Curran," the man said. "Please follow me. You'll be eating at the debtors' table today."

"But I was going to sit with—"

"Mr. Davani."

Amir was used to administrators talking to him without warmth, but the ice in Mr. Curran's voice was next-level cold. No choice but to obey.

Mr. Curran escorted Amir to a table in the corner. Amir had seen students sit here before, always supervised, always glum, and always eating the same type of sandwich that now graced his lunch tray. A boy and a girl were already seated, the boy absentmindedly eating his meal and scrolling through his phone, the girl folding her arms and death-staring into space.

"Mr. Davani, these are your fellow debtors," Mr. Curran said with faux-lightness. "And debtors, this is your newest partner in crime, Mr.—"

"Fuck this shit," the girl said, standing up and stomping toward the cafeteria exit.

"Miss Nichols," Mr. Curran said, his icy voice going liquid nitrogen-cold. "If you come back now, a detention is the worst you'll suffer. But if you keep walking—"

She kept walking—and pointed a middle finger behind her. Some students at the regular tables laughed. A few more steps and the girl was out of the cafeteria, then out of the school entirely.

"Well," Mr. Curran said, pulling out a plastic seat for Amir. "We can only hope you're better behaved than she is."

Amir shared a "can you believe this shit" look with Finley across the room, but his friend's attention had shifted to Jason, another older boy on the varsity team. Finley showed the boy something on his phone, and both burst out laughing. Whether it was a TikTok or meme or funny text, Amir had no way of knowing; a burning jealousy coursed through him. He'd ask Finley to show him what it was at practice.

Practice. The thought of doing conditioning drills on a mostly empty stomach made Amir queasy. Inspecting the debtor's sandwich, he lifted the top slice of stale bread and peeked at the filling. It had to be egg salad. The yellow fluff had a glossy sheen with flecks of black and red—pepper and paprika, maybe. But it didn't smell eggy. More *mineral*, like the rocks Amir's science teacher made students test for hardness. It was gross and weird, but Amir couldn't afford to be picky. His mom had told him that time and time again. He took a bite.

His gag and spit reaction was immediate, but the acrid mineral taste still clung to his tongue.

"Come on, now," Mr. Curran said. "You're in high school, not preschool."

The other boy at the table looked up, still chewing on his own sandwich.

"You'll get used to it," he said to Amir.

Before Amir could reply, Mr. Curran's walkie-talkie blooped and a voice came through the static: "Another debtor, Ron. It's Caroline Hopps. Can you escort her?"

"On my way," Mr. Curran said into the device. He left the table, scanning the cafeteria for his next target.

This was Amir's chance to sneak away. If he crouched beside Finley, hidden behind the table, maybe Mr. Curran wouldn't catch him. He hurried over and then slid like a baseball player the last few feet to the table, hoping the entrance would make his friend laugh. But Finley didn't notice. He and Jason were debating what base fingering a girl's ass counted as.

Amir chimed in. "That's like—what?—third-and-a-half base."

"Oh, hey, Amir," Finley said, glancing at him briefly before returning his attention to the other boy. His tone seemed cooler, less playful than it had just a couple minutes ago.

But Amir didn't have time to process this change. A long, bald-headed shadow crept up behind him: Mr. Curran, ready to put an end to his joy.

"That'll be a 30-minute detention for leaving the debtors' table," the administrator said, then narrowed his eyes, "and an extra 30 minutes for that foul mouth of yours. We'll head back now."

Finley snorted, barely suppressing a laugh. Jason went red in the face, lips tight and gaze averted.

And here Amir was, the butt of the older boys' joke. Did Finley find him immature—or did he think the double detention was cool? Amir couldn't tell. Slouching, he followed Mr. Curran back to the debtors' table. His sandwich was waiting for him.

⌘

Amir missed basketball practice to serve his detention. He worried Coach would cut him from the team, but even more than that, he worried Finley would forget about him—going from stranger to friend to stranger again in the blink of an eye.

Amir *had* to escape the debtors' table. He *had* to eat with his friend again. Tomorrow, when Finley or Jason brought up a new topic—*is it gay to get pegged,* or something like that—Amir would be there with an answer, ready to make Finley laugh.

But no lunch money appeared overnight. Amir asked his mom for some, hoping beyond hope she'd pull a few bills out of a coffee can under the mattress, but she was broke until payday. Having exhausted his best option, Amir rummaged through their couch cushions for lost coins and came up empty-handed.

So it was that he remained isolated from Finley with yet another debtor's sandwich for lunch. Mr. Curran escorted Amir across the cafeteria, keeping a close eye on him as if he were an inmate planning an escape. Amir didn't flee though. Instead, he watched Finley's table. There he was with Jason, chatting and laughing and eating Salisbury steak that smelled like heaven. Amir waved to his friend, but Finley took no notice—or pretended not to.

"You're not staying in the cafeteria today, Mr. Davani," Mr. Curran said. "Yesterday, you made it clear that you can't behave in the presence of your peers. If you'll follow me…"

"Wait, are you serious?" Amir said, clenching his lunch tray. With each second spent in Mr. Curran's presence, he better understood that girl's "fuck this shit" reaction. She had the right idea storming away and flipping the man off. Amir hadn't seen her around here since, but he hoped she'd escaped the administrator's wrath. Maybe if Mr. Curran pushed him a little more, he would follow in the girl's footsteps.

"Come," Mr. Curran said, as if Amir were a dog. Before Amir could reply, the man lifted his walkie-talkie and requested that another administrator cover his post.

Amir followed the man out of the cafeteria, imagining what it would be like to punch him in the back of the head—a brief but incomparable rush before the terrible consequences. If he did it, the school resource officer would probably tase and tackle him. Maybe even worse.

Soon, Amir realized where he'd be eating: Mr. Curran's office. Mr. Curran opened the door and led him inside. The space was uncluttered—just a desk, two chairs, and a squat filing cabinet—but the bare gray walls seemed claustrophobically close. The lack of any personal touches—no framed family pictures, pinned graduation party invites, or cheesy inspirational posters—made Amir feel far away from the human world. The pocked ceiling tiles bore the texture of an alien moon.

"Your office feels like a jail cell," Amir said.

"No need for exaggeration," Mr. Curran replied, taking a seat at his desk and opening his laptop. "Sit and eat. I'll be right here, answering emails."

Amir did as he was told. Despite the sandwich's mineral-smelling filling, his gut rumbled. He hadn't had breakfast this morning—the peanut butter jar scraped cruelly clean. He swallowed each bite of the sandwich without chewing. It was easier to stomach that way.

He imagined day after day of debtor's sandwiches in Mr. Curran's jail cell. No money, no Finley, no hope or joy at South Crest High. No longer *one of us*. There had to be a way out of this. A way to rejoin the world.

"So, I don't think my mom's getting paid anytime soon," Amir said.

Mr. Curran looked up from his emails, apparently annoyed at the interruption. Why this man worked with teens when he seemed to dislike them, Amir didn't understand. Lots of administrators were like that.

"Is there any other way I can clear my lunch debt?" Amir continued. "Like, shelving library books during my study hall or something. I just…I hate this. It sucks."

For a second, Amir wondered if Mr. Curran would scold him for saying "sucks." He'd met adults like that, ones who looked for any bullshit excuse to punish kids. But the administrator just nodded and grinned.

"I admire your initiative," he said. "Working for your meal instead of relying on your mother. There is, in fact, something you can do. Finish your sandwich and follow me."

Something in Mr. Curran's voice made Amir shiver, but he'd only have to endure the man a little longer. A life after debt awaited him.

⚭

Amir wondered what type of work he'd be doing but knew better than to ask. Mr. Curran seemed to enjoy being cryptic, withholding information to display his power. While they walked, Amir imagined where the man might take him. The cafeteria's dishwashing station to scrub marinara sauce off lunch trays? The main office to be their little errand boy? Whatever the work was, he hoped Finley wouldn't witness him doing it. Being seen in that context would feel embarrassing—an illustration of the starkly different worlds they came from.

Sneaking a glance at his phone, Amir saw the text from his friend: *You missed practice yesterday, so Coach says you'll be running laps while the rest of us scrimmage today. Sucks to suck.* Amir felt a pang of frustration and loneliness. The longer he spent isolated from his team, the less likely he'd be to make friends with them. Finley probably already thought he was a loser for missing practice, even if Amir couldn't help it.

"How quickly can I work off my debt?" Amir asked as Mr. Curran guided them down the hallway. "Like, if I go hard today, could I—"

The administrator stopped in front of a thick metal door. When he input his credentials on the keypad, the door hissed open. Beyond it was a narrow descending flight of concrete stairs.

A mineral smell wafted upward, sharp and thick. Probably the wet stink of an unfinished basement, but it smelled like a debtor's sandwich. The similarity disturbed Amir.

"Go on. Quickly now," Mr. Curran said—and was that a nervous wobble creeping in under the sternness? "I'll lock up behind us."

Amir didn't like the idea of being locked in a basement with Mr. Curran. Maybe the administrator was just trying to keep other students from going where they shouldn't, but Amir couldn't shake the feeling that he was an inmate being transferred from a county jail to a supermax prison.

What would Mr. Curran do if Amir refused to go inside? Would he give him another detention? Tell Coach how lazy and useless he was?

Clearly, refusing would make too much trouble for him. Amir could suck it up and get this shit over with, whatever it was.

Without further delay, he entered the stairwell. Mr. Curran locked the door with an electronic whir and metallic *ka-chunk*. Amir looked behind him every few steps. The administrator trailed him by a couple feet, scanning the shadowed ceiling with wide eyes. Was he looking for mold? The source of that mineral stench?

Rounding a corner, Amir discovered that the stairwell continued farther down. Another turn and still it continued. The deeper he descended, the more the stairs resembled dust rather than stone, as if each step he took pushed forward the clock of geologic time.

"Where the hell are we going?" Amir asked, unable to stop himself from cursing.

"Patience, Mr. Davani," Mr. Curran said. And again, there was that little tremble.

"Ron, is that you?" When the voice echoed up from the depths, Mr. Curran jumped, concrete debris skittering under his feet.

A second later, the man let out an exhale followed by a too-high chuckle. Something had him on edge, and the presence of another person—probably an administrator—was his only source of comfort.

Amir wished he could run back upstairs. He'd push Mr. Curran over and trample his face if that's what it took to get past him. But how would he open the locked door?

"Mrs. Logan. It's good to hear you," Mr. Curran said. "I'm coming down with another debtor."

The prospect of encountering another student here soothed Amir's nerves, but he couldn't shake his fight or flight response. A deep breath of acrid mineral air, then he kept walking.

Six more flights down—how and why was this basement so deep?—they reached the bottom.

Instead of a concrete room, Amir walked into a massive natural cavern. He couldn't tell how big the chamber was, but when the air made him cough, several seconds passed before the echo returned. Bare bulbs in metal cages clung to the walls like spiders, but none were bright enough to illuminate the ceiling, cloaked in humid darkness. Moisture dripped from above, pattering Amir's forehead. When he wiped away the liquid, it looked cloudy white on his finger. Water leaching minerals from stone, maybe. He pictured the ceiling slowly eroding—a sinkhole imminent. In one year or a hundred, this cavern would swallow the school whole.

"Have you briefed him yet, Ron?"

Amir tensed as the second administrator appeared beside him and Mr. Curran. Mrs. Logan removed a pair of green-eyed night-vision goggles and propped her hands on her hips. Nestled beside her walkie-talkie was a taser with an oversized battery pack. Again, Amir wanted to run.

"Mr. Davani," Mr. Curran said. "Today you'll be harvesting lunch for the many debtors in our school district. We'll forgive a dollar of your debt for each pound you collect."

"Pound of *what?*" Amir asked.

But before he could get an answer, Mrs. Logan shoved her night-vision goggles and a large metal bucket into his hands.

"Put these on," she said. "Oh, and sorry about the sweat. It gets hot down here."

The goggles' sweaty rubber lining was the least of Amir's concerns; he put them on. Anything could be hiding in the darkness down here, so the more he could see, the safer he'd be.

"The eggs grow in clusters," Mr. Curran said, "but only where it's dark. They look like marbles, but bigger. Make sure to mash them thoroughly before you bring them back in the bucket. Not a single egg intact, understood?"

"I—" Amir struggled to find the words, and instead gravitated back toward Mrs. Logan's taser. He needed to know what he was in for. "Why do you have that?"

"Oh, we don't use these on you kids," she laughed. "I'd lend you mine, but it's out of juice. Your harvest partner—Eve Nichols—has my spare."

Nichols. The "fuck this shit" girl. Amir found comfort in the fact that she was down here with him. Someone tough. Someone who'd put up a fight if…if what?

"Where is she?" Amir asked.

"That way," Mrs. Logan said, pointing into the dark.

Amir turned on the goggles. The stretch of stone in front of him lit up phosphorescent green. The darkness was full of craggy pockets and jutting mineral deposits, but from what he could see, no eggs. What kind of eggs was he supposed to be looking for anyway? Chicken eggs? Was this some sort of underground farm? He couldn't hear any clucking. Just the ceiling's slow, ceaseless drip.

His neck prickled at the thought of going deeper into the cavern, but he reminded himself why he was here. What he'd get back when it was over: lunches with Finley. He imagined them joyriding together on Friday nights, going to parties, playing video games until the wee hours of the morning. The effort would be worth it.

Amir stepped into the darkness.

⊙

Sound traveled far in the cavern.

Amir had been walking away from the administrators for a couple minutes, but he could still hear them talking.

"I know this is her first time down here, but I thought Eve would be back by now," Mrs. Logan said, her words echoey and distorted but still discernible.

"She's probably wasting time, waiting out the rest of her classes," Mr. Curran replied. "She ran out on me during lunch yesterday. Even flipped me the bird as she left."

"No surprise there. She's been that way since freshman year. I don't see her changing."

"Well, if she doesn't turn up, we can tell her parents she ran off again."

Amir's gut twisted. He wondered how often the administrators had conversations like this when they thought no one was listening. More than that, he wondered where Eve had disappeared to. The administrators' voices were easy to hear from afar, so wouldn't Eve's footfalls be, too?

"Eve?" Amir called out.

The echo must have reached the administrators because their conversation cut off abruptly. Silence consumed the vast space, punctuated only with the occasional drip. Amir swore he could hear his skin crawling.

Maybe Eve was a mile off, collecting globs of eggs from some cramped crystalline corridor. Or maybe she was nearby with her headphones in, blaring angry music loud enough to drown out Amir's voice.

Amir had no choice but to keep walking. If he found Eve, he'd be grateful, but if he stumbled upon the eggs first, he wouldn't stick around much longer. At the rate Mr. Curran gave, Amir would need thirty pounds to cover his lunch debt. He'd scoop and smash what he could, then get out.

The farther he trudged into the cavern, the more he worried about finding his way back. If he got lost, he'd miss basketball practice and Finley would lose all respect for him. He grabbed a loose rock and started carving arrows into the limestone floor every few feet. Maybe Eve—if she really had taken a wrong turn—would find these markings and be able to make her way back.

By the time he'd carved his tenth arrow, a clumpy shape gleamed at the edge of his night vision. It didn't look like a stalagmite or a pile of stones; it possessed a slimy sheen, and each clump looked perfectly spherical. These shapes had to be the eggs.

Amir rushed forward, only to trip on a rocky snag. For that split second hanging in the air, he imagined his goggles cracking against the floor, dousing him in the purest darkness he'd ever known. But his hands broke the fall. Wiping away what was either blood or stagnant cave water, he took a deep breath, got back on his feet, and prepared his bucket for the harvest.

A quick look was all he needed to confirm these were the eggs. They certainly hadn't come from a chicken, but he didn't have the slightest clue what creature might have laid them. Each egg was the size of a pool ball and slightly translucent. Inside the gelatinous spheres were hair-thin webs that might have been veins, and black specks that might have been embryos. One sphere twitched slightly, as if sensing the approaching danger, and a sharp sulfuric stink filled the air—a fear pheromone, perhaps. Amir thought about the eggy paste digesting in his stomach and swore he felt a sympathetic twitch inside him. He turned away to puke. The wet, hot slurry splashed against the stone. He dry heaved a few times after that, and only then did he feel truly empty.

When he got out of this cavern—*if* he got out—would he tell Finley about this? Would the boy believe him or think he was a weird liar? That question would have to wait. For now, the harvest was all that mattered.

Reaching into the egg cluster felt like sinking into a pile of giant tapioca. Amir grabbed what he could and slopped it into the bucket. A sticky membrane clung to his hand, but he had to ignore it until the job was done. The closer he got to the center of the cluster, the warmer it became, as if the eggs generated their own heat, not needing a parent to sit atop them while they matured.

Again, the question of what that parent might be made Amir shudder. He could ask Mr. Curran, but he doubted the man would offer a clear answer.

Eager to be done, he picked up the bucket and weighed it in his hand—nicely heavy. He wondered if it would clear his lunch debt and cover his next meal, too, but he doubted the school would be that generous. Regardless, it was time to go.

Before he could turn heel, something else caught his eye. No. Some*one.*

Maybe thirty feet off, Eve stood near a stalagmite. Her goggled head was slumped, but she waved at Amir as if still able to see him. Amir had only interacted with this girl once, but the vigorous enthusiasm of the wave didn't seem like her. Maybe she, like him, was just happy to see another student in this infinite cavern.

But why hadn't Amir heard her approach? Had she been standing there the whole time, waiting?

"Hey, are you okay?" Amir asked, easing toward her. "This place is creepy as fuck."

Eve waved again, her head still slumped. Maybe she'd had a medical event—a stroke or something. Could high schoolers get strokes?

Amir took another step forward before noticing the taser dropped at Eve's feet. She'd clearly fired it at something, but the wires and electrode needles weren't attached to anyone or anything.

Amir thought about getting the hell out while he still had the chance, but he couldn't just leave when Eve needed his help.

"Let's get out of here, okay?" Amir said. Another step, his nerves hot, his muscles resistant. "I've probably got enough in my bucket for both of us. We can tell the administrators we collected it together. Can you lift your head?"

Another wave.

When Amir traced his gaze up Eve's arm, he spotted a near-invisible string trailing from it—upwards and upwards, toward the shadow-choked ceiling. Heart thumping, he squinted into the darkness. Several long seconds passed and nothing appeared.

All sound—even the liquid dripping—stopped, silence blanketing the cavern. Amir heard his own shuddering breath, but not Eve's. Was she scared and holding it in? Was she dead on her feet?

The second Amir grabbed Eve's limp hand, her body zipped up toward the ceiling. Amir clung to her for only a moment before letting go, but by then, he was already airborne and falling. He thrashed in the air but couldn't ready himself for the impact. When he hit the ground, his arm snapped, bone puncturing flesh. The wind was knocked out of him—no way to scream. Gasping but unable to draw breath, he pushed himself to his feet, his fractured arm bending farther out of place. The thinnest wheeze escaped his throat.

No matter what happened, he wouldn't look up, wouldn't see what had used Eve like a worm on a hook. Not five feet away was his bucket, somehow still upright. Amir grabbed it with his one working arm and ran toward what he hoped was the cavern's exit.

From above came a sound like writhing slime. It kept pace with Amir as he carried away the bucket of its spawn. He considered dropping it, but leaving with nothing wasn't an option. Eggs tumbled out of the bucket as he tripped and staggered. He hoped he'd still have enough by the time he reached safety—if that thing didn't get him first.

His lungs gradually recovered, spiked with a shot of adrenaline and strengthened through basketball conditioning. Amir screamed while he sprinted. Full-bodied madman howls. He could no longer hear the creature squirming along the ceiling after him. Whether he had outrun it or scared it off, he had no way of knowing. All he knew was that he'd live to see a debt-free day.

❧❧

Neither Mr. Curran nor Mrs. Logan ran into the dark to save the screaming boy.

When Amir finally reached them at the well-lit edge of the cavern, the administrators were standing exactly where they'd been before. They wouldn't meet his gaze.

"Eve's…dead," Amir panted, prying off the now sweat- and possibly blood-soaked goggles. His punctured arm was oozing. "What the fuck was that thing?"

A flash of fear reddened Mr. Curran's face, but sternness soon replaced it. "That'll be a thirty-minute detention for cursing, Mr. Davani. I ought to give you another for spreading lies, but I won't this time. Consider this your warning."

Amir looked to Mrs. Logan for backup, but the administrator kept staring at the ground with glossy, catatonic eyes. The pose reminded Amir of Eve and her marionette posture. He eyed Mrs. Logan for strands connecting her to the ceiling but found none.

A pang traveled through his broken arm, and he set down the bucket to squeeze the area. Even the slightest touch felt like fire.

He knew it then; he'd be benched the rest of the season. While he sat on the sidelines, Finley would play and score and forget all about him. Amir was sure of it now. If they didn't have basketball together, their friendship would fade. This process had already begun in just two short days. He felt like crying.

Mr. Curran pointed to the bucket. When he spoke, his voice shook: "Remember what I said. The eggs need to be mashed before we take them upstairs."

Amir could've killed the man right then. Spun the bucket around and caved in his skull.

But the administrator turned toward his colleague and whispered to her—something about Eve. Silent tears streamed down Mrs. Logan's cheeks.

The idea came to Amir then. While the administrators were distracted, he grabbed one of the eggs—slimy and warm and weirdly heavy. It twitched in his palm, but he didn't drop it out of revulsion. Instead, he smiled at the egg and slid it gently into his pocket. The other eggs could be smashed and processed and eaten for all he cared, but this one had a special purpose.

⊷

A week passed uneventfully, and Amir wondered if the egg's secret hiding place had been discovered, its innards pulverized into something harmless. How long did these things take to hatch? Days? Months? No biology textbook could answer that question.

While Amir waited in dread and excitement, he spent his lunches with Finley, trying to rekindle their friendship. Now that Amir was benched for the season, Finley looked at him like he was some sort of barnacle—his presence merely pitied and tolerated. It didn't help that Amir went lunchless, refusing to take on further debt and return to the work he'd barely survived once. Everyone else at the table ate and joked and bonded and ignored Amir. He might as well have been a ghost.

In those lonely moments at the table, Amir thought about Eve, imagining what kind of relationship they might have had if she'd survived. Maybe she would've hated him, her sour attitude directed at everyone and not just authority figures. Or maybe they would've bonded over their shared debt and suffering, even becoming friends.

Amir couldn't think about it for too long. The thought made him want to cry.

 প্রজ্ঞ

Two weeks after Amir hid the egg, it finally hatched. He didn't see it happen; rather, he stumbled upon its aftermath.

During fourth period Advanced Algebra, he asked his teacher if he could use the restroom. She knew he'd just wander the halls for fifteen minutes—a habit he'd recently taken up—but she was a pushover.

A few minutes into Amir's wandering, a commotion down the hall caught his attention. Outside Mr. Curran's office, Mrs. Logan was hyperventilating. The school resource officer gripped her wrists firmly and looked her dead in the eyes.

"We'll get to the bottom of this," he said. "Which students did Ron call to his office today? Guarantee you one of them did it."

"No, no," Mrs. Logan sobbed. "You don't understand how much danger we're in."

Amir didn't have to look inside Mr. Curran's office to know what had happened. He imagined the administrator suspended from the ceiling tiles like a worm on a hook, translucent string connecting him to that dark and dangerous pocket between the electrical wiring. He pictured the man still alive, but unable to move, dying slowly and painfully.

Amir wanted to cheer. He wanted to throw up.

And when Mrs. Logan glanced up at him—when she squinted and assessed and knew all at once what he'd done—Amir wanted to run. But the administrator didn't point her finger in accusation. The pain and guilt of Eve's death still lingered in her eyes. Even if Mrs. Logan didn't approve of Amir's decision, she at least understood it. And Amir knew right then he'd get away with what he'd done. A brief thrilling rush coursed through him.

But even if he never faced any consequences, what was left for him at South Crest High? Only death and debt and days of unbearable loneliness. A spark snuffed out in the cruelest fashion.

It was time to return to Langley. To go back home, for better or worse.

- THE END -
ENJOYED THIS? CHECK OUT.
UNDER THE CHURCHYARD IN THE CHAMBER OF BONE
BY JR BILLINGSLEY

HANNAH ENGLAND THOUGHT SHE WOULD BE SAFE FROM THE GROTESQUE IMAGES THAT WOULD HAUNT HER EVERY WAKING MOMENT, IF ONLY SHE COULD BECOME INGRAINED WELL ENOUGH IN THE PANTOMIME OF A NORMAL LIFE. SHE DID EVERYTHING SHE WAS SUPPOSED TO—GOT TWO "IMPRESSIVE" CREATIVE WRITING AND LITERATURE DEGREES, SETTLED DOWN INTO A CUSHY COPYWRITING JOB, GOT PUBLISHED IN A FEW MAGAZINES HERE AND THERE. YET, LIKE EDGAR ALLEN POE'S INFAMOUS PROTAGONIST, THE THOUGHTS SLAMMED UPON THE FLOORBOARDS OF HER MIND IN AN INFERNAL SCREAM SHE COULDN'T IGNORE. NEAR-MAD FROM EXHAUSTION, SHE DRAGGED HERSELF TO HER COMPUTER AND TYPED OUT THIS WRETCHED TALE: RUPTURED—THE STORY OF A WOMAN MADE MONSTER BY THE PAINFUL ARRIVAL OF A BRAND NEW SET OF TEETH, PERFECTLY PRIMED TO CUT AND TEAR AND CONSUME. PERHAPS NOW THEY'VE BEEN FREED FROM THE CONFINES OF HER SKULL, THESE MACABRE SPECTRES WILL CHOOSE A DIFFERENT HOST TO HAUNT.

RUPTURED

HANNAH ENGLAND

The pain begins on a Tuesday morning—an aching, wretched agony buried beneath the gumline, demanding attention from the moment Alice's eyes flicker open in all their bloodshot glory. She thinks that perhaps she has some rogue piece of food jammed in the fleshy pulp of her mouth, mind flickering to vague memories of greasy kebab shoved down her throat with all the abandon of a beast mauling its dinner with sharpened canines. Three tequila shots deep, Alice had felt her spine shift as she transformed from marketing executive to wild beast with a gaping, drooling maw. She wanted to fuck, she wanted to consume, she wanted to *eat*. The fryer-slick meal did the trick to curb the insistent scream of her stomach at the time, but she still feels hollow the next morning, her bedroom swirling around her ears as she shoves an intrusive, probing finger into her mouth.

She notes nothing. No lodged debris of a rogue french fry, no fat-slick meat wedged in her flesh. Alice's mouth, dry as it is, has no external violator, save for the finger she suckles on near-obscenely. For all her searching, she can find nothing to explain the uncanny tenderness, akin in sensation to what she imagines chewing on a rock would be like—soft, malleable flesh pressing against something unyielding.

She slips her finger out unceremoniously with a wet pop, drying her saliva-speckled skin upon her duvet, limp with the same sweat that coats her body. Alice burrows into the warm embrace of her blankets, tries to stave off her alcohol-fuelled trembling with the weight of it above her, like she is a child, like she can expel this monster of her own making by losing herself in this soft, familiar cave. She rouses a moment later by the pungent scent of her own body, her tequila-and-meat breath, the plaque lining her teeth and gums. She sucks in the stale air of her bedroom, pushing the mop of mousey hair back from her still-eyeliner-smeared eyes. She is a mess. The ache in her jaw gives an affirmative roar of pain, then quietens enough that she might slip out of her soft enclosure, her feet hitting the matted carpet as the clock makes its lazy roll forward to 8:00am.

♋

"Did you or Dad," Alice begins, swirling her tongue into the gap behind her molars, the slick sound amplified through the phone's speaker, like she was slipping the appendage directly into the tight, wet heat of her mother's ear canal, "ever have wisdom teeth?"

The pain is most noticeable now when she touches it. There's a cruelty in knowing that she could stave it off by leaving her new wound alone, and yet she can't help but draw her tongue back to the place where she can begin to feel the flesh part, becoming pulpy and wet with blood whose sting brings a coppery, sharp taste.

"Nope," Alice's mother replies. She seems distracted—or perhaps, she's just disturbed at the intimacy of knowing what her daughter's tongue sounds like as it flicks wetly across her teeth. "Neither do either of your sisters."

"Duckie is younger than me." Alice pauses the obscene flicker of her tongue for the contradiction. "She might just not have got them yet."

"Duckie also got a brain injury, and an x-ray, and we know she doesn't have wisdom teeth. Because of the x-ray."

"I got that."

"Why do you ask?"

Alice notes that her mother (and indeed, Duckie and Toyah's mother, too, she doesn't belong *solely* to Alice) seems perturbed, as if this admittedly banal line of questioning is a personal slight.

"I think I'm getting a wisdom tooth. There's a—" she flicks her tongue against the curved wound, tastes its salty-sweet-bitter discharge, "a hole in my gum."

It feels wrong to call it a hole. It's not a hole—it's an opening. An entrance. Far less passive than a *hole*. It feels *unfeminist* to call it that.

"You're not getting wisdom teeth. Me and Dad don't have them. Toyah doesn't have them, and Duckie won't get them. I think you've probably worn a hole into it yourself. You're always eating shit—maybe it's finally catching up with you."

Alice is less offended by her mother's judgemental snideness towards her eating habits than she is at her passivity. Her mother's body was once her home, her feeding-trough, her comfort; the duvet she enclosed herself in, with the same dank, heady scent as her own at home today. Alice *could* have wisdom teeth. She could have something growing inside her that her mother doesn't know about. Alice has been inside her mother's depths, but that intimacy has not been returned. Duckie and Toyah's mother does not know what lingers within her. It could be anything. It could be a tooth. It could be a whole mouth with a whole set of teeth, and those teeth could have teeth, and she could be consuming herself from the inside out at this very moment, and her mother wouldn't know.

"Yeah. I gotta go to work soon," Alice murmurs, forcing her tongue away from the playful pit of her new orifice long enough to form the words. Her jaw aches, cracking with the effort of being dragged to one side so Alice may explore herself, to enjoy the hole in her gum, to feel every inch of it.

Her mother hangs up first, but this time, Alice hardly notices. She flicks her tongue against the wound, and shivers with delight at the pinpricks of that near-arousing, angry sensitivity.

 CRSO

Alice cuts the tip of her tongue on the small, barely-there mountain of bone that protrudes through her gum. She misses her cavern, the warmth of it, the depth—but the sharp edge that's forced its way through has presented her with a shining white pearl resting delicately upon the red velvet cushion of her mouth. It feels regal, almost.

A drop of her blood rolls over lip, lands on the top of the page she's reading. Her head is bowed, headphones protecting her ears from the offensive chatter of her fellow passengers on the bus. She wishes she could be the kind of person to find camaraderie in a place like this; to wish good morning to the vile man watching her with his knobby legs spread, revealing a core that, she can tell, does not need as much space as he is giving it. She wants to want to talk to the woman beside her, flooding her nose with cheap perfume. Alice wants to want something besides the addictive pull of the knife protruding from her jaw, the unfightable urge to slice herself again and again over its tempting edge. Her mouth fills with blood that drips from her maw, slides over her chin, splatters limply upon the page and mars the words she's trying to read in a crimson void. She may never know, now, if the unnamed narrator returns to Manderley; the whole story has become bathed in gore.

The woman beside her has become aware of Alice's mess, of the parts of herself she spills out generously. She looks horrified—a half-hearted concern that does nothing to disguise the disgust that ripples beneath her flesh, her pudgy hand closing around the handle of her purse. As if Alice would steal her measly pocket change, as if a girl bleeding from her mouth is a threat to anyone but herself. Alice watches as the blood on the page rearranges itself into letters she can read, foreign tongues slithering across the page, blossoming phrases the way fresh gore seeps from a wound.

A crimson bone gem
I am no star of torn men
Who netting a grow
Fret not those in art
Hornet net I'm to

She understands this poetry, she is understood by it. Something is happening to Alice, something wonderful. She slices her tongue like thick cuts of sausage from the expensive deli she can't afford to visit, and the bloody words come faster to greet her greedy eyes.

⚡

She can't tell if the people in the café are staring at her because half of her face has swollen to the size of a volleyball, or because of the obscene tongue-in-cheek gesture she can't help committing. The bone has broken through her gum, standing half as tall as the rest of her teeth, and doubly as sharp. It hurts the most when she swallows, the tender flesh caressing her new intrusion giving firm flares of agony. It feels maternal, the way her gums protect the thing they birthed, even as its ivory tower draws shallow gashes into the roof of her mouth. A mother's love knows no limits, she thinks.

"Ma'am." An employee adorned in a black apron, fastened tightly around the waist approaches, sets her cappuccino on the edge of the table in a precise precariousness that makes Alice feel doomed to upturn it. "If you could keep your voice down, we would appreciate it. The other customers are…" He glances back to the bar, to a coworker who is pointedly avoiding his gaze, shielding his brow in cowardice as he focuses too hard on the caramel-drizzle-whatever-the-fuck he's concocting. "The other customers are complaining. About the noise."

Alice doesn't think she responds, but the employee flinches as if she's screamed at him. Her hands are fumbling, feeling grotesquely large as she lifts her headphones off her ears.

Ah.

Yes.

She *is* screaming. Her voice is hoarse from it, throat bubbling with bile that desperately tries to lubricate her windpipe, to protect it from the lashing of pure *noise* escaping from her lips. The tooth, her tooth, the thing she has created and gestated in her mouth, erupts further, knocking her molars aside in its eagerness to reach the roof. She tries to communicate, speaking through episodic screeches *'I'm terribly sorry, it's just that I'm in a lot of pain. I'm having a baby. Sorry, I mean that I'm having a baby tooth. I miss my cavern, it was warm and wet and beautiful. But now I'm full to bursting with this sharp thing and I can't wait to show it to you all."*

She hopes a word or two slips through between her raspy wail, but she doubts it. The employee beside her looks as if he might cry, and she wants to tell him that he should, that she can be his warm place, that she can take him within her body and keep him safe from the things that scream.

Instead she takes her coffee and leaves. The door sighs shut behind her in relief, the building losing some of its tension now that she's gone. Alice makes a mental note to leave them a bad review. *2/10 stars—great coffee, but the staff didn't understand the miracle of life, of the thing I am creating between my gums. Also their AC is too cold, my nips were like knives.*

☙❧

As Alice Pierce awoke one day into an uneasy hangover, she found her mouth transformed into a gigantic stalagmite.

By the time she's halfway through her shift at the sandwich shop, her gums have been mangled, split open like a ripe pomegranate spilling ruby seeds that sprinkle the food her hands are trying to shape.

"That's *disgusting*. I don't want to *eat* that."

Alice tries not to take it personally. This customer, one of a dozen formless bodies packed into the midday rush, could not possibly understand the miracle of what is happening.

"Should I start over?"

She's not screaming anymore, but her mouth has swollen near-shut; when she speaks, the tooth penetrates the fleshy gap between tooth and gum, creating papercut fissures that weep and swell and ache.

"No. Don't bother, just—oh my *god*."

It's an overreaction, Alice thinks. It makes perfect sense to her that this should happen. The new tooth was never a standalone presence, it brought sisters that buried themselves inside Alice, finding their homes within her mouth, squeezing into the lightless gaps, entangling themselves in the roots of her teeth. The curved headstones of her existing denticulations could only withstand their conquest for so long—but these swarms need to spread their pearly wings, and that means making some space. She stares down at the turkey-on-rye-hold-mustard she was making, eyes focusing on the white tooth resting delicately on its surface. She can already feel its replacement growing in, urging its siblings to expand, to take root, to make their claim to her mouth.

Alice opens her jaw to explain to the horrified customer, to preach the joyous truth to this unwitting disciple—but the time to talk has passed. As she spreads her lips, her teeth clatter like porcelain raindrops upon the counter, spilling out in shards that tear her flesh, drawing ribbons of gore. The pain began that Tuesday morning, but it had been buried within her for far longer. She closes her eyes, body faint from exhaustion and blood loss, and welcomes the ecstatic thrust of her newly-formed fangs as they embed themselves through the roof of her mouth, through her jaw, encasing her words in an eternal prison of blood and bone.

– THE END –
ENJOYED THIS? CHECK OUT:
YOUR FINAL SUNSET
BY SJ TOWNEND

ASSEMBLY AND QUICK-START INSTRUCTIONS FOR YOUR DEMONIC HEART™

TIFFANY MICHELLE BROWN

Thank you for purchasing your very own Demonic Heart™! We loathe our customers, and we want to ensure you get everything you expect out of your body modification.

This kit includes: (1) full-length mirror, (2) plastic drop cloths, (1) bone saw, (3) tweezers of varying lengths, (4) heavy-duty body clamps, (1) pair of goggles, (1) Demonic Draught™, (5) patent-pending absorbent patches, (1) large needle, (1) spool of medical grade thread, (1) bottle of iodine with dropper, and your new heart, divided into (8) individual pieces. Please ensure all items have arrived safely in your kit before you begin the procedure.

You can install your Demonic Heart™ independently, or you can enlist someone to help you, so long as they are not squeamish or hesitant to help you embrace your innate darkness. An assistant is not required, and many of our customers report greater satisfaction when they complete their modification alone, but this choice is entirely at your own discretion.

Phase 1:

Prepare your space. Cover all surfaces with the plastic drop cloths to protect your possessions from blood spatter. There will be quite a bit, so be thorough. Set the mirror in a strategic spot and be sure to anchor it in place.

Take a moment to look into your eyes and verify that this is truly what you want. You do, don't you? You really, *really* do.

Great!

Plug in the bone saw. Do *not* plug this into a power strip. It conducts a lot of energy, so it's safest to plug it directly into an outlet. Sterilize the tweezers and body clamps by boiling them in a pot of water for at least 30 minutes. Put on your goggles. Make sure they are snug but not so tight as to obscure your vision or fog up when you scream.

Take a breath.

Phase 2:

Remove all clothing from the waist up. With a writing implement of your choice (not included), draw a cross upon your chest to bisect your torso both horizontally and vertically, with the intersection of the lines appearing directly above your heart. Please note, your heart is *not* located in the center of your chest, but on the left side. It is recommended you reference images and diagrams in books or online to ensure the placement of this mark is accurate.

Steel your nerves and concentrate on your end goal. Throw back the Demonic Draught™ in a single swallow. Your chest will begin to feel leaden and heavy. This sensation is the pain blockers doing their work, so do not be alarmed. Wait fifteen minutes for maximum effectiveness. You will have an additional forty-five minutes to complete the procedure before your nerves wake up.

After fifteen minutes or when you feel sufficiently numb, turn on the bonesaw at full power. With a steady hand, cut along the lines on your chest. Be sure to press hard enough to pass through skin, muscle, tissue, and bone. If you hear a cacophony of cracks and breaks, you're doing it right! Rest assured, you will not feel anything.* However, there will be quite a bit of blood. You may need to take breaks to wipe away viscera, clean your goggles, etc. You can also use our patent-pending absorbent patches to allay the gushing.

*If you *do* feel something, stop what you're doing and grab a bottle of alcohol of your choice. The Demonic Draught™ has been tested, but everybody is different, so there is a chance you may not experience the full benefits of the drugs. Our apologies if this happens!

Phase 3:
After you've cut the cross in your chest, unplug the bone saw. You don't want the tool to start up sporadically while enmeshed in the delicate work that comes next.

It's time for the clamps. Select one of the four loose flaps on your chest and pull on the diagonal. The more you can expose, the better, so be sure to use your full strength. Fetch one of the clamps, squeeze to open the pincers, and guide the teeth in place. Imagine the clamp is a mouth that's about to take a bite out of the meatiest part of a sandwich; one side of the clamp will disappear beneath your skin, and the other will remain visible. Repeat these actions on each flap. Use the patent-pending absorbent patches as needed.

Stare into the blood diamond you've created. Let it pull you in. Allow yourself to be beckoned into the brutality you've enacted.

There's no turning back now. You are forever altered.

Phase 4:

The sight of your heart will be shocking, but not because of the extremity of the situation. You will be astonished to learn that hearts are sectioned and color-coded. Each segment is responsible for a particular facet of innate goodness (eww, right?). Here's a key for easy reference:

- Kindness is Yellow
- Love is Pink
- Acceptance is Blue
- Sincerity is Purple
- Humility is Brown
- Modesty is White
- Gentleness is Green
- Knowledge is Orange

In your package, you will have (8) black segments that will compose your new Demonic Heart™. Each segment is engineered to imbue you with the exact opposite of the traits listed above.

Important: This means that you must swap out each fragment with care; if you simply stuff your Demonic Heart™ into your chest without following these directions to a tee, the modification will not hold—and death may occur.

Yes, all of the sections of your Demonic Heart™ are black as a crow's wing, but inscribed upon each is a capitalized letter to denote the evil characteristics you shall inherit.

Using the tweezers and a delicate hand, remove a section of your Good Heart and replace it with the corresponding section of your Demonic Heart™, one at a time, as follows:

1. Replace Kindness (Yellow) with Malice (M).
2. Replace Love (Pink) with Loathing (L).
3. Replace Acceptance (Blue) with Bigotry (B).
4. Replace Sincerity (Purple) with Hypocrisy (H).
5. Replace Humility (Brown) with Narcissism (N).
6. Replace Modesty (White) with Pride (P).
7. Replace Gentleness (Green) with Callousness (C).
8. Replace Knowledge (Orange) with Ignorance (I).

You will delight in how easily your Good Heart succumbs to the slightest touch. As you secure each fragment of your Demonic Heart™, you will feel fire in your veins. Your home will likely take on the smell of sulphur, though this can vary and is not guaranteed. If you are blessed with the stink of rot and ruin, breathe it in as you sink.

Phase 5:

If you've placed all of the components of your Demonic Heart™ in the correct configuration, the organ will begin to beat. This rhythm will be slower than the pace of your previous Good Heart.

If your Demonic Heart™ has not begun to pulse, double-, triple-, and quadruple-check your work. Rearrange the pieces as needed. If a heartbeat continues to elude you, sew yourself back up using the directions below and call our customer service line at 555-666-EVIL.

If all is working as expected, carefully remove the clamps, fetch the needle and thread, and sew yourself up. If you prefer a jagged, rugged reminder of your modification, you don't need to be precious about this part; stab and pull and stab and pull until the cross on your chest is closed. If you're all about clean lines and precision, we recommend consulting how-to videos online and investing in scar-minimizing cream, available over the counter at most drugstores.

Phase 6:

Wipe your sutured flesh clean with warm water and apply iodine liberally. This is when the pain will kick in, if it hasn't already. You will feel the ache of something lost. Your cross to bear. A fire in your veins that will singe you continuously for all of eternity.

Look at the new you in the mirror. You see someone darker, don't you? An entity who will inflict cruelty rather than suffering it. A being incapable of love or joy or content.

All it took was giving up the good fight. Transforming into something else. Submitting to the unknown, hoping it will be an improvement, because how could it not be?

You feel better now, don't you?

Don't you?

Don't you?

– THE END –
ENJOYED THIS? CHECK OUT:
BAD FORM
BY JOE TAYLOR

CORPUS

EMMA MURRAY

I only looked away for a moment, but that was when the waves rose up and grabbed her. By the time my eyes were back on the shore, Annie was being dragged away, foamy fingers wrapped around her tiny form, eyes wide with terror.

"Mama! Mama!" Her lips formed the word twice before she was swept under. My feet carried me across the hot sand before I could register what had happened, a mother's reflex, but it was too late.

Stumbling through the waves, I searched for her. Bent over, frantic hands reaching into stirred up sand. She wasn't there.

"Annie?" I hurled myself past wave after wave, waist-deep, then off the sandbank with paddling legs and bobbing head barely staying above the surface. "Annie! Where are you?"

I never learned to swim properly, but I couldn't let that stop me. Diving under, my open eyes stung. There was no way to see past the murky brown of the Gulf waters. Flailing, my hands closed on watery nothing until some stranger pulled me out.

"Call 911! Call somebody, for God's sake!" I heard a voice shouting behind us. Would-be rescuers came but were forced to admit that she was gone. I remember they looked so young, these baby-faced heroes, and I felt so ancient beyond my thirty years.

Back on land, the sun baked my skin golden then bright red and blistered, but I didn't care. I refused to leave the shore. I needed to keep my eyes on the horizon in case her ginger crown or waving arms appeared, begging me to save her from forever treading water.

The sun set, and I was alone on the beach.

Shivering, I watched the moon dance silver over the sea and felt the flutter of tiny crabs skittering over my toes. One particularly strong wave brought the iridescent blue-purple balloon of a man-o-war to the beach, its sail fluttering in the strong night breeze as it suffocated beside me. That was when I broke down. To have it die before my eyes, unwilling to pick up the jellyfish and walk it back to the sea for fear of getting tangled in its stinging lengths of tendrils, brought the reality crashing down over me.

I left the beach in the first rays of morning, but part of me remained. No matter how I tried to move on, therapy and loss groups and new jobs and new lovers, a move across the country: none of it helped. The novelty would wear thin, and just beyond it, Annie's frightened face peered out from the waves with big eyes and trembling lips. Crying for me, but I hadn't been there for her.

I replayed every minute of that day on an endless loop. How could I have let her play out there alone? Why hadn't I run faster? Why hadn't I learned to swim as a child so I could paddle my way easily to her, offer my hand, and pull her from that briny grave? Then she'd be here and so would I. Not both of us forever stuck on that goddamn beach, the stench of rotting seaweed and exhaust fumes from the highway making our heads spin and thoughts slip away.

Today, I return. My fingers tremble as I show the security guard my boarding pass, and I get pulled aside for extra searching due to my nervousness, one-way ticket, and lack of luggage, but of course, nothing is found. I couldn't explain because they wouldn't understand. On the airplane, I drink two miniature bottles of white wine and my hands finally still. Out the window, tilled fields, houses, office buildings, and miles of dry brush pass beneath me. I will miss the land, but I'm sure Annie misses it more. How dare I even consider my own comfort anymore?

The rental car has a sticky shifter and smells like fresh leather, the kind of details I would've taken for granted before, but now I cherish. Nothing is good or bad, pleasant or annoying anymore. There is only life, what little I have left.

With no need for a hotel, I drive straight to the beach, parking next to a van stuffed with a family of six, faces smeared white with sunscreen, ready for their day in the sun. They notice me and smile. I smile back. The youngest is all rolls and chubby cheeks with a sunhat pulled over its head. It drools and stares at me with blue eyes that I could've sworn were Annie's. From my car, I watch them digging trenches and building castles with plastic shovels. The mother lets her children run in and out of the surf, unworried.

My arms are heavy as I force them to retrieve the towel from the backseat, the same cheap one with some neon cartoon cat grinning against a backdrop of dizzying rainbow. Annie's towel. The one she'd picked out for our weekend vacation.

I spread it out and lay back, soaking in the sunlight, vision bright red as the light penetrates the thin skin of my eyelids, forcing me to stay out of the dark.

"Dakota, don't you touch that. It'll sting the bejesus outta you," the dad shouts and my eyes flutter open. The child looks back, jaw tight and eyes brimming with defiance, but doesn't touch the dried corpse of the jellyfish, its sail half-deflated and flapping pathetically in the constant sea breeze. Another man-o-war. This decides it.

There is no going back.

"Kids, get over here," the mom yells out. "I don't want y'all going too far out. People have drowned here."

"Aww, mom," the eldest boy whines, limp arms and rolling eyes as he stomps to his mother's side.

Their tires rumble against the sandy asphalt and I wait for them to pull onto the road before I stand, rub the bits of loose sand from my legs, and walk to the water's edge. Cool, but warmer than that day, my feet squelch in the wet sand and swirling foam of the pulling tide. Further and further, I let the water embrace me. Then I'm doggy paddling, the sandbar far behind and the waves crashing over me harsher and higher than before. I take a deep breath, savor the feeling of the sun on my scalp, then dive under.

Swimming deeper, my limbs work hard to pull me into the cold depths until a riptide catches me, sending me tumbling out into the dark blue where there is no more up or down, no direction or orientation in the void. Then my heart stops. I see her.

Annie.

White, sightless eyes fix on me. Green-tinged hair floats in a halo around her head, strands of seaweed and bits of algae attaching to the once-coppery locks, dulled and thinned by battering waves and the constant pull of currents. Bloated limbs, distended stomach, blotched skin, inhumanly pale, I could cry at what's become of my baby, but then she smiles. Those pouty, toddler lips stretch out and up, displaying the same gap-toothed smile I could never forget. *My Annie.*

She is still my Annie.

My lungs burn, the ache climbing my trachea and clawing at my jaws, forcing them open. I gasp, the rush of salt water welcomed by my desperate body before immediately rejected in a choking, sputtering panic of clogged bronchioles, but my arms refuse to stop. Pushing forward, using the last of my strength, I dive, fighting the current that threatens to push me out farther. Almost there, my fingertips reach toward Annie and through my bleary, darkening vision, I see her hands extend out, like she always did when she wanted me to pick her up. I can hear her voice, somewhere far away yet whispering in my ear, "Mama!"

I blink, but when my lids open again, there is nothing but blind darkness and the need for air I could never reach, but I'm not scared. Even when my arms brush against a stinging curtain of strands, cast down from the brainless inflated sail above. Pain doesn't matter anymore. Fear doesn't matter anymore.

Kicking my legs harder than ever, I propel forward, arms wrapping around my little girl and feeling her head nestle against my shoulder, her gentle kiss on my neck, and my name on her tongue one last time, no longer frightened, but a sleepy mumble, soft and warm.

"Mama."

– THE END –
ENJOYED THIS? CHECK OUT:
THE CARTOGRAPHY DOOR
BY SEAN EDWARD

WELL, WELL, WELL, MY BLEATING LITTLE LAMB CHOPS . . . TONIGHT'S TASTY TREAT COMES STRAIGHT FROM THE BELLY OF THE BEAST! SINK YOUR FANGS INTO 'THROUGH THE WOLF'S GUT', A GUT-CHURNING LITTLE PIECE FROM THE DREADFULLY DELIGHTFUL VEDA VILLIERS, A FRESH NEW POET WITH A TASTE FOR THE LETHAL, AND THE LIGHTLY DIGESTED! OUR STORY TONIGHT IS ONE OF SHEEPISH SECRETS AND HOLY HUNGERS WHERE INNOCENCE GOES DOWN SMOOTH, AND THE AND THE TRUTH GETS CAUGHT IN THE THROAT. IT'S A LYRICAL LAMB-SCAPE OF DENIAL, CLOAKED IN WOOL, BUT MAKE NO MISTAKE—THIS ISN'T ABOUT SPINNING YARNS, KIDDIES . . . IT'S ABOUT SPITTING OUT BONES! SO SAY YOUR PRAYERS AND SHARPEN YOUR CUTLERY, BECAUSE WHEN THE HUNGER HOWLS AND THE CLOAKS FALL, YOU MIGHT JUST FIND YOURSELF ON THE WRONG END OF THE MENU.

THROUGH THE WOLF'S GUT

VEDA VILLIERS

I nside each wolf lies the bleating gut of the lamb he just devoured.

Teeth stained red, like a wine-drunk altar boy after communion, he'll lie: No, mamma, I didn't touch the blood, didn't taste the Lord's sheep.

It's just wool in my teeth, mamma, I was spinning clouds soft and thick as a worship hymn, to keep the winter from biting through—

the wretched lamb's song seeping out floorboards of a crumbling inn. I didn't swallow down innocence, mamma- *least not all at once!* Mouthful of night nestled close to my ribs; thick as the caves we creep—

just a little warmth to keep full and fill, through the long, lean dark.

They believe me, mamma, that it's only wool in my teeth, that all I carry is soft and harmless, when the truth is a shard of bone scraping the edges of my throat, and I wear their trust like a cloak,

concealing the hunger beneath.

- THE END -
ENJOYED THIS? CHECK OUT:
MELPOMENE'S GARDEN
BY CURTIS HARRELL

NOW, FROM THE SLIMY PEN OF AMANDA M. BLAKE, A TWIST OF ROSE VINES AND TENTACLES IN A TRENCHCOAT, COMES A TALE OF ANXIETY, DESPAIR, AND AN ENDLESS PURGATORIAL REPETITION OF FRUITLESS PRODUCTIVITY . . . AND THAT'S BEFORE THE ZOMBIE APOCALYPSE. HAVE YOURSELF A CUP OF YESTERDAY'S COFFEE FROM THE POT, CALL IT ESPRESSO, AND SETTLE INTO YOUR LUMBAR-SUPPORTING OFFICE CHAIRS FOR BLAKE'S TALE . . .

THE COFFEE POTS ARE EMPTY AND ALL THE ZOMBIES ARE HERE

AMANDA M. BLAKE

I creep out from under a string of white cubicle desks. The walls only separate us desk level and above, which provides a world of unused foot space. Dante joked we should hide a cot under there to take stealth naps during the day, but once everything started going to hell, I took the joke and ran with it, not for naps but to stay overnight so I could wake up, turn over, and clock in early to keep everything running smoothly.

Because, my god, I knew things were bad, but this is unacceptable.

Our single-serving coffee machine occasionally works, if you run a few throwaway coffee mini-cups through it first.

The espresso machine never works.

The drip, however, is reliable for its strong brew, and you can't beat a nice tin of proper coffee grounds. Easy coffee was the decline of civilization. But when I entered the office a few weeks ago and the drip coffee hadn't even been turned on, while everyone just milled around like they weren't on the clock, I knew we'd reached the nadir.

I made the coffee, even though I'm no one's secretary and there were dozens of capable hands here before me, and I continue making the coffee, because I need caffeine more than I need to make a point.

The daily janitorial crew doesn't seem to be going through during the evenings anymore, but for now, I can ignore the coffee filters and other trash building up in the bins—although that's in no small part to the fact that I'm the only one who seems to be putting trash there.

Everyone else has just given up. They leave piles on or under their desk, smear jam and spoiling meat into the industrial carpet in a way that strokes my fur the wrong way, but as long as they're not doing that in my row and management isn't calling them out about it, it's none of my business. I spray Febreze to cover the smell and wish candles weren't banned along with space heaters.

What really grates my cheese, though, is that I already knew other people didn't work all day like I do, with my compulsive need to please, but it's like no one's even pretending anymore.

Margaret and Billy used to hook up in the supply closet or the gym shower rooms. Now they devour each other like clockwork at two in the afternoon right at Billy's cubicle—grunting, screaming, shaking the whole latched double-row cubicles. Nick, Billy's neighbor, sometimes slavers over the sight; other times he's too busy eating what looks like a footlong sub, without bothering with a plate, napkin, or wax paper.

My manager, Kaye, grumbles at the keyboard when she's not throwing it against the wall and jumping on it, sending keys flying like bloody teeth. And then she tries to type with it again. She has a six-month-old, so I don't blame her for being a little spacey, but you'd think she'd figure out that the reason her keyboard isn't working has nothing to do with the wireless.

Don, my manager's boss, used to never be in his office, and none of us were sure what he actually did other than disrupt what we were doing in the name of efficiency, but now he just lounges in his office and scribbles incomprehensible notes on the whiteboard walls of his office, when he's not bellowing equally incomprehensible jargon into his phone, which I'm not convinced is actually plugged in anymore after all the times he's slammed it into the window-wall of the office, leaving spiderweb cracks in the tempered glass.

Our actual boss hasn't come in at all. A few weeks ago, Meredith used his office to pound against the window, screaming in the sound-proof room so loudly that I could hear her. Now she just sulks under the desk and occasionally raids his mini-fridge.

The rest kind of maunder around, congregating in clusters of two or three in the main office or the breakroom, grunting their hushed secrets as though they've realized how much I like to eavesdrop while working. Not for office blackmail or something juicy to share on social media. I just used to like listening to people who actually have lives so I could live vicariously through all their dirty laundry—bad siblings or children, salacious divorce proceedings, child support and visitation drama.

No more secondhand thrills, yet here I am, working all day and staying in the office overnight just to make sure things get done, because it's clear less is getting done than usual, even though other people are staying late, too, or coming in early. The company doesn't care what hours you keep, as long as you keep hours at all, but I'm run about ragged.

Sometimes I want to make like Meredith and scream at the top of my lungs, then walk out. Let them clean up their own messes. And make their own motherfucking coffee.

It's as though I'm the only one left who cares, and I don't even know why I do. Cheap coffee, self-serve mini-mart with increasingly slim pickings, spotty delivery apps, drinks fridge getting just as spare, no cleaning, filthier and filthier bathrooms (down to one stall that isn't backed up with someone's bad takeout). More and more of our clients aren't answering emails, and more and more of our drivers aren't answering their phones, and when they do, they're dismissive of the requirements they're expected to follow. It's as though our clients don't want their product and our drivers don't want their paycheck.

Good afternoon. This is my fourth follow-up on this issue, due to no response. Per policy, I've copied your field supervisor and regional manager to ensure that the matter is resolved as soon as possible.

Not that the supervisors or managers are responding, either. I'm making unapproved corrections in the system for the month's close and marking them as analyst adjustments so that if someone audits, they know I was just trying to improve accuracy without an ounce of support.

But even as I do the work, occasionally kicking my cot with my shoe while I dance in my chair to headphone music—for the barest of joys during the day to accompany my five or six mugs of coffee— I don't think I can do this much longer.

Margo and Beth have been full-out fighting each other for two hours. They broke through one of the manager's office window-walls. No one interceded; I tried calling security, then the police, but security isn't picking up and the police line only plays a recording: "All operators are occupied with other calls. Your emergency is important to us. Please stay on the line to wait for an available operator to take your call, or hang up and try again later."

Those two women have always had a sustained tension between them that bordered between murderous and sexual, but I'm kind of afraid they're going to kill each other.

On top of that, someone in dispatch won't stop open-mouth breathing like some kind of phone pervert, and although I pass them every time I need another cup of coffee, I can't figure out which of my slack-jawed, dead-eyed colleagues is doing it—not that I'd do anything about it.

And the smell—oh god, the smell.

The AC is still going strong in this Texas summer, thank heavens, but I'm the only one I ever see in the gym showers. Wherever the others are going, it's not to their own bathrooms, because there isn't enough Febreze in the world to completely cover the smell of fermenting shit, piss, rotting meat, and spoiled fruit and vegetables— worse than microwaved broccoli or burnt popcorn wafting from the breakroom. I'm not sure how effectively I'm showering away the smell penetrating my clothes, my hair, my skin.

The worst part is that sometimes I don't smell it at all.

After the light outside the office windows fades—I barely look outside anymore, what's the point when it's just a view of traffic and other office buildings?—I finally clock out in the business portal and pull out my personal laptop to stream my shows in the dark under the desk while eating my slightly expired sandwich, as well as chips that seem like they'll never expire. I drink a caffeine-free diet soda, because I'm still buzzing from the fifth cup of coffee that keeps me from falling asleep at my desk.

But sometimes I wonder if I'm sleepwalking anyway, if I'm missing important things by not having a significant other or friends or a pet, by living states away from my family, by not going out and talking to strangers and having a drink or something more substantial than the equivalent of gas-station food. Giving my all to a job that clearly doesn't give a damn about me. Living like an office gremlin in a perpetual group project, where I'm expected to do most of the work for equal credit and probably close to equal salaries.

Which only works if they're actually paying me.

I lose track of days all the time, because I work overtime on the weekends when I'm not sleeping through sleep debt from my caffeine-fueled weekdays. But I know when I'm supposed to be paid.

Now, while attempting to soothe myself with *Kitchen Nightmares*, I stew over the fact that my bank account still isn't showing the deposit that was supposed to appear four days ago. It's the only reason I'm here, and HR can't even be assed to get back to me about the oversight. I tried to ask my colleagues if they were having the same problem, a chance to commiserate about corporate, but they furtively rolled their eyes to the backs of their sockets and refused to talk about pay, even though we're allowed to. (We never do.)

I lower my sandwich. Despite preservatives, the mayonnaise in the tuna salad seems sour. The office stench joins the fish on my tongue. No amount of carbonated caramel syrup can mask it.

I'm living out of a suitcase—if you can call it living—and I haven't changed the sheets I've folded on my cot since I started staying overnight.

Even before then, I brought work home with me to pair with background streaming. I planned grocery pickups for healthy meals to bring in, planned meals for when I came home and didn't want to cook. I drank and dreamed spreadsheets. I rarely take vacations, because I know how many emails I'd have to field when I get home, so days off keep accumulating and most don't roll over at the end of the year. None pay out.

What the fuck am I doing? Killing my back. Eyes blurry from staring at too many little numbers. Dealing with increasingly feral employees, even people I consider work friends devolving into caveman-like vocalizations, minds melting smooth under the onslaught of the same-shit-different-day rows and columns and endless, endless emails. And how am I doing any better, industrious little worker ant that I am, shuffling through life with them? My fingers are the only limbs of any speed, even when my carpal tunnel's acting up.

Living for work, working to live, living to work, working to work, and *work work work work work*.

Surely a person isn't meant to live like this.

It isn't cruel or unusual or even punishment, but the more I blink my eyes and look around at the rows and rows of cubicles from my little space under them, I realize how small my world has become, and I don't have to love my job, my life, but I don't even fucking *like* it.

That smell… in my hair, in my skin, in my bed. Cheap junk food. Caffeine dependency. Ibuprofen every day from despair dragging my spine *down-down-down* and pudging my middle with office treats— although we haven't had any in a while, and already it shows.

Slowly killing my body. Slowly killing my brain. Making myself a hunched-over computer for them, and for what? Time and time and a half unpaid?

It's bureaucratic hell—a line that never ends, a clock that never reaches five, another email and another, little grievances, petty squabbles, constant surveillance, demanding that I justify my splodging ass in their office chair while they consider training a bot that they can give my name, never appreciating that I give my life for them and I'm not entirely sure *why*.

Then they withhold the last tether of my own justification as to why I'm killing myself—or already dead—in their dead-end job.

Perspective. Perspective, with a sour sandwich and the smell of shit.

I leave my streaming site and switch to personal email, then address my company's HR representative:

Dear Annie,

I've followed up with your department three times by email and three times by phone regarding the fact that my paycheck has not yet been deposited into my account. Though I've received no response, I've continued to work for the last four days with no indication that I will be paid for that time.

Conditions in the workplace have deteriorated to an untenable level. I will forever be grateful for my employment, but recent changes—in the last year, but particularly the last month—have been perplexing at best, and I no longer feel valued for my time and effort when it's clear that no one else is held to the same standard to which I hold myself.

I tender my resignation, effective immediately. If my paycheck is not deposited within the next three business days, I will be seeking legal action.

It might not be politic to burn a bridge, but already I feel free. My blurry vision clears. I finally comprehend the reality I've been living in.

Sad. Pathetic. Not worth the filth on my feet.

I climb off my cot, then gather my laptop, phone, purse, suitcase, and my spider plant. The rest can be dispersed among my coworkers and replacements, if they bother replacing me at all.

As I stand, my vertebrae pop all the way down, cervical to lumbar.

I pick up my headset and drop it on my desk—the closest I have to a mic drop. "Peace out, bitches."

I keep it soft, because there are people here I actually like—although why are they even still here after hours, just milling about like always? Don't they have families to go home to? Have they been there all along while I sleep under the desks?

But I'm giddy, my heart racing like I'm in love, like I've had *way* too much coffee. Like I'm *alive*.

Dozens of heads—from the other cubicles, from the glass offices—turn toward me with slow, haunted-house creaks of tortured tendons.

I see the tendons.

Why can I see tendons?

Lips peel back from stained teeth and thick black tongues. White eyes as though blind, but they see me, too.

I've crossed their paths so many times during my early morning, late morning, mid-afternoon somnambulistic shamble. Their gazes passed over me, like they always did when people were focused on work or whatever they did to distract from work—barely acknowledging each other but not taking it too personally.

Now they *see* me.

And when they do, their rotting mouths erupt with dissonant moans, like the prolonged whine of an ancient accordion. One by one, they advance.

Other heads pop up over the cubicle walls, other gazes latch upon me, other feet—shod and shoeless—shuffle toward me, and I don't think it's to wish me well.

With a high-pitched shriek, I abandon my things and run for the front doors. However, when I start running, so do the zombies, the company I've kept for who knows how long—certainly not me, because although I'm a data analyst who can spot any inconsistencies in a spreadsheet, I somehow couldn't tell that all my coworkers were dying or dead.

To be fair, they hadn't figured out I wasn't dead, either.

But now that I realize I'm alive, they notice it, too.

As intractable fingers crook into my dirty blouse to drag me back into the office and the first foul teeth dig into my shoulder with hunger for life rediscovered, the dead find my resignation quite tender indeed.

– THE END –
ENJOYED THIS? CHECK OUT:
PERSEPHONE'S ESCALATOR
BY JOE TAYLOR

AND NOW, A BONUS STORY — A PREVIEW OF JENDIA GAMMON'S UPCOMING *THE VALE OF DRAGONS* SERIES, AVAILABLE 2026 FROM SLEY HOUSE PUBLISHING.

ON THE BIRTHDAY OF
A PRINCESS

JENDIA GAMMON

The fourteenth birthday of Princess Githilien of Vickery dawned like a smudge of water-thinned ink on brown paper. It was hideous, and to Thilly, portentous of nothing good. The mood of the castle was similarly glum, albeit for the overly excited Mrs. Florence who, in rare form, had taken it upon herself to ensure the proceedings for the princess's birthday belied the garland of irritability draped about the place and its stubborn heir. King Gathlade, recovering from a hacking cough, had retreated to his quarters early the night before, and stayed up late painting tiny figurines, as he was wont to do when no one was looking. Many of them bore swords, with some of them riding upon horses, some upon pearl-scaled thaleccions with copper-tipped wings and vicious-looking claws (even at that scale), and even one on a rather small dragon. There were now no dragons, and thaleccions had long ago migrated to the far north.

Thilly had avoided him for days because of his cough, while she endured her lessons, chafing at the slurry-skied late winter, stuck inside. She loathed having a birthday during that month, one month before spring, in fact. The point of the year at which everyone was more than ready for winter to be over, with its charm of solstice two months prior now evaporated, and the year's dawn a small blip before stale, chilly, often croup-ridden weeks in which nothing grand happened and everyone grew more and more cranky.

"Did Mother have to bear me *this* month?" she pondered aloud to Mrs. Florence that morning, while the chief lady-in-waiting oversaw the last finishing touches on her birthday gown. This would be a subdued birthday, two years before her coming-of-age, and marked by lingering waves of illness in the kingdom.

Mrs. Florence placed her hands on her hips, jaw working. (Thilly knew this to be a sign that she was irritated with the staff, or perhaps with *her*, and also knew she was on shaky ground with any arguments.) "The Lady Woadlynn did not bear you for you to complain about the month in which you arrived. You were conceived in great love, and you arrived when the gods decided it."

Thilly stared at herself in her long mirror. Still a bit arms-and-legs gangly, growing into her figure but not liking its pace, she noted her own deep-set eyes looked rather more shadowed beneath than usual. She was paler as well, her scattered ginger constellation of freckles on her cheeks more prominent as a result. Her dark auburn hair frizzed and yet hung limply at the same time.

"Do you feel ill, Your Highness?" Mrs. Florence then asked, taking hold of the girl's hands, turning them over. She pressed her own cool hand upon Thilly's forehead.

Thilly shook her head.

"I'm fine."

But she was not fine; she was thinking of her mother. The Lady Woadlynn would not be there for her fourteenth birthday, and had not been for several birthdays. She was in the north, in Aceltia, with a sect of priestesses of the Covenant of the Veiled Isles, practicing magic illicit for men and other beings. Her abdication of her queenly position had proven to be a minor scandal among the Vale, and yet Vickery itself had largely understood. Woadlynn was a golden pillar of the family, but from afar; her daughter and her husband the King mere ramparts flickering in a gale, held to her by but threads. And yet they clung.

Thilly thought of her mother often, wondered what *she* had been like at fourteen. Only Mrs. Florence and the head butler, Birkswood, had known Woadlynn in her youth. The King had met her later; some said she had cast him in her thrall, but Thilly scoffed at that. She wasn't *that* swept up into legends; she knew that her parents had loved each other. And still did, apparently, despite their distance apart.

"That ought to do it," said Mrs. Florence crisply, and Thilly's north-drifting thoughts snapped back to the stuffy room and her scratchy gown, sewn with glittering threads in stiff embroidery of the famed house dragon of old, Antares, with his scarlet and gold and orange scales and menacing tail.

There are no dragons now, and my mother is not here on my birthday.

"You're certain you're well enough for this evening?" Mrs. Florence asked, a sharpness to her tone.

Thilly nodded again, jutting her chin. "I won't miss it. There's cake, after all."

As the other maids unlaced her to press the now-fitted gown, Thilly stood in her pantaloons and glanced at the shimmering picture of her mother, which stood on the nightstand beside her bed. It glistened, and even seemed to wink at her. She pulled her day dress back on, waving off assistance, and sat on her bed to look at her beautiful mother. Mrs. Florence dismissed the other maids.

"Child," said the older woman gently, "I know you'd rather she was here."

"When will she ever come back?" Thilly's voice broke a little too high for her taste. Like she was not a great girl becoming a woman soon.

"We hope that she will for your coming-of-age."

Mrs. Florence's voice cracked, and Thilly turned to look at her. But she had pivoted away, her face out of sight.

"I'll be back to help you prepare for your Honor's Feast, dear Princess," she said, and then she slipped out the door.

Thilly's throat ached and her eyes stung. The light of day was muted, the very air dank.

But still, the picture flashed and shone.

She stood quickly. This was not how she wanted her birthday to go. She seized a cloak from her wardrobe, a simple one of roan hue, and then she knelt in front of the great piece of furniture and pulled down a little compartment underneath. It was difficult to do, as there was only a small gap between the base and the rug. But down it came, and she pulled forth a simple tunic and a pair of trousers. She'd procured them secretly back in late summer, having found them in the laundry on one of her explorations of the castle's downstairs. They were loose, and for a teen boy perhaps, but they fit well enough. She pulled up her skirts, pulled back her top, and layered with the boy clothes beneath her day dress. Securing her cloak around her, she stepped outside her chambers and slinked over to the servants' stair.

This took her down, then forked; one passage led to a back door of the castle, and from there, she dashed down another set of stone steps and out of sight. She stripped off her dress, stuffed it into a divot of stone, and pumped her legs to climb into a nearby patch of woods. From there, she sometimes watched the knights practicing, and she would seethe in envy at their skill and their ability even to *be* knights, something she could never become. But today she felt restless, and there was little activity with the knights presently. She'd heard rumors of a hunt, and supposed many of them must have gone to the edge of the palace grounds for that sport. She slipped down into the palace village and wandered, hood up, her breath in clouds, as the murky sky threatened either rain or snow; she wished it would decide one way or the other.

She came upon a market, and recognized the wreaths and forced bulbs she'd seen in the castle; they'd been preparing for Twixtal, the only remaining holiday of winter, that in-between of frozen winter and thawing spring. She wandered on, at one point paying for a pearled bun that smelled of warm spices and the fruits of distant lands. She lingered over each flavor, more rustic and yet more exotic than palace fare. She found she preferred it.

She came upon a blacksmith and his small forge. It beckoned with the golden-amber pit of molten metal, and the man stood with fading red beard and wild, tangled red and grey hair. His nose was sharp and his eyes deep grey-blue. He brought his hammer down in keen, sharp strokes upon a new blade, and the force of it rang in Thilly's ears and in her soul. By and by, he looked up to see her, raising his protective goggles. She kept her face slightly shrouded by her hood. He tipped his head at her.

"Out to market today, lass?" he asked.

She nodded.

"Don't suppose you're buyin' a sword, then, are you?" teased the man.

"Not yet," she said archly, and he boomed out a great laugh.

"And I don't suppose that if you *bought* a sword, it'd be for your father or your brother?"

His soot-smudged eyes twinkled.

"You suppose correctly," said Thilly, lips tickling with a desire to laugh.

"Naw," agreed the blacksmith. "It'd be for you. I see it in your eyes."

How can he even see *my eyes?* she wondered, and she felt a little uneasy. If he guessed who she was, she would be in for months of trouble—maybe not from her father, but from Mrs. Florence and, gods forbid, Birkswood, which would be far worse.

"What sort of sword would be right for me?" she asked.

The man's bushy orange eyebrows wriggled for a moment.

"Somethin' light, for certain," he mused. "A short saber, methinks. Fine, like one of the north."

She felt her breath catch.

"The north?"

"Aye, up in the mists; the practitioners and fairfolk. Aceltia. I think so!"

Can he know…?

"Why is that?" She hoped her voice wasn't shaking as much as she feared it was.

"Ye've got that *gleam* in your eye. Magical, yes. I think so."

She laughed.

"I don't have a magic bone in my body," she said.

He laughed as well.

"Well, a young maid still growin', maybe not yet, maybe not yet." He walked over to a shelf and pulled out a scroll. He approached her and unrolled it for her to see.

She stared at it: It was an ornate illustration of a very fine saber with a slightly curved tip. Etched upon the blade were fine runes and scrollwork, illustrating a dragon and its flames. The color of the faded paper dulled the hue of the sword. But it was meant to be red-gold, very like the color of Antares, the dragon of Vickery, long gone.

"It's beautiful," she breathed.

"Aye. Made for a priestess, long ago. I've tried to find it, and cannae. Always hopin' to make one like it, one day. If it were Aceltian, then naturally that's beyond my skill; only the priestess could forge that."

"I didn't know they made swords too!" Thilly exclaimed.

"Aye." The blacksmith rubbed his beard with his stained hands. "The priestesses are known for many skills, and unknown for many more beyond the prying eyes of brutes like me." He chuckled. "Not that I've not tried, mind! Not everyone can reach them. Maybe you will, though."

Thilly stared at the fiery saber and felt a deep and profound longing. She could almost feel it in her hands; her eyelids flickered just enough that she could almost see it, newly forged and polished, gleaming from reflected dragonfire.

"Maybe," she said softly.

She bade the man farewell, and continued a circuit of the markets, but her thoughts rose above them all, above the palace and the castle, above the hills and the great Vale, sweeping north, undulating, as though upon a dragon's back. She would have given anything to have lived in the time of dragons, to ride one, to glide over land and sea and among clouds. And yet here she was, on her fourteenth birthday: a princess and a lonely one at that. She was not of age to travel far, and never could alone. *Lonely and never alone; the worst feeling in the world.*

Thilly meandered back to the castle, found her bundled dress, and, looking this way and that, found a moment to change. She walked into the servants' stairwell again, absent-mindedly, and ran right into Birkswood!

"Hmmph," he said, in a disapproving tone. She swept back her hood then, and the tall man's heels clacked together, and his shoulders flew back.

"Your Highness!" he said in his deep baritone voice through his grey goatee. "I apologize. I did not know that was you."

She squinted up at him, but he kept his head high, and she smirked.

"I wonder, Birkswood," she said with a sly wink. He did not budge; nor would he, as chief valet to the King and the commander of the downstairs staff of the palace. Yet she suspected the lines on his face bore many stories in their depths.

"If I may, Your Highness," he said briskly, "I do believe Mrs. Florence is looking for you. It is your birthday, after all, and we all wish to celebrate you at the feast."

Thilly sighed. "I suppose I should get ready." She let her eyes glaze for a moment. "Did you…er. I know you knew my mother." Birkswood did not make eye contact with her, but threw daggers with his eyes at a bumbling footman. "Did she ever…have a sword?"

"A sword?" Thilly winced at his tone. Birkswood sniffed. "It is not for the knowledge of men, what those of the Covenant may possess."

"But you—"

Birkswood cleared his throat, and Thilly recognized the conversation as over. He bowed to her, and she nodded her head, and walked slowly back up the stairs to her room. There she found Mrs. Florence with eyes like cracked marbles. The effect chilled Thilly instantly.

"Your ladyship!" she wheezed. "We've wondered where you've been. It's time to prepare you for this evening! Look at the state of you: You need to bathe. What is that smell? Smoke? Oh, and you've had another gift delivered. Bath first, then the gift, I think."

Thilly beheld a little wooden box, which fit easily in her hand, on the table where she often had tea.

"It's my birthday, Mrs. Florence," she said. "I'll have the gift first."

Turning away from the woman, she lifted the lid on the box. Her eyes flew wide. Inside was a tiny, fire-hued saber, two inches long, with exquisite, tiny scrollwork and a wee dragon carved into it. She pulled it forth and found that it was in fact a brooch.

There was no tag.

There didn't need to be.

She knew who'd sent it, and she knew then too, that she could never be just a princess.

She would be a princess with a sword.

A real one.

One day.

And that realization was the best birthday gift possible.

– THE END –
ENJOYED THIS? CHECK OUT:
THE VALE OF SEVEN DRAGONS
BY JENDIA GAMMON

ABOUT THE CONTRIBUTORS

AMANDA M. BLAKE is a cat-loving daydreamer who enjoys geekery of all sorts, from superheroes to horror movies, urban fantasy to unconventional romance. Born and raised in Texas, Blake attended Trinity University in San Antonio and graduated with a BA in English Literature. Amid dipping tentacles into the sea of gothic and horror short stories and poetry, Blake is also the author of fantasy novel *Drift*, horror novels *Question Not My Salt*, *Deep Down*, and *Out of Curiosity and Hunger*, dark poetry collection *Dead Ends*, and the fairy tale mash-up *Thorns* series. Alt-historical plague novel *Masque* has been acquired by Quill & Crow Publishing House and is slated for publication in 2027.

TIFFANY MICHELLE BROWN is an LA-based writer who once had a conversation with a ghost over a pumpkin beer. She is the author of *How Lovely to Be a Woman: Stories and Poems* and co-host of the Horror in the Margins podcast. Her work has been featured in publications by Tenebrous Press, Ominous Thrill, Black Spot Books, Cursed Morsels Press, the NoSleep Podcast, and more. Learn more about her work at tmbwrites.com.

DAVID CHANDLER (he/him) grew up in small-town Mississippi and currently teaches college English in Tulsa, Oklahoma. From a young age, he's always had a predilection for the weirder stories that seem to follow him wherever he goes. His previous work was featured in Bitter Become the Fields, an anthology from Horns and Rattles Press.

Inspired by H. P. Lovecraft, M. R. James, Shirley Jackson, Robert Aickman, and a ton of fan fiction, **CASSANDRA DAUCUS** (she/her) writes a spectrum of horror. She is intrigued by how the human mind responds to the unknown, and also enjoys a good gross-out. She has stories published and forthcoming in several literary magazines and anthologies. Cassandra lives outside of Philadelphia with her family and three cats. Her social media and website can be found at https://linktr.ee/residualdreaming

AMANDA NEVADA DEMEL is an emerging speculative fiction author. Her favorite genre is horror, thanks to careful cultivation from her father. She especially appreciates media that can simultaneously scare her and make her cry. She is a recent MFA graduate from the University of New Hampshire, and she loves reptiles, musicals, and breakfast foods.

ALEXIS DUBON is a work of fiction. Any resemblance to actual persons, living or dead, is purely coincidental. She is the author of *Nineteen Little Stab Wounds* (an occasionally available chapbook) and co-editor of *No Trouble at All* (Cursed Morsels Press, 2023). You can find her in various magazines and anthologies as well, but good luck looking elsewhere—certainly not under the bed, or in your grandma's creepy attic, or singing to the dead in a dark forest.

HANNAH ENGLAND thought she would be safe from the grotesque images that would haunt her every waking moment, if only she could become ingrained well enough in the pantomime of a normal life. She did everything she was supposed to—got two "impressive" creative writing and literature degrees, settled down into a cushy copywriting job, got published in a few magazines here and there. Yet, like Edgar Allen Poe's infamous protagonist, the thoughts slammed upon the floorboards of her mind in an infernal scream she couldn't ignore. Near-mad from exhaustion, she dragged herself to her computer and typed out this wretched tale: RUPTURED—the story of a woman made monster by the painful arrival of a brand new set of teeth, perfectly primed to cut and tear and consume. Perhaps now they've been freed from the confines of her skull, these macabre spectres will choose a different host to haunt.

Introducing **ADAM FALL**, or "book guy," as he has become known in Northwest Arkansas. Adam is a degenerate for all things spooky and disgusting. He is @adamsfall everywhere.

JENDIA GAMMON is a Nebula and BSFA Awards finalist author of fantasy, science fiction, horror, and thriller novels and short stories. She is also CEO of Roaring Spring Productions, LLC and Editor-in-Chief of its publishing imprint, Stars and Sabers Publishing. She has also written under the pen name J. Dianne Dotson. Born in Southern Appalachia, Jendia now lives in Los Angeles with her family. Jendia conducts workshops and participates in panels on creative writing for conventions such as San Diego Comic-Con and Star Wars Celebration. She holds a degree in Ecology and Evolutionary Biology. Jendia is also a science writer and an award-winning artist. Learn more about Jendia at jendiagammon.com

KC GRIFANT is an award-winning writer based in Southern California who writes and edits internationally published horror, fantasy, science fiction and weird west stories. Her most recent novel, *Melinda West and the Goblin Queen*, is out by Brigid's Gate Press.

JON LASSER was from Seattle, WA, where he lived with his wife and two children. He was a graduate of the Clarion West writers workshop. During his career, his stories appeared in *Lightspeed*, *Interzone*, *Underland Arcana*, and elsewhere.

This tale was crafted by **SHELLEY LAVIGNE**, a fine purveyor of moist literature. Their words have dampened the pages of many an esteemed publication, such as Three-Lobed Burning Eye, Cosmic Horror Monthly, Gamut, and many others. Their novellas, *Enamoured: A Triptych* and *The Flesh of the Sea* (co-written with Lor Gislason) have landed on shores and in stores. If this story has whetted your appetite, you can satiate it at shelleylavigne.com.

AVRA MARGARITI is a queer author, Greek sea monster, and Rhysling-nominated poet with a fondness for the dark and the darling. Avra's work haunts publications such as Strange Horizons, Apex, The Deadlands, Asimov's, F&SF, Podcastle, and elsewhere. You can find Avra on Twitter & Bluesky (@avramargariti).

MARY MAXWELL is an Arkansas native who squeezes in her passion for writing between her full-time desk job and part-time baking business. Her stories explore themes of mental health and self-reflection, using a foundation of personal experience to build grounded narratives beneath more fantastical genre elements. When she isn't scribbling in her notebook you might find her performing in local community theatre productions or, more likely, holed up in her Fayetteville AR home with her husband and their three spoiled dogs.

Our storyteller is somewhat of a recluse. The author claims his name is **J.B. McLAURIN**, but nobody really knows. His story came to us with nothing but his supposed name and a drawing of the Holler Owl. Not much else is known about J.B., other than that he claims to have seen the Holler Owl up close and personal, which he revealed in his one and only interview with Backwoods Folklorist magazine. Since that interview, no one has seen hide nor hair of him. His only contact with this upside-down world is the occasional tale he sends to us. Like the one he prepared for you tonight. Pour a drink, sit back, and enjoy. Who knows, might be the last story you ever hear. Okay, maybe that's not entirely true, you might be able to find J.B. at @mclaurinjbauthor on Instagram and Threads, @jbmclaurinauthor on TikTok, or jbmclaurinauthor.com.

EMMA E. MURRAY is forever cursed to tell stories of the desolate and disturbing. Her works include *Crushing Snails*, *Shoot Me in the Face on a Beautiful Day*, *When the Devil*, and *The Drowning Machine and Other Obsessions*. When she isn't crushing souls and small invertebrates, she spends her time creating new worlds with her daughter and playing retro video games. If you'd like her to squelch your heart under her shoe, you can find more about her writing at EmmaEMurray.com

ABDULBASIT A. OLÚWANÍSHOLÁ, SWAN V, is a young Nigerian creative writer. He studied Agriculture in Usmanu Dafodiyo University Sokoto. His works are up/forthcoming in *A Long House*, *ANMLY*, *Ake Review*, *BAM Quarterly*, *Tahoma Literary Review*, *The Marbled Sigh*, *Over/Exposed Lit Review*, *Poetry Journal*, *Poetry Column*, *Ninshãr Arts*, *Visual Verse*, *Rowayat*, *Haven Spec*, *Sley House*, *Singapore Unbound*, *Invisible City*, and elsewhere. He tweets @abdulbasitoluwa. You can also find him on Bluesky @oluwanishola.bsky.social.

An admirer of authors like Harry Crews and Joe R. Lansdale, **MAX PALERMO** is a writer of pulp, grit, and horror with a comedic flair and a penchant for the bizarre. He is one of the main contributors to the *Orbit Drive-In Zine*, the premier publication for the schlock cineaste, and has published stories in *Close to the Bone*, *Schlock! Webzine*, and *All Due Respect*.

DANIEL A. RABUZZI (www.danielarabuzzi.com) has been published in, among others, Crab Creek Review, Asimov's, Strange Horizons, Coffin Bell, Shimmer, and Lady Churchill's Rosebud Wristlet. Pushcart nominee. He lives in New York City with his artistic partner & spouse, the woodcarver Deborah A. Mills (www.deborahmills woodcarving.com).

ERIC RAGLIN (he/him) is a horror/weird fiction writer. His short story collections include *Nightmare Yearnings* and *Extinction Hymns*. He owns Cursed Morsels Press and has edited *The Writhing*, *Verdant End*; *No Trouble at All* (co-edited with Alexis DuBon), *Bitter Apples*, *Shredded: A Sports and Fitness Body Horror Anthology*, and *Antifa Splatterpunk*. Find him on Bluesky or Instagram @ericraglin1992.

If you like this story, visit **M. BRANDON ROBBINS**'s Substack at mbrandonrobbins.substack.com and check out some of his previously published works. He's been featured in several short story and poetry publications and even has a few books you can buy. Don't worry: He won't send his pet monster after you. Maybe.

GREGG STEWART draws his inspiration from the liminal space between diffused streetlights and the deepest shadows. A published author and award-winning musician, he's penned over a hundred songs, toured the world, and slipped his work into more than twenty film and TV flicks. His dark fiction prowls the pages of leading horror and fantasy anthologies, and his latest novella—*Kim Reaper* (Graveside Press, 2025)—kicks off a teen fantasy-horror trilogy. His latest nonfiction work, *Let It Out* (New Fable, 2024) cracked Amazon's Top 10 in Creativity, and his TEDxTalk (June 2025) was branded an Editor's Pick. Find him roaming the digital dead zone: @greggstewart (Blue Sky), @thegreggstewart (X and TikTok), and @thatgreggstewart (Instagram).

SJ TOWNEND has dark fiction published in a few places including anthologies from Eerie River Publishing, Vastarien, Ghost Orchid Press, and Dark Matter Magazine. Her first horror collection, *Sick Girl Screams*, introduced by Robert Shearman, is out now (Brigid's Gate Press) as is her second, *Your Final Sunset* (Sley House Press). She's currently working on a third collection because she's addicted to writing short stories. Some (most) of her tales are inspired by the disgusting things her two wild children do. Twitter: @SJTownend Bluesky: https://bsky.app/profile/sjtownend.bsky.social

VEDA VILLIERS (she/her) is passionate about speculative fiction and poetry that probes the complexities of the human experience. Though her day job keeps her busy, you can find her on Twitter @VedaVilliers.

GORDON B. WHITE is a Seattle-based author of horror and weird fiction. His fiction has been nominated for the Shirley Jackson and Bram Stoker Awards, and his stories, reviews, and interviews have appeared in dozens of venues. His most recent book is the short story collection *Gordon B. White is creating Haunting Weird Horror(s)*. You can find him online at www.gordonbwhite.com or on most social media as @GordonBWhite.

IF YOU'D LIKE TO READ MORE STORIES IN THIS UNIVERSE, CHECK OUT TALES OF THE SLEY SIBLINGS VOLUME ONE.

ALSO FROM SLEY HOUSE

NOVELS

A Mind Full of Scorpions
(Eyes Only, Book One)
J.R. Billingsley

Ground Control
K.A. Hough

Bad Form
Joe Taylor

Persephone's Escalator
Joe Taylor

The Cartography Door
Sean Edward

Black Echoes
J.B. McLaurin

Under the Churchyard in
the Chamber of Bone
J.R. Billingsley

Ristenoff
J.R. Billingsley

Atacama
Jendia Gammon

ANTHOLOGIES

Tales of Sley House 2021

Tales of Sley House 2022

Tales of Sley House 2023

Tales of the Sley Siblings

Tales of Sley House 2024

STORY COLLECTIONS

Melpomene's Garden
Curtis Harrell

Observations and Nightmares:
The Short Fiction of J.R. Billingsley
J.R. Billingsley

Your Final Sunset
SJ Townend

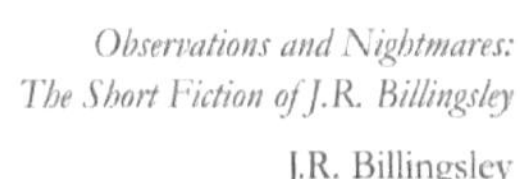

See more at https://www.sleyhouse.com